HIGH IMPACT INSENSITIVITY

Jonathan McQuillan

Published by Lasavia Publishing Ltd.
Auckland, New Zealand
www.lasaviapublishing.com

Copyright © Jonathan McQuillan 2025
Cover image by Steven Taylor
Edited by Rowan Sylva
Designed by Daniela Gast

ISBN: 978-1-991083-28-9

For Megan, Leo and Oscar

"Whoever fights monsters should see to it that in the process he does not become a monster. And if you gaze long enough into an abyss, the abyss will gaze back into you."

Friedrich Nietzsche

ACKNOWLEDGEMENT

Creating this book has been a journey, and I'm deeply grateful to the people who supported me along the way.

First, I want to thank Steven Taylor—my friend since school days, from sitting in classrooms to seeing The Stone Roses at Spike Island. Thank you for reading my short stories over the years, for your unwavering encouragement, and for designing the stunning cover art. Your talent and friendship mean so much. You can find more of Steven's work at: facebook.com/LazyBoyArtStore

To my old band mate Dominic Buzugbe, thank you for your early cover mock-ups, reading two drafts, and standing by me as a true friend.

A special thanks to my friend AM for an incredibly detailed beta read, which changed the course of this book. To Karen Skews of Wellington, Euan Kirkland of Dunedin, and Mark and Sally Ewens of Waiheke Island: your feedback helped shape this story, and I'm grateful for your insights. My thanks also to Gina and Shane Cotton and Steve Cumming for your thoughtful input and suggestions.

Rowan Sylva of Lasavia, thank you for your honest and thoughtful editing, which sharpened this work. And to Daniela Gast, Mike Johnson, Leila Lees and the rest of the Lasavia team, thank you for your patience believing in this project.

To Colin and Christopher Wood and the Wood family in Manchester: I'm forever grateful for your love and encouragement. To Bruce, Rhonda, Ian, Linda, and the Ritchie whānau in Tāmaki Makaurau: thank you for welcoming me with love and acceptance.

To my parents: your influence runs through every word of this book. My mother, Gloria, is an extraordinary woman who changed the world for the better for so many people. Her tireless work and passion inspired me to persevere, even when it felt impossible. She couldn't have done it without the support of my dad, Peter, and my brother, Mathew, who have always been there for her—and for me. I wouldn't be where I am today without your belief in me. And to my sister, Estelle Jones: thank you for your critiques and for being my greatest cheerleader.

My deepest thanks go to Melissa Barge (Porter) for introducing me to my wife, Megan Ritchie. Megan, without your love and patience, this book simply wouldn't exist. For six years, you've supported me as I engaged in one of the most antisocial things a husband can do: writing a novel. Through the late nights and long ferry rides, you've been my anchor. You are the cleverest, most thoughtful person I know, and you've given me the greatest gifts of all—our boys, Leo and Oscar, who fill my days with laughter and humility. This book is as much yours as it is mine.

This story is not about hate or division—it's about Love. It's about what we can achieve when we give each other the time and space to understand our differences.

And to all the people who told me I was wasting my time writing this book: the last two words in it are especially for you.

Part One

Chapter 1

THE SACK

Monday, 28th October

It was the biggest fuck up in the history of Kiwi sports broadcasting, and fifteen minutes earlier, Mark Goodenough, had just made it. He'd bugged out. Grabbed his bag and gapped it. Bolted through the station's exit door, hoping no-one saw him go.

Right Shoulder – If no-one sees you go, maybe no-one'll give you the sack.

Muddled thought, yes.

An irrational plan, yes,

Piling it down Queen Street on a chill October night, sprinting past the New World and down through the Britomart concourse. Gunning it to catch the last ferry home. He makes it, just. Scans his pass, trots down the landing bridge and parks his arse in a plastic seat on the boat's top deck.

Twenty minutes later the word 'WORK' flashes onto the face of his iPhone, the handset vibrates in pulses. 'WORK' just one word, but it reaches inside him and drags another wave of anxiety up over his shoulders, pinning him down through the chest. A singularity of dread spinning at his sternum. The phone carries on ringing but Mark is frozen again, hovering his index finger over the green mnemonic.

Pausing for a time.

And then he taps it.

"Goodenough!" The voice on the other end of the line knows his name and it is raging.

"Where the bloody hell are ya?" The voice doesn't wait for an answer,

"You've ruined the broadcast ya fucken clown. The World Cup Final and you've ruined the fucken broadcast," moving up an octave, the voice implores "the best bit of the game too, and now you've flaming well gapped it ya bloody idiot. Where are you?"

"Erm, who's is this?" Mark replies.

"Who is this? Who is it? Who the fuck do you bloody well think it is?"

"I..."

"It's your *fucken* boss's boss cunt," Gordon usually has a rapid speech rate, though, in cases like these he'll slow down when he introduces himself because he thinks it better communicates the intellectual mana that he thinks his job commands him. The thicker he thinks you are, the slower the delivery of mana. "It's the Executive Programme Director here, Gordon fucken West."

Back to the usual speech rate, spewing, "Five minutes of it ya clown. Five fucken minutes of it. Dead air! Dead air! Five fucken minutes! Ya fucking clown! Have you any idea how much money those spots were worth?"

Contrite, "A couple of thousand?"

"A couple of thousand? And the rest. You're a bloody clown. Try two hundred thousand fucken dollars Goodenough. Try two hundred fucken grand." Then, self-reflecting, "That's *my* fucken bonus. That's *everyone's* fucken bonus, it might even be the end of next year's Olympics coverage. Those were the most valuable spots we've had in years, and you've bloody well fucked it. Why didn't they just call you Notgoodenough when you were born," he's practised that bit, "ya bloody idiot."

"Notgoode.."

"You've fucked it Goodenough, shoved it up your arsehole and fucked it. You've pissed on your chips and danced on the ashes. You'll never work in this industry again. Not while I've got a hole in my arse, do you hear me, Sunshine?"

There is little recourse for excuses here. Mark Goodenough is unable to talk about spilled coffee and accidents, of short-circuiting mixing desks and panic attacks. None of it would've mattered anyway. He'd gapped it, leaving the station off the air. You just can't do that in the radio game. Gordon's voice goes up another octave again, pleading, "'ken half a million listeners, Goodenough, half a fucken mil' and 'cos of you, all they got was silence!"

As a matter of fact, that last bit wasn't strictly true. Listeners hadn't 'got' silence at all. What they had 'got' was a live broadcast of novice producer, Mark Goodenough's nervous breakdown as he struggled to deal with a short-circuiting, mixing console. A freeze up, a debilitating anxiety attack. Three voices in the broadcast, (and five all up for Mark). Two different telephone calls. The channel carrying the live cricket commentary, totally fried and silent.

Listeners had waited their whole lives to experience moments in life like these, but the sound of the commentary wasn't being broadcast and now they weren't living this *once in a lifetime moment* with the rest of the nation.

People started phoning the station. Normally, the producer would answer the call and park the caller on one of two lines on the broadcast console where they wait to go live to air. Here, the haywire broadcast console had caused lines one and two to by-pass human intervention, answering themselves and dropping each caller live to air simultaneously.

'Ropeable as fuck' was how best to describe the caller on line number one. Raymond Schist was his name, and Blockhouse Bay was where he was calling from, a regular caller. "He likes to be called Schisty," is what the profile note says in the station's telephone system against the old boy's number. Well, old Schisty was spewin' alright. Drunk and spewing. His voice, indignant and gruff, rattling down the telephone line with the burn of the 750,000 durries he'd nailed down the years, coating the airwaves with a slew of industrial language for a duration of about five minutes or so. The sound of a heavy door slamming near the end of the episode.

On line number two, for the last half of it was Mark's AWOL line manager Jay Dicks. 'Your Boss' is what the profile note against Jay Dick's phone number says in the station's telephone system. At first Jay seemed calm. Uncharacteristically nice. Maybe someone had died. He wanted to know where the cricket was. Within twenty seconds his tone changed, and he was raging in a cocaine fuelled tirade against Mark, and latterly Schisty.

That's right, contrary to what Gordon West says, listeners hadn't 'got' silence at all instead they were privy to a Schisty and Dicks swearing masterclass. It was a massive audience too, easily the biggest in a decade, in fact, a staggering one in five New Zealanders were listening to Mark Goodenough being carpet bombed with a selection of extreme profanity that more modest people would initialise and link to the word 'bomb' via a hyphen.

The *'F-Bomb.'*

The *'S-Bomb.'*

The *'C-Bomb.'*

It was all there. Present and correct. There'd have been loads of kids listening to it too, but Mark flipped, he flipped, and he gapped it, you could tell that he gapped it because the sound of the door closing was there on the logs. It was the single greatest five minutes in New Zealand cricket history and 20% of the country's population, didn't get to hear it because Mark Goodenough is a klutz.

Yes, Gordon West's overview on what was actually broadcast some fifty minutes earlier is largely meta. What *hadn't* been broadcast, how long it *hadn't* been broadcast for, how much money it was worth, how many listeners would've been listening. Hence his question, "And where's Jay D..cks ..n all of th..?" As usual, when the ferry passes through the Motuihe Channel, the signal starts to get patchy.

"Sorry, you're breaking up. I, I can't hear you."

"Wh... pen... ay.... is...shi... de... m..assel... echa..."

"No, I can't hear you."

"..hall......mi..shum....di...di...di...ba," even though he can't hear the words, Mark is increasingly aware that Gordon is screaming. It sounds like Morse code transmitted by a Dalek, "...om. ..ot....ick, y... flami... diot...tou... Fu.... bas... d... an... I'll ram that pho... up y... flaming ar... ...oody idi..."

"I can't hear you. You›re breaking up."

"..all... avin... mm....Fla....ing... rongo. Ag ...i..p e..ithouse"

After twenty seconds, the signal starts to return, and Gordon, still shouting, adds, "Jay Dicks, Jay fucken Dicks, your bloody line manager, where's he in all of this?" If Gordon West had have listened to the broadcast logs himself, he'd need not have asked.

"I assumed he was off, you know, on leave or something."

"He was fuck! I'm not giving my PD a day off for a big game like that, am I?"

"Well, I didn't see him at the station."

It sounds like Gordon is straining when he says, "he should've been there."

"I don't know what to tell you, Mr West, I didn't see him at the station."

"What! Well, he was rostered on. Where was he?"

"I dunno," by now, it's clear to Mark that Gordon West likes calling spades 'spades' and Gordon continues to call spades 'spades' until he reaches the last two words of the call which are "you're" and "fired."

Even though Mark Goodenough saw it coming, it still shocks him. Never in his wildest dreams had he expected to be given his marching orders in 'shout', on the boat ride home. The sacking Mark had imagined had been a corporate one. Wednesday morning. Tea and biscuits. Jay Dicks a rattlin' through the facts and the failings. Done by the book, a she/her from People and Culture should nod away at the line manager's side and ensure that everything is fair. Being compromised, she does this with the sincerity of a plastic-dog on a car's rear-dashboard. Eventually she'll hand Mark an offboarding-pack. These are made from glossy cardboard and are branded with the company's logo. Packaged inside the offboarding-pack there'd be a copy of his employment contract (highlighted at the breaches), a letter of dismissal and a parachute payment of three vouchers to see a shrink.

Right Shoulder – You're a fucking idiot, let's have a drink.

Using the handrail, Mark walks down the twelve steps from the upper deck then pushes the main cabin's blast-doors open. Inside, it's chock full of about two hundred pissed up cricket fans. They're singing along to Queen's, *We are the Champions*, but it sounds more like a field full of farm yard animals with Freddie Mercury on lead. Mark listens detached, waiting in line at the beverage kiosk.

"And bad mistakes, I've made a few..."

"MMMM Captain's Club," the man one place in front of Mark in the queue, says to the hostess He speaks with the aid of an electro-larynx, a buzzing tool that's placed next to the jawbone acting as a voice-box for people who've had their larynx removed. He doesn't smell too good. It's best to stay away. Electro larynx is with a Priest. You see the Priest all the time.

You don't know him, but you feel like you should, for some or other reason.

Mark is next at the bar, "Heineken please," he says over the din as he reads the word 'Joy' on stewardess' name-badge.

Right Shoulder – Knackered, would've been more apt.

"A what?"

"Heineken."

"Run out,"

"What?"

"Run out."

"You've run out?" Mark says in disbelief.

"Yeah," such a din.

"Any wine?"

"Nope," Joy says, pointing towards the man with the electro-larynx.

"They've drunk the bar dry?"

"Yeah!"

"In twenty minutes?" Mark is shouting in amazement.

"Yeah," Joy pauses and says, "been to the cricket?"

"Sort of."

"Well, only just fund out we won. We tried to listen to the radio for it, but then this weird CB radio thing came on instead of it. We missed the best bit."

"So did they," Mark says motioning to the room. Being the last boat home on a Labour Day Monday, they had missed the best bit too.

"We've got hot chocolate, but you know, we are close to Mātiatia."

"Yeah, nah, I'll have a hot chocolate," and then he says the two words required for the five percent resident's discount, "Captains Club." He is confident saying "'Captain's Club'" because he has the card to prove it in his wallet.

As Joy turns to prepare Mark's drink, he pays the balance using the Eftpos machine then leans against the counter. He picks up a copy of the *Gulf News*. There's a photo of a crashed car on the front page, the headline 'Death on the Onetangi Straight' lays it bare. On the right side of the page, there are three smaller, framed images stacked above one-another. The top image is of an angry toddler and carries the slug-line, 'Triggered'. The slug-line is pulled from a quote from the child's mother about the cancellation of this year's Oneroa Santa Parade. Her four-year-old had raged on it.

The second framed image, the one in the middle, is of a neatly prepared hamburger, and it carries the slug-line, 'Burgered.' It refers to a petition against fast-food giant, Carl's Junior's application to open a drive-thru in the carpark by Placemakers. The last of the three images, features the logo from Mark's alma mater, *Waiheke Island Radio,* with the slug-line 'Tune in.' It directs readers to a two-page spread on the centrefold.

Mark leafs straight to the radio piece and he skims it, learning that staff at the station are fund-raising, helping pay for the renewal of their frequency. There's a colour photo with five people in it. Mark scrutinises it, seeing who he knows. A pretty woman with a resting bitch face, another with pink hair, glasses and dungarees, a short blind man with a guide-dog by his side, and a smartly dressed chap with a beard. The only person in the picture Mark knows from *his* time there is Big Bill Tong, the distinctive South African pensioner of six feet and seven inches.

When Joy returns with Mark's hot chocolate, he puts the *Gulf News* back on the top of the pile, takes the drink, and walks outside to the back of the boat. At the rail, he stops, cold, looking out on the blackness of the water, the neon glow of the Auckland City skyline beyond it. Hypnotised by the churning water and the path of white foam it has braided through the sea.

Right Shoulder – Jump! Go on jump. No one will know. No one gives a fuck about you anyway. Jump! Jump! It's not like you've got any kids, it'll be quick, a head injury.

Left Shoulder – Nah, don't do that. You're too young. There's too much to do. You don't want to go out like that. Drowning in the dark. Sharkfeed.

With his mind in two, and his feet tingling from the vibration of the turbines below him Mark does his thinking, stubborn to the temperature, reducing the evening's events to a two-word descriptor, proceeded by the word 'The'. Mark did that with all his most embarrassing moments. This new one would be known as *The Dead Air Incident*, and it would rank alongside *The Walk-In* as an event that Mark wished had never happened to him.

Chapter 2

THE WINZ OFFICE

Wednesday, 30th October – 13:20

Two days have passed since *The Dead Air Incident* and Mark sits in the WINZ office in the seaside village of Oneroa. It's a curious little WINZ office, this one. Hidden off the street like a dirty little secret. Moved back from the rest of the shop frontage, the upmarket tourist boutiques, the fancy restaurants, and the la-di-da art shops. The Hamptons of New Zealand is how some like people refer to this place. Nevertheless, this is where you go when you don't have a job, and you live on Waiheke Island.

Trying to be proactive, Mark Goodenough turned up ten minutes early and pulled a number off the number peeler. 76 is what he got. He waits on a couch in an area with three other people. One of them looks like he's on P, he has that unhinged look in his eyes, that, and he's rocking backwards and forwards like he's got pinworms. Moving pin worms, writhing up his back-pipe. The two other people on the couch, Mark remembers from the boat ride home. Electro Larynx and the Priest. Electro Larynx stinks of ammonia. Could be his clothes though, maybe a cat pissed on his dirty red football shirt, late 40s, long greasy hair, bushy eyebrows, grey and black. His unkept stubble fails to hide his hippo-neck double-chin. Electro Larynx is a rotund specimen, unfit, bad back, the rosy cheeks of a secret pisshead.

The Priest, Mark recognises from the paper and the Countdown. He was on the Six o'clock news once. Something to do with a funeral. Always rocks up to a protest. You could imagine that it wouldn't take much for him to start chucking the Molotov cocktails in a good riot. The priest in his 50's, he is sharper than Electro Larynx. Looks like he'd wear his sunglasses at night. He has a dog collar, a clerical one. Polished shoes. Electro Larynx and the Priest are together. You can see it.

There is music playing at twenty percent volume. It is coming from ceiling speakers. It is the same kind of music they play at the Tax Office when people phone up about their rebates. Musical sedatives which knit nicely with the humming sound made by air conditioning units, and which enhance the monochrome aesthetic of grey wallpaper. A playlist of Hayley Westenra, Stan Walker, and The Feelers has so far cycled. Bic Runga is on now. She is singing her number *Sway* and all of those waiting, (except for the P head) have heavy eyelids.

Mark blots it out. All of it. All of *them*. Head down, trying to stay awake. Whiling away the wait by picking at the scab. The same old scab he'd been inspecting for months. Scrolling through the fake profiles to spy on the ex, surfing the comments on her virtual walls. Fingering through them. Scratching at them. Peeling the scabs back. Seeing what's underneath them. Thumbing at the heart, dialling it round in circles, and all from the comfort of the Waiheke WINZ wait room couch.

Mark is looking at a photo of his ex, Liz, she is with her new man Gavin. They're on the ferry in it. They're all happy and the sun is shining in it. Mark is seething. The word 'KEVIN' interrupts him from it, flashing on the face of the iPhone as it buzzes alive. An incoming call from the older brother, a welcome intrusion. Since Dad died, the family had atomised. Mum had run off to Australia with an octogenarian fitness guru called Merv. Merv was from Perth. They met on a cruise. The older brother, Kevin is married to a Wellingtonite. He lives in Upper Hutt with her and their two kids. He's been there for five years now. Mark misses his brother. The last time he'd seen him was eighteen months earlier when Mark and Liz, had spent five days in the capital. In hindsight, it's proven to have been a pivotal trip in the life of Mark Goodenough. Going into it, Liz would've married him, by the end, not so much. She brooded on Kevin's two young boys, but Mark was oblivious to it, dismissive even. She was at her crossroads and Mark hadn't even noticed.

"Hello."

"Whaddup brother? Heard your cricket game."

"You did?" Mark, speaking in a hush.

"Yeah," sniggering, "your boss called you a 'cunt' on the radio."

"You heard that?" Mark wouldn't know, how could he? "But how?"

"I dunno, but everyone heard it, bro. The cricket commentary stopped. It was you and two other fellas talking."

"Oh Jesus no."

"Yep, and the auld fella on the phone called you a 'fucken clown' too. Fucken heard it all brother. Then, *your* boss phones up and calls *you* a 'cunt' and then *his* boss phones *him* and *he* calls *him* a cunt too; It all went off. You couldn't make it up. You'd be mortified, eh?"

"Well to be honest I didn't realise the whole country was in on the joke. Now I know that, of course I'm am. Fuck. I didn't realise it was this bad. This is a lot to process; man, it'll take a bit of time to sink in." He pauses for air, "So, just to be clear, you could actually hear *me* talking, and the two telephone calls that came in?"

"Yeah. The cricket wasn't playing though. It was dead."

"Fuck."

"Man, but they were harsh with you brother, it wasn't nice to have to hear, as your brother. I mean are you alright about it?"

"Fuck knows."

"I'll bet they sacked you."

"Yep."

"Well, who sacked you if the boss was at a party?"

"The boss's boss."

"The boss's boss? Oh, that's not good. Well, you can't exactly blame them can you, I mean, a World Cup Final bro. How much would do you reckon those spots were worth? A hundred G? That's a lot of money to lose?

"Try two hundred G."

"Oath?"

"Oath."

"But Brother yeah, you can't be letting people talk to you that way. Ever. Much less have it broadcast to the country."

"Well, what else was I supposed to do?"

"Start by telling these cunts to go and fuck themselves. A man's got his pride. And anyway, why wasn't the prick there with you, at the studio? The boss should always be present in case something goes wrong, right? That's a massive game and he was AWOL; you'd have thought he'd have been there?"

"Someone said he was off."

Kevin sniggers, "oh yeah, he was 'off' alright. Off his head. Old mate was out partying. You could hear voices and splashing sounds in the background of his call, I even heard the clink of glasses and the *cht* of a beer can opening."

"Nah bro, I don't remember any of that stuff," Mark is bewildered by it, "probably a panic attack or something."

"Pfft, I don't see how you couldn't have noticed that bro?"

"I was working Kev. I wasn't tuned into the background noise, and I didn't know it was going to air until you just told me now."

"Brother, it was clear as day. You could hear him snorting something too. Maybe he's on the coke. You could hear his mate, Birdie, telling him to get it 'round his beak'. You never heard that?"

"Dude, I was in the middle of a panic attack."

"You and your panic attacks, bro," Kevin paused, "hey and actually, why was *The Benny Hill Theme Tune* playing in the middle of it all?" Incredulously, "what *was* that about?"

"Oh, that. It's just the boss's ringtone."

"Boss's ringtone?"

"Yeah."

"But how could his phone ring if he's on the phone to you?"

"Must have another phone."

"Two phones? That's a bit sus."

"I guess."

"So, what're you gonna do now?"

"Well, I'm sitting in the WINZ office as we speak, bro."

"Blessing in disguise, mate. Pay in radio's shit, *you* know that. Just go back to IT man. Money's way better in IT. It's not brain surgery."

"I don't need that much to get by," Mark snaps.

"Yeah, only 'cos mum's too soft to ask you for rent. Pfft. There's no way that'll carry on. She'll be all over you soon. I'd be proactive there if I were you."

"Yeah, whatever."

"Hey er, you've not forgot about the Sun Festival, have you? It's in a couple weeks. I've got a flight booked the Thursday before it. Catlove's letting us use the yacht. We're gonna sail there."

"Who's coming?"

"My old crew from school. Oh, and Bento's back too, he wants to come with us."

"What? Ben Tony."

"Yeah."

"Back on the island, is he?"

"Yeah, and he's looking for a place to stay too. Maybe you should rent out one of the old rooms to him, there's plenty of space in that old house."

"I'm not fucking living with him. He's mental."

Kevin sings the next bit "Five hundy, back pocket."

A WINZ analyst calls out the number 76. It's Mark's ticket, so he terminates the call, gets to his feet and walks the small number of steps to the desk of the woman who'd motioned towards him. Sour of face is the WINZ lady. Zesty. Like a bulldog licking piss off a nettle. Badge says Shelley, Shelley Spakfilla. Using body language alone, Ms Spakfilla offers Mark a seat opposite hers, then, she seems to scan him from top to bottom. It is as if she is trying to place him on the *Layabout Spectrum*. Figuring out whether this one is a worker or a shirker. A bludger or a grafter.

"Name?"

"Mark, Mark Goodenough."

"Address?"

"Thirty-five Wairua Road, Ōmiha."

For the next few minutes Mark willingly imparts all of his relevant personal information to Ms Spakfilla who hammers each letter into her computer via her beleaguered keyboard. Fast, loud, impersonal. At no point while doing that, does her gaze leave that of the Dell monitor into which she is staring.

"And what are you looking for Mr Goodenough?"

"I'll do any casual work on the island in the short term, but ultimately, I'm looking to a career in radio."

"Lost your job, have you?" Ms Spakfilla says with the side-eye. It is clear to Mark now. She's pegged him as a bludger.

"Yeah,"

"*UNZMedia*, correct?"

"That's right."

"You were a part-time producer, correct?"

"That's right."

"Weren't there very long, were you?"

"Three months."

"Mmm, says here you used to work at Radiohub too."

"Yeah."

"Didn't last long there either." Suddenly Ms Spakfilla looks enthused, "wait, hold on," she says, "but you've three years' experience in IT. You worked at Mussell Dekker Biggs. That's a top tier law firm. Why aren't you looking for work in that area?"

"Well, I mean I could, but you know I just finished a degree in radio and I mean, it's in the blood, my dad was a music programmer, my brother does it too. I just think that IT might be a step backwards for me."

"No, no, no, you're mistaken Mr Goodenough, that's not a step back, there's loads of work in IT."

"But there's nothing in radio?"

"Mmm, not sure it's wise to limit yourself like this Mr Goodenough. I mean I've got at least three jobs doing IT support, these would be perfect for you, we could have you interviewing next week." Ms Spakfilla then looks up from her monitor, taps her pencil on the desk and performs another virtual MRI scan of Mark. Top to bottom. The Bullshit Detector this time.

"Mr Goodenough, you've been let go by Radiohub and UNZMedia. Why was that?"

"Oh, it's a long story."

"Walk-out, did you?" Flint face.

"No."

PING – On the Bullshit Detector.

"Please tell me you're not one of them," air-quotes, "Attitude People, are you?"

"No."

PING – On the Bullshit Detector.

Left Shoulder – What the fuck?

"Riiiight, 'cos you dress like one."

"Are you even allowed to say stuff like this?"

"Look, Mr Goodenough, I've got a job to do. Let's get you processed, shall we?"

Mark doesn't say anything.

"Right, you've been fired from the two major players in the New Zealand radio industry," then, shaking her head, she returns her gaze to the monitor and continues to clack away at the keyboard. She stops and after about fifteen seconds of silence, she says, "between them UNZMedia and Radiohub control twenty-eight of the thirty-two radio stations in Auckland. I'm afraid you've got no chance in radio. You're damaged goods, Mr Goodenough."

"Can you at least check?"

"OK, I'll have a look," again Ms Spakfilla returns to the keyboard and pummels each key like she fucking hates it. Hitting the Enter key like she is about to call it a 'cunt' and offer it out for a fight, "OK, well maybe you might be in a bit of luck. There's a job here at Radio Christ in Eden Terrace. I assume you're Christian and you're happy to commute?"

"Yeah."

PING – On the bullshit detector.

"Look, I'll print out the particulars, and you can get your application away."

"How about jobs on the island? Anything casual going?"

For this Ms Spakfilla doesn't need to do any typing, she's been trying to palm this one off for a day or two, "there's a mowing job going down at Passage Rock, shall I print this one out for you too?"

"Yes please."

Chapter 3

THE SAUSAGE SIZZLE

Saturday, 2nd November - 11:34

Mark's ex-girlfriend Liz is diligent on the socials. All of them. Her work demands it, and her life is on show. Duly, Mark engages with it. Vigorously lurking, he scrutinises her feeds with the laser-like precision of Ebenezer Scrooge at his counting table. It's ironic then, that in real life, he goes out of his way to avoid her, sneaking out to the supermarket. Scooting along the road by the beach at Kauakarau Bay. Past the end of Valley Road, he goes. On up to the bus stop where, he takes the right turn up Glen Brook Road.

He is going the long way round so he can avoid Liz. Going the normal way is much quicker, but *that way* goes directly past her place on O'Brien Road. Her place / their place. The place Liz now shares with Gavin Gregson. Gavin Gregson, Mark's oldest friend. Mark had gone to kindy with Gavin Gregson. School, rugby, scouts, all that. Best mates they'd been. Stabbed in the back though. Ended in violence. The pair coming to blows during *The Walk-In*. A proper fight it was too.

A tooth-taker.

A dry-wall damager.

Mark convinces himself that taking the detour isn't so bad, especially at this time of year. It's only a minute or so, and it's fun to ride along the ridge and see the views out west towards the city skyline and the Waitākere Ranges. A road that takes you down and back onto O'Brien, at the end of the detour.

Right Shoulder – Where you should've been in the first place, pussy.

He drives over the brow, and around the S-bend, it turns at the top by the vines at Frenchman's Hill, and the view over ANZAC Bay at high tide.

Right Shoulder – How demeaning though, doing this detour.

The road winds its way down and across the face of the hill, along the edge of the bush where the trees don't fully block out the view. Descending and running parallel with the back straight at the Waiheke Dirt Track, holding the curve by Waster's Corner and the Gordon's Road turn off.

Right Shoulder – You've been emasculated.

Through between the clubrooms and the bus stop by the entrance to the dog walking park, the gates of the Waiheke United football fields, and the colony of stray roosters that've been dumped there.

Right Shoulder – Mug.

Up the hill the road goes, and on into the village of Ostend, where all life on Waiheke Island comes together. The 'Countdown' it's called. The supermarket. Underneath it, down in the carpark, a voice echoes off the concrete rafters. It's one of those voices that people stop for. Jolly, and booming, grizzled and gruff. The Mad Butcher on super strong Dutch skunk.

"Breur! Howsit?"

It's the voice of moustachioed Capetonian, Bill Tong. A retired builder with a house in Blackpool. A man of leisure, and one with that air about him too. Dresses like he's going on-safari. Kits himself out in white. White shorts, white T, white socks, white veldskoene. The only deviation from the white being the blue of the text in the words 'Waiheke Island Radio' that span the chest area on the front of his T-shirt. In his right hand, Bill holds a large tub of Olivani margarine. In his left, a red money box with the word 'FLOAT' written on it.

"Billy!" Mark shouts, craning his neck to accommodate both of Bill Tong's metres, "saw you in the paper." It's not entirely unusual to see Bill Tong in the paper and it is accepted that after Graham Henry, Peter Leitch, Princess Chelsea, Hinemoa Elder and Paul Rutherford, he is easily the Island's sixth most famous person.

"Ugly as mince, eh?" Bill undersells it, chuckling "Hey er, we're doing a sausage sizzle for the station, you'll buy a snag won'cha, boy?"

"Shit yeah."

The pair lock step by the trolley lift and walk on up the ramp. On the left-hand wall, four large posters decorate the concrete – four images of four different foodstuffs, with four different words stencilled on each, Juicy, Sweet, Crisp, and Fresh, in that order. The pair walk up and on past them.

"Still working in radio?" Bill asks.

"Well," Mark says, trying to form a lie, "my contract just expired at UNZ, but you know, between gigs. Hard market."

"What about that girlfriend of yours?"

"Split up in April."

"April of *this* year?"

"Yeah," and by July she'd cut him from her life, as if a malignant tumour. Turned off the tap in the language of TikTok.

"Ey nah breur. You would have been together a long time then eh?"

"Eight years."

"Still hurts, I'll bet?"

Notwithstanding the detour, the fake social media profiles and the hours of internalising what had happened between the three of them, it did hurt. Mark, keen to change the subject says, "You were raising money for the station, right?"

"Yeah."

"But I thought the government paid for Access Radio."

"Well, they used to, but ever since that new Broadcasting Minister came in, they want us to raise ten percent of the costs to renew our frequency."

"Saddleback?"

"Yeah."

"How much does he want?"

"A hundred grand?"

"Reckon you can do it?" Mark says with a raise of his eyebrows.

"Yeah."

At the top of the ramp the pair double back to the bench where people tie their dogs up. In front of the bench there is a sausage sizzle station. A barbecue, and a trestle table. On the trestle table, sits a plate of stacked bread, another of napkins, and bottles of mustard and ketchup. There is someone at the barbecue. They're lost in sausages. Bill, using jazz hands, calls out to them loudly.

"*Wendy! Wendy!* Please let me introduce to you, one of our esteemed alumni. The one, the only, the legendary..." it's as if Bill Tong is giving a Las Vegas style introduction but has forgotten the name of the person he is introducing. A group of teens pivot by the coffee shop and stop what they are doing to listen and still Bill hasn't clicked, until eventually he shouts "DJ Skidmark!"

A peal of laughter ripples through the concourse.

Mark is embarrassed, "no, not Skidmark. Marksman. DJ Marksman, Mark Goodenough, Chart Attack, I did the top twenty on the station there."

"Oh! That's right!" Bill says face-palming.

Immediately, Mark recognises Wendy Metcalfe from the previous week's paper. Nose piercing, short pink hair, turquoise shell suit, square-rimmed glasses. Like Bill, she wears a white T-Shirt with the station's name in blue on it. Socially and emotionally, Wendy doesn't offer much, just a clipped smile.

Once upon a time, there'd have been a bit of a chat. Maybe Wendy would have asked Mark to re-join the station, get Chart Attack going again. Lately though, for Wendy, there've been more important things to think about.

Chapter 4

THE MANCATION

Tuesday, 5th November - 13:50

Excepting the anxiety, the uncertainty and the dread, what a cracking lifestyle this is for a man! Up when you want, shower if you like. Media overload. Weed, beer, takeaways. Wankery, solitude, bliss. The rare air between losing your job, and the biting of its fiscal consequence, the suspended life, the golden living. He's given it a name. *The Mancation.* Today's Mancation had started at 11 a.m. with the morning episode of *The Chase,* which, during a cash-builder, is rudely interrupted by the sound of gravel crunching underneath the tyres of a car. It is on the driveway, and Mark gets to his feet to look out of the window.

Benjamin Tony, or Bento, is known to his friends and family as the most tactless person you're ever likely to meet. Bento is now bringing his blue Toyota Prado 4x4 to a halt in the family spot at the top of the drive that hasn't been used in the eight years since Dad passed. Mark watches on from the window as Bento gets out of the car, walks around the side, opens the boot and pulls a large travel bag out of it. As he does this, the passenger side door opens, seemingly on its own, and then, a monkey gets out of it.

Left Shoulder – A monkey!

A real-life monkey. A rhesus macaque wearing blue shorts and a white t-shirt saying 'Banana for scale'.

Right Shoulder – No one mentioned any monkeys.

The monkey is following Bento and running to hold his hand as the pair climb the steps to the front door. He's only five foot five is Bento, and

Mark has to bend down to give him a pound hug. He's got a black eye and a plaster on his cheek, other than that, he still looks the same, the face still riddled with acne scars, the hair still jet black and scruffy. Bento has aged in the years since Mark last saw him. More lines, yellower teeth. He is wearing blue jeans and an ironed white T-Shirt. Green military fatigue jacket and Dr. Martens. He's clean shaved, trimmed out, and giving off a Travis Bickle vibe.

Within five minutes of arriving, Bento is lying down on the couch, talking to the ceiling, while the monkey explores the house, "want to hear a cool story, bro?" Bento, the quick-talker, the words rattling out of his face like bullets from a machine gun. The tempo dictated by excitement, indignation, or the concern that he might lose his train of thought. He's always tended to answer his own questions. This is one such occasion. "Fucken blocked in at the petrol station by an electric car. *Dude!* Who takes an electric car to a petrol station?"

Mark looks at him blankly.

"Nissan Leaf. Red it was. Had one of those stickers from your radio station on the back bumper. You're still doing it aren't ya?"

"What?"

"The radio?"

Mark hesitates to answer, "Erm, well, no, I stopped doing it ages ago. Well, I stopped doing it *there* ages ago."

"Oh, that's right you got fired, didn't you? Yeah, your brother told me." Bento, half-chuckling, "Yeah, I heard your cricket game. Fella said his name was Jay Dicks, eh? Called you a cunt live to air. What happened there?" Without waiting for the answer, "buzzy as fuck it was, I mean, Benny Hill, what the fuck man? I'd been smoking weed all day too and that comes on." He pauses for breath, "I didn't realise it was you until your Kev told me. Bet you'd be mortified, eh? Being called a cunt on the radio like that. There'd have been what? Half a million people listening to it too? Think about it, half a million people. That's a million ears, and they all heard you getting called a cunt. Yeah, anyway, what were we talking about? I've forgotten."

"The car, electric car at the petrol station, it had a sticker."

"Oh yeah, so the sticker was from your radio station."

"On the island?"

"Yeah."

"So?"

"Oh, no," Bento chuckles, "it gets better. Right, so the driver, she comes back right and she's bought this KitKat," he pauses for a second, then draws out the first word of the next sentence for expression, "well, I say 'she'," leaning in, lowering the voice to a hush, "might've been a man though, 'cos er, you know, she's, she's in a dress, earrings, eye makeup," Bento says grinning.

"Trans? So what? Get with the times man, Jesus."

"No, no, no. I'm not saying anything bad about it, dude. Just, you know, remarking on it, 'cos, well, you know, it was remarkable, wasn't it? Well, it was to me anyway 'cos, I mean, she had this big fuck-off beard, mate. A proper one, like Conor McGregor's. She had his muscles too. Cut to fuck she was. She'd have battered you," a pause. "She'd have battered us both," another pause, "at the same time, man. But you know, on the other hand, there's the short dress, the perfume, the necklace, the earrings, and then, there's, this big fuck off beard, man. Looked like a cross between Captain Birdseye and Taylor Swift. I mean I'm all for it, man, go for your life, but let's not try and pretend that that's not remarkable. 'Cos it is." It had always been like this with Bento, a stream of consciousness without any filter.

"Anyway, I cracked a little joke with her. She gets all dark on me, thought she was going to batter me. All I said was she'd 'forgotten to put the petrol cap back'. Rarked her right up. Told me to 'remind my own business'." Then he laughs, "said I shouldn't mess with 'cycle-paths' like her."

"Psychopaths?"

"No, cycle-paths. Said she was a," Bento laughing now, "stone-code twisted cycle-path."

The monkey who has returned to Bento's side chitters as Bento stops talking. There's another train of thought approaching the station in Bento's head. A heavy goods train, a-coming in hot. Here, most people would stand back from the platform edge. Not Bento. "Is it true you walked in on your bird fucking your best mate?" Before Mark could answer, "In your own bed too, wasn't it?" Bento, totally matter of fact about one of the worst moments in Mark's life, *The Walk-In*. "What position where they in dude?"

"Ahh," utters Mark, stunned, suddenly transported back to that excruciating moment nearly eight months earlier. The same moment that had been haunting him. The frayed edge. The loose bit. The scab that he picked at. The image of arriving home early from uni, seeing the familiar black Raptor and wondering why it was parked at the bottom of the drive. Remembering the voices.

"You fucking love it."

"Yeah, harder, harder."

The sound of the headboard banging. The rhythmic slapping of skin on skin. The grunting and the panting and the moaning. His girl. His bed. His home. Then, the red mist, the dry throat. Steaming up onto the deck and into the kitchen. Throwing open the bedroom door to find the love of his life, naked, and his best mate drilling her. Pillows under her hips, being done from behind. Loving it.

"I really don't want to talk about it, mate."

Chapter 5

THE PIVOTAL DECISION

Sunday, 10th November - 23:50

That Sunday night as Mark is dozing off in Rocky Bay, fate is wrangling his job prospects on the other side of the island. The wheels turning in a one bedroom rented bach at fifteen George Street, in Surfdale. For this is the home of the sausage-sizzling, nose-bolt programme director from Waiheke Island Radio, Wendy Metcalfe. They and their husband, Royce, (Calfie to his mates) are working through the repercussions of a three-month-old email that Royce had received in August.

The message was as unexpected as it has been destructive. He was just a sparky before it arrived, now he's a bigot. It was a heads up from across the Tasman, sent by an old colleague Royce hasn't seen in years. Its contents speak of work in the mines near Perth, of cheap accommodation, cheap food, and three times his usual pay rate. It is enough money to solve all their problems and two *Zoom* interviews later, a generous contract sits upon the breakfast bar in the Metcalfe rented kitchen. Now their marriage is taking strain about it.

Royce is itching to sign it. Wendy isn't convinced. They like the sound of the money but their job as programme director at Waiheke Island Radio is more of a wrench. It'd be hard to leave a job like that behind. It was causing confusion and strife. In the 12 weeks since Royce first mentioned the mines, Wendy has dyed their hair pink, driven a bolt through their nose, shaved a quarter eyebrow off, and come out as non-binary. Now, they have new friends. Royce feels intimidated by one of them. The hard cunt in tights and heels. This one is chipping in on his missus, or so it seems. *Real sus.* The dates all line up on it too. Tallying off with her acquisitions from Waiheke Island Society for the Care of Animals (WISCA), the dungarees and the 90's shell suits. He feels like he is losing 'her' and on one level it's already too late.

Tonight, Royce Metcalfe is playing his last hand, and he'll need all the persuasive strategies available to him. Still, if anyone knows Wendy's pressure points, Royce does. Wendy's most sensitive pressure point is property, they might have changed their gender lately, but they still aspire to the Kiwi dream and the material accoutrements that go along with said dream. Royce rips at it, saying.

"No house, no kids, no savings, no SUV, no boat, no bach, no money."

Wendy hates renting. The weekly contribution to someone else's nest egg. Someone else's dream. Never mind the instability, Rocky Bay, Blackpool, Surfdale, three moves in four years. And the cost of it too, moving between rentals on Waiheke Island is an expensive business. It really ground their gears.

"Paycheque to paycheque, we've fallen behind," is Royce's favourite line.

Lately, it has become more urgent for Royce Metcalfe. There were a lot of questions from a lot of his workmates about what was up with his wife. They've been taking the piss with it too. Even the apprentice had a pop. The cheeky bastard. Well, people talk. That's what you get when you work with the same team of tradies on the same jobs on the same small island. Hammer Hands was what the crew was called. They worked as a team, and they sponsored a show on the local Access Radio station. They were at their most candid at Friday drinks. It was always good natured, but they all wanted answers about Wendy.

"Hey Calfie, Leeroy says your wife's been hanging around with a crew of gays. What? is she a Lesbian now eh? Drive her to it, did you?"

"Fuck and that tranny boxer's always with them now too, eh?" said Leeroy the apprentice, whose Ritalin has just worn off for the day.

"Hey you!" From out of nowhere and without any irony, "don't you use words like that. This is an inclusive workplace. I won't have transphobic attitudes like that on my site!" Shouts foreman Randy, who is also the oldest man on the site, "besides, happy wife, happy life, eh Calfie?" he pauses then adds, "Good luck to you though Calfie, no one's judging you here mate. I've got a nephew who's gay. He's a lovely lad, works in banking. Didn't tell his wife about it for years."

Leeroy cuts in, "sorry boss. Probably shouldn't tell you they got in trouble for rating dildos on the radio a few weeks ago, eh? Hear about that?" Leeroy furthering the subject.

"Who did?"

"A Crew O'gays."

"A Crew O'gays?"

"Yeah, a Crew O-gays, I think that's what they're called."

"That's not what they're called," adds Royce.

"Still got in trouble for rating dildos in a show at dinnertime, though, didn't they?"

"Well, they're allowed to," said foreman Randy.

"Well, no, they're not and anyway, my Wendy wasn't a part of that show. It had nothing to do with her."

"Yeah, but she's involved at the station though, isn't she?"

"She's not in every show."

"Signs off on it though, doesn't she?"

"Well, that show was live, and anyway, why don't you mind your own business?"

"Well, I mean we did see you on TV at that Pride march last month," said Jesus, the Argintine gib stopper. "Is there something you want to tell us, we'll still love you."

It was true. Royce, as a show of acceptance of his wife's new way of being, had gone along to the Pride festival with her. A trans-pensioner gave him LSD, painted rainbows on his cheeks, and put his hair up in pigtails. A camera crew stopped him. Guy Williams it was, in Royce's mind, a large praying mantis was where his acid trip went. The Mantis Williams had a microphone and glasses. Lights and a camera. The light was warm, batheable. It was shown on prime-time television. Now he's getting hit on by men all over the island for drugs and gay sex.

"I'm not gay," he says.

"Well, you never know until you give it a try."

"No thank you, I'm not interested."

"Aww but you might like it."

It happened enough that he lost his patience and snaped in a perceived homophobic outburst, in which he said to a man in the biscuit aisle at Countdown "Look man, truth is, I couldn't suck a dick. The idea makes me want to wretch. I'm not a gay, I'm only going along with it for my wife, she's into all that stuff. Just like I'm into synth pop."

These hurtful words of trans and homophobic language could damn Royce to the dustbin of the heretic. His words, however fleeting, mask a feeling of jealousy and anger. Of insecurity. Allies like Royce can be tarnished forever, judged by words over actions, never to be reformed, never to be free of the spectre of those words and that hate. The green-eyed monster is loose upon the streets of Bethlehem now. If Royce is going to be hung for a sheep, he'll be hung for a lamb. He's hammered and he's about to turn those words on his wife. Thank God 'she' can't hear it.

"What the fuck was 'she' thinking with that fucken nose-bolt, man? It's like waking up next to livestock, fucken looks like a cow now. And I'm not sleeping. The fucken thing whistles when she snores too."

"What does?"

"The fucken nose bolt. There's no escape from it. It's like something off of Frankenstein. She's all like, 'nose bolt in, apnoea out'. All night long it goes. It's a fucken nightmare, and you know 'she's' shaved half an eyebrow off now too. I mean, how do you tell the love of your life 'she' looks like a fucken weirdo."

"At least you can use the disabled parking at the Countdown."

"Yeah," mirth.

"Even a stopped clock tells the right time twice a day, my dear Watson," says the labourer.

"Well, you try living with someone who only wears shell suits around the house. I mean, the noise of it. 'She' sounds like tin foil. It's like living with Metal Mikey. Oooh, it cuts through me that noise. And those glasses aren't real. It's all a fucken put on and I'm taking shit from you lot because of it. Maybe, I should start dressing like a masculine lesbian. Like that tranny boxer friend of 'hers', or whatever it says it is this week. Yeah, maybe 'she'll' respond to that. I mean, this whole non-binary thing man. What the fuck?

26

Look, I'm not saying it's not a real thing. I'm sure it is, but Wendy? It's just a phase with 'her', she was a goth once, 'she'll' probably replace it with knitting or something. I've just got to get 'her' away from it."

"Hey you!" Shouts foreman Randy, "What do you mean 'it'? I've warned you before about transphobic language on my site."

"What? No, I was talking about 'it', the influence."

"Oh, right I thought you were talking about the boxer."

"My friend," says Jesus, "chor wife, isa packen a, how do you say? a suitcase. She er, she movin' of a da island. You know where she going? She a goin' a Hatemanistan, buddy. Big houses, free buzz cuts, and overactive thyroids."

"Mobility scooters and ample parking," Leeroy adds.

"A place where the scent of a ballbag is just a blip," Randy.

"A faded memory," Jesus.

On this, Jesus was wrong, Wendy hadn't packed for Hatemanistan at all, she'd not even packed for Australia.

Back on George Street, in the here and now, it is now or never for Royce. Save his marriage, save his dreams. All night and into the early hours he turns the screw in a rhetorical masterclass. How come a sparky knows *Munroe's Motivated Sequence*? By the end of it, Wendy is sold. Royce is right about Wendy's deepest wants, and once he's convinced them to make their mind up, they start to mentally de-couple from the radio station with five key questions running through their mind.

How secure is the station really, anyway?

What if we get some more complaints?

What if we lose the frequency?

And what of that new broadcaster, the rich conspiracy nut, what was with her?

Who needs this shit anyway?

Chapter 6

THE FERRY TERMINAL

Thursday, 14th November – 12:00

Mark, Bento and the monkey are waiting for Kevin in the Prado, they're parked in one of the expensive bays at the ferry terminal carpark, neither has paid for the space. *Paper Planes* by M.I.A. is playing and the monkey is doing the Rubix Cube on the back seat of the car. Mark in the passenger seat, looks out past the boats that are moored in the bay, then out beyond the channel and over at Rangitoto's green volcanic slopes. Bento fidgets in the driver's seat. He is contrasting the widespread availability of disability parking spaces against the dearth of them in the standard parking section. Just then a Ferrari Testarossa hyper-car pulls up in one of the mobility spots. As it does, a muffled rendition of Simply Red's *Fairground* ceases with the engine.

"Ohhh you'd better be crippled," says Bento in an accusing tone, focusing on the Ferrari.

"What!?" Mark replies with outrage.

"This joker here, sports car, disability badge."

"And?"

"Well, you get these rich pricks who can afford the fine don't you?"

"You do?"

"Fuck yeah. It's nothing to them, a forty-dollar fine."

"So, what are you saying? You can't be rich and disabled?"

"No, but it's important to be across these things, and anyway, it's hardly wheelchair accessible, is it?"

"What?"

"That car." Bento pauses, then with a small amount of authority says, "It'll be gout," before singing the next bit, "the disease of kings."

Mark gags on laugher and says, "let's hope he's not vision impaired."

The man in the Ferrari hangs disability badge off his rear view mirror.

"Nah, it'll be gout."

Without adding anything, Mark shakes his head and continues sniggering while the pair scan the boat's human cargo as it spills from the wharf and onto the pavement. The hi-vis tradies late for work and just back from the k-hole. The cruise-ship day-trippers. The packed lunch pension crew, riding the ferry for free on Winston Peter's Gold Card Cruise whilst aiming to pump a grand total of nil dollars into the island economy. No sign of Kevin though.

"Phone him, bro."

"Give him a minute."

Twenty more seconds, "Come on, call him, bro."

Mark obliges. "No answer, went straight to voicemail."

"Must be on a call."

After two minutes, just 150 paces ahead, a man with a big black beard and familiar green backpack is approached by a couple of local activists. One is short, flinty and old. He wears a Lenin cap and a smug grin. The other looks equally like a cunt. They want him to put his name on a petition against an application to open a new Carl's Junior in the car park next to Placemakers and he obliges them.

"He's grown a beard?" Bento laughs.

"Yeah," Mark says, smiling.

Kevin's beard suits against the black Levis jeans, his green Lacoste polo is sharp with the green soles and green laces of his sand-coloured Clarkes Desert Treks.

"You reckon he's a hipster now?"

"What?"

"You know. Short hair, beard. He'll have a neck tatt next."

"It's only a beard man, chill out."

"Well, you never know, they're all like that down there."

"Where?"

"Wellington."

"Like what?"

"You know, craft beer, chilli, Wu Tang, Miley Cyrus, fire pits, sudoku, Pokémon."

"What are you trying to say, Bento?"

"Well, it's not the beard capital of the South for nothing is it?"

The monkey chitters but Mark is already out of the car and walking towards his brother by the time Bento reaches the word 'beard'.

"What happened to you?" The younger sibling shouts to the older.

Before he could answer, Bento bellows from the open car door. "*Dude!* Customs, was it? Sniffer dogs?" The intonation rising through the word 'dogs', "rubber gloves?"

"The fuck are you on about?" Laughs Kevin, addressing Bento while in an embrace with his brother, "phones munted. Dropped it on the boat, landed in some water. I think I've broken the SIM card, seems to come on, but the screen goes blank. I wonder whether it's shorted or something."

"Clone it."

"Clone it? That's a bit extreme, eh?"

"Well, you can still clone it even when it gets shorted"

"I know but, cloning it? What is this? Communist Russia?"

"Nah, you can clone it? Even if the SIM *is* shorted, you can just clone it, can't you? You have to put a blank SIM in another handset. You can send a full copy of it. You don't lose any data. Even what's stored on the phone itself. I've got the cables and the software for it. We can use my laptop."

"Well, if you can."

"You can have one of my old handsets. I've got loads. Probably got an iPhone in my drawer if you're lucky. And then we can get a blank SIM on the way home. It's easy."

As the four of them pile back into the Prado, Kevin calls shotgun and opens the passenger door. He sees the monkey on the back seat. "What's with the monkey?" he says.

"I rescued him from a cigarette factory."

"Did he just finish that Rubix Cube?"

"The monkey does what it wants."

The Beatles are playing *Come Together* on the stereo, it soundtracks the drive up Ocean View Road, past the radio station, the library and the WINZ office in Oneroa.

"Hey, I got a promotion at work," says Kevin.

"At the Tax Office?" says Bento.

"Yeah, I'm on rebates now and I look after wait-room programming too. It's hardly quantum physics, but I do seem to have a knack for it. Anyway, what about you Bento? I've not seen you in ages. What are you doing now? Is there a woman? What about your job? What do you do?"

"Oh, you know, a little bit of this and a little bit of that."

"Go on."

"I write software freelance, so I'm doing that all the time. In my last job, I was working at this place that investigated insurance claims. You know, getting phones and computers going again. Forensics. Security"

"What about a woman?"

"Nah, no woman. I seem to repel them, not sure why."

The monkey mocks crying by rubbing his eyes and sticking out his bottom lip as the road dips and snakes its way through Surfdale, down Alison Road and on up to the roundabout by the school. It crosses the causeway, turns by the boatyard and the statue of the Ram with the bollock-bells that stands by the parking at the League fields. A quick stop at the Countdown to buy a SIM and then home.

Let the good times roll.

"Who's Yolanda Samant?" Bento is leaning against the kitchen counter pulling on a fat spliff.

"Eh?" Mark suddenly off-guard, "What? Well, erm, oh er, just, you know, an old colleague, yeah. Worked with her at Radiohub. What of it?"

"Oh right," nodding the head, eyebrows raised, bottom lip protruding, "'cos erm, she's signed into Facebook over there on your computer. That's a bit weird don't you think?"

"Who, w, w, what the fuck are you talking about?"

"Yeah man. *And* Yolanda has been stalking *your ex-girlfriend* on that computer," pointing, "*there*." The sarcasm drips from Bento's voice.

"What's this?" Kevin joins in.

"Your Mark's a stalker."

"Nah."

"Stalking the ex online, he's been." Bento passing the joint to Kevin.

"No, I haven't."

"Yeah, ya have. I mean. *Please.*" Bento, incredulous, palms up, face screwed up in mock indignation. "This m'brother, is textbook stalking. You see it all the time in the forensics game. This Yolanda Samant right, I'll bet it's one of Liz's old colleagues, a schoolmate or something." He's right.

"Oh, I don't know about that man. I wouldn't say it's stalking."

"I would."

"Pfft."

"Nah man it's stalking. It's text-book stalking. I'm not judging you for it. I'm just telling you what it is. Don't shoot the messenger," Bento says, laughing. "You're pretending to be Yolanda Samant so you can stalk Liz, that's clearly what's happening here. I bet you've got her profile on your phone too."

He does. "Oh, fuck off."

"I never knew what you saw in her anyway. I mean, she wasn't all that. She had a humpback for a start. Going around looking like Quasimodo," then switching to a voice mocking of a stroke victim, "It was the bells, Ezmerelda. It was the bells that made me deaf." Nobody says anything and Bento continues, "she had that thing with her nose and her face too. You know. Like she had shit on her top lip and she's trying not to smell it."

"Stop talking," snaps Mark and Bento does, for about seven seconds until, resisting it no more.

"Put a bit of weight on though, eh? Absolutely piled it on. What if she's pregnant? Hope not. I mean, she'll never get her figure back after that. You only have to look at the mother," Bento, riffing, "arse like a rhino. I saw her out jogging on The Strand the other day. Black yoga pants. Looked like a looped GIF of couple-a bulldogs fighting in a bin-bag. Should'a seen it man. Shit's hypnotic. Should'a put it on TikTok."

"And you wonder why you're single," says Mark.

"What do you mean by that?"

"You sound like a misogynist talking about women like that."

"Talking about women like what?" he replies, "this is all stuff I'd say about a man. I mean, I'm an equal opportunity offender. I don't care that it's a woman, man. I just don't want my eyes being drawn to the movement of the mass. You know, especially when I'm trying to drive the car on a tight road with a bus oncoming. It's dangerous to be distracting drivers like that. You can't stop looking at it. And anyway, I say what I see man, say what I see. It looked like a block of black jelly in a mega-thrust earthquake."

"Please stop talking,' says Mark.

It doesn't stay quiet for long, then Kevin speaks up, addressing his brother, "You need to focus on the things that you can change, brother. Get a job. Get some exercise. Get out more. Be happy."

"Well, I've got one job at least."

"You do?"

"Yeah, I've got a mowing job down at Passage Rock on Tuesdays. Oh yeah, I've got that interview on Monday too."

"Interview?" Kevin says surprised.

"Monday?" Bento equally so.

"Yeah."

"Doing what?"

"Adverts at a radio station."

"Really? I thought you'd pissed on your chips with radio," Kevin says.

"Which station?" Bento.

"Radio Christ."

"Jesus! Radio Christ?"

"They'll be trying to convert you, won't they?" Bento asks.

"Yeah, that's what I'd heard too, compulsory God-bothering."

"I'll just say, I am, if they ask."

"When's the interview?"

"Nine."

"Nine in the morning?"

"Well, it's not going to be at night, is it?"

"Yeah, but nine's pretty early."

"Duh."

"Aren't they in Eden Terrace?"

"Yeah."

"But you'd have to be on the 7:30 boat for that one. There's no chance you're making that."

"'Course I will."

"I thought we were getting on it this weekend though?" says Kevin.

"Well, *you* can. I might rein it in. I need that job. I'm broke."

"Whatever, man, stop being a pussy," Bento says, "we're crashing on Catlove's boat. We've got a kitty going for piss and Nikehead's organised some MDMA and an ounce of weed."

"Really?" Mark says with some interest.

"Yeah, but you know, you're reining it in, so you won't want any will you?" Bento says.

"Well, I'll smoke a bit of weed, but that'll be all," Mark says, suddenly tempted.

"You'd better be dressing up, you're not getting out of that, I've already ordered the costumes," Bento says.

"And what are we dressing up as?"

"It's a surprise."

Chapter 7

THE SURPRISE

Saturday, 16th November – 05:30

Exercise has always been important to Bento, *and* just before dawn, come rain, come shine, he does his training. He'd developed a new routine since moving in. Starting the day by running around the block four times, then doing fifteen-minutes of exercises on the playground, a twenty-minute swim in the ocean, and all before dawn. When he finishes his exercises, he stretches on the edge of the beach where McMillan and Wairua Roads meet. The Tamaki Strait is in front of him, seven kilometres of open water, Maraetai on the other side. Half a click to his left, the sky lights itself, shimmering over the rocky ridge on Okoka Road. Metres to his right, a large Pohutukawa is crouching in over her mutant relative, the wooden bench.

With his routine done for the day, Bento accepts the day's mail from the local postman and walks up the driveway opening all the envelopes as he goes. He's happy. It's the day of the Sun Festival. The old gang is getting back together and sailing to Tāpapakanga Regional Park, some, twenty K's south.

Four hours later, just around ten, the three make their way to it. Clambering into the Prado for the ten-minute drive to meet the rest of the crew at Pūtiki Bay.

"Can we make a quick stop at the Countdown? I need to get a couple of things." Mark says as the car waits by the T-Junction where the quarry is.

"Yeah, bro."

Three minutes later, two K on, Bento has parked his car in the loading bay by the entrance at the shops. Over on the bench where people tie their dogs up, a white busker with ginger dreadlocks approaches the chorus of

Nirvana's *Rape Me*. A young mother and her toddler twins, exiting the shop, fail to notice. Mark skips past them, and through the sliding doors.

Dance Monkey by Tones and I is playing on the inside, 'Radio Countdown, bustin' loose,' goes the sting over the top of the song's middle eight. On a subconscious level, the music is programming Mark with the urge to buy more goods than what he'd gone in for and he eyes the specials in the chocolate section as he walks on by it. He feels good, for once, excited for the day, content even. He'd not felt as happy as this for ages. Maybe things were changing. A job interview on Monday. Laughter around the house. He'd even refrained from using Yolanda Samant's Facebook profile for a good 24 hours.

In the seconds that follow, Mark is standing at the personal hygiene section, facing the shelves, when he feels a presence behind him. A familiar one. A dear fragrance. He turns and it is her. Liz. Bento was right. She *does* look pregnant. Her boobs look enormous. She's radiant. Beautiful. Her red hair, longer now, wavy, just around the shoulders. The skin, milky white with freckles. Those deep sapphire eyes, the ones he'd met on the bus to school all those years ago. The ones he'd spent hours gazing into.

"Liz."

"G'day Mark, how ya goin?" Her voice is soft, exuding pity.

For a second, he's unable to form the words. It's as if a finger is pressing on his Adam's apple. "Okay. You?" Clipped.

"Yeah, good, yeah, well we just got back from Queenstown yesterday. One of Gav's conferences."

Right Shoulder – 'Gav?' What wank.

"Oh, right, and?"

"I heard your cricket game."

"You did?"

"Yeah. Jay Dicks called you a cunt on air."

"Oh, you heard that?"

"Yeah, everyone heard it. I hear they fired you, you poor thing."

"Yeah," an awkward pause.

"Erm, well, I've got some big news, not sure you're going to want to hear it though."

"But you're going to tell me, anyway, aren't you?" Arms folded across his chest.

Left Shoulder – Here it comes.

"We're having a baby."

Nothing now, just numbness, "Congratulations." His heart had just been scooped out of his chest with a rusty auld spoon in aisle eight. That was supposed to have been *his* baby. He was the one who'd put in the hard yards for that little fucker. Now it was Gavin Gregson's. Gregson the snake. Cucked by his best mate, could it get any worse?

"She's due in May, I'm terrified." The ache pulses. He's missed her so much. "So, what are you going to do for a job now?"

Right Shoulder - None of your fucking business, you insincere bitch.

"I don't want to talk about it."

"We should probably get together for a coffee some time eh, have a little catch up, a debrief, I'd like that."

"A debrief? What? Of our relationship? For future learnings? Probably not eh," incredulously.

"Oh well, er, I hope one day we can, Mark. I've missed you."

"Yeah, and I've missed you," he could have cried.

Left Shoulder – Hold it together.

"I've got to go. Kev's on the island. He's outside. We're on our way to the Sun Festival."

"Oh, the Sun Festival, cool. Well, tell him I say hi, eh?"

Right Shoulder – Yeah, whatever.

Walking away, any spring that Mark may have had in his step is gone. Replaced by the gait of the zombie dragging its bad leg behind it as it lurches up the street in rags. Mark Goodenough has been gutted out here and as he operates the self-service checkout, his head buzzes. The scab has been pulled. It will most definitely be leaving a scar.

Right Shoulder – Harden up, soft cock.

Bento pulls up at the Wharf Road boat ramp in Pūtiki Bay by the 'All You Need is Love' sign, and then, from shore by dinghy, the crew of seven shuttle aboard *Yesterday* in about ten minutes. This is Kevin's crew, his old mates from school. Dominic Catlove has the boat, Conrad Shoulderpuss, the big lad with the soft touch and the rhotacistic speech impediment is the security. Nikehead gets the drugs and Bento, the funny cunt, organises everything else. No one really knew what Kevin Goodenough did. Today, Mark is the tag-along of the most expendable.

An hour out, *Yesterday* sails the south flank of Waiheke Island. She cast right at Te Whau point and skimmed the rocky headlands at Whakanewha, Awaawaroa, and Te Matuku Bays, sailing past secret mansions with manicured lawns and five-mile driveways. This is where the real money is. Aboard, in the galley Bento changes up the music, and the opening peal of *Fanfare for the Common Man* starts playing.

"Attention please!" he says in his kingly accent pulling three bulging black bin bags in close, "Fancy dress time!" He opens the first of the bin bags, "Ladies and gentlemen, boys and girls, let me present to you, your evening wear. For one night only!" A pause, "emu jockey!!" he sings those last two words, "Observe."

He then climbs into this strange costume, which, at first glance looks like a cross between a tutu and a snake, the silks of a horse-racing jockey. Bento's silks are blue and have a red star at the sternum. Next, he puts the tights on, nylon, brown. It looks like he likes it. More than he should.

Above the tights, there's a wide brown plumage from which a fake pair of legs dangle and rest in a pair of pretend stirrups at each hip. The pink emu neck protrudes from his groin. It is long and attached at the jaw by a leather rein and when moved, it looks like it's got a mind of its own. It is indeed an emu jockey. Everyone is laughing. Everyone except for Mark, who has been distant since the Countdown, and is already on his fifth beer, where everyone else is on two.

Another half hour has passed and in *Yesterday's* galley Bento and Kevin sit opposite at the table, dressed as emu jockeys. The monkey, also at the table, is skinning up a big fat bifta, after popping two Tuis open for the boys. The monkey has a beer of its own, but don't tell anyone at WISCA, they'll hit the roof. Still, has the odd cig too here and there, but he does that on his own dime. People say it's animal cruelty, but the monkey is living his best life. The radio is on 95bfm which is carrying psychedelic pop and irreverent chat.

"The fuck's wrong with your brother?" It was unusual for Bento to show concern for anyone other than himself, "he's been acting weird ever since we got on this boat."

"Fucken oath he has."

"Hardly said anything since we got aboard and he's fucken caning it, eh?"

"Well, I mean, these are *my* friends. That'd be a bit awkward for him."

"Nah man. He's dark. Something's bugging him. He's tanning the piss a too bit much eh."

"Reckon?"

"Yeah, man. I'd be keeping an eye on him."

Once, there'd have been a time when Kevin would've put his arm around his little brother. He'd have taken him to one side, and they'd have had a quiet little chat. Unfortunately, Kevin's judgment is also impaired, in so much as he is several Tuis deep himself. Besides, programming hold music at the Tax Office has hardened him emotionally, "Oh, fuck it, she'll be right, give him some of that MDMA. That'll cheer the cunt up."

Viewed from above, *Yesterday* sails steady on the drink, raising a wake of white bubbles behind her as she threads the needle between Ponui and Pakihi Islands. Aboard, the scene is loose. Her crew bathing in an orgy of beer, weed and selfies. All of them wearing emu jockey outfits. One and a half slabs of Tui, ransacked. Mark, the thirstiest of the shipmates.

"What about those contact lenses? Didn't you say there were lenses coming too?" Shoulderpuss says.

"Ah yes, the wenses, I almost forgot about the wenses." Bento receiving a dirty look from Shoulderpuss as he fingers the inside of his wash bag. Then, in no time, he is randomly doling out six pairs of lenses to the group, each getting set to claw them onto their eyeballs. When Mark checks himself in toilet mirror a moment or so later, he slurs loudly.

"Hey, mine are dollar signs."

Everyone else had emu eyes.

"They must have made an error at the lens place," offers Shoulderpuss.

"An ewwow at the wens pwace? Cool story, bro," Bento mocking, and pulling at the loose bit, trying for a reaction from Shoulderpuss.

"Why don't you just fuck off I can work through my speech impediment with a therapist, but you'll always be a short cunt. You need shoe risers, you fucken short man syndrome, weirdo."

"Thewapist."

The monkey chitters.

🐨

At dusk, *Yesterday* takes her place in a flotilla of fifty vessels a hundred metres from the beach at Tāpapakanga Regional Park and Catlove brings it to anchor. On the beach, adjacent to the sea stands the main stage, before which hundreds of people mill about aimlessly. The six crewmates are raring to go. Just one more photo, one of the group in their emu jockey gear, then, one last job. Nikehead drops to the galley, pulls out the stash of MDMA then proceeds to split the powder into five smaller piles.

"Do a sixth one," Bento says.

"What for?"

"For him," he says pointing at Mark.

"I thought he wasn't having any."

"Course he fucken is."

"You know I am here," says Mark, who looks ridiculous in his green and white, hooped racing-silk, white cap, and emu jockey fancy dress.

"Well, do you want some or not?"

"Yeah man," Mark says slurring, "I'm not watching you cunts get munted, while I sit there drinking water like that tool from Coldplay."

"Which one?"

"The singer."

"Guy Martin?" Kevin says.

"No."

"Steve Martin?" Nikehead offers.

"It's Chris Martin, you fucken retards," says Shoulderpuss.

"Chwis Mawtin?"

"Dickhead."

"Yeah, whoever the fuck it is, cut me in."

Nikehead then fashions six small envelopes out of paper, into which he pours each of the six piles that have been made. Then, leaning in he says, "now you need to be careful with this stuff. It's as strong as fuck. Don't do too much at once. Just do a quarter to start with."

"How long does it take to kick in?"

"About an hour."

About an hour later, the emu jockeys are standing together ahead of the left side of the stage.

"Feeling it yet?" Asks Shoulderpuss.

"I don't think so," Kevin replies.

"Nah, nothing. I hope it wasn't fucken chalk man," says Catlove.

"Nah, didn't taste like chalk," Nikehead says.

"You'd know, would you?" Bento.

"I might take some more," Mark says.

"Wooaaah, I wouldn't do that if I were you," Catlove pleads, pushing his palms out.

"Nah, fuck it," Mark says wasted and unfazed, and he wraps the remaining three-quarters of his MDMA into half a Zigzag cigarette paper which he then forms into a small ball. Then he takes a swig from his beer, drops the parcel in his mouth and swallows it.

A flash of concern flashes across Catlove's face as he jogs from foot to foot on the spot. It is funny, because it makes it look like the emu is eager to get going. "Shouldn't have done that eh. You'll be munted," Catlove says, stretching the word 'munted' out, so as to emphasise how munted he thought Mark was going to be.

Ten minutes later.

"It's coming on," Shoulderpuss quips.

"Yep," says Kevin.

The monkey chitters.

"Yeah, I got it," Catlove, tingling down his spine.

"Mmm mmm," Bento.

It's starting to work on Mark now too. His first indication is a wave of nausea creeping up his back. It's the Tuis. They want out.

"Man, you really shouldn't have taken the rest of that E dude."

"I'll be ok. Look I'm just off to the water station, wait here," and with that, Mark drifts off into the melee. It is the last anyone will see of him until he swims up to *Yesterday* at eleven the following morning drenched and still wearing the emu jockey suit.

Chapter 8

THE VIRAL SHAME

Sunday, 17th November – 17:32

"Wake up dickhead, you're famous!" Kevin says, from the foot of Mark's bed. At his side, Bento squats holding hands with the monkey, offering out his phone while grinning. They're all still buzzing from the early afternoon MDMA chaser they'd shared on the way home. Not the monkey of course. By contrast, Mark is splayed out eastwards on his mattress. He's only been asleep for an hour, ample time for a new variance of moss to start flourishing about his gums, for his teeth to turn to sandpaper and for his eyes to burn like piss-holes in the snow.

"What?" Mark spits with nauseous indignation.

"Here, look," Bento enthusiastically thrusting the phone out again.

"The fuck are you waking me up for, dickhead?"

"Take it."

Without looking at either of them Mark reluctantly reaches for the phone and watches the video that's been primed. Then comes the response, when, with the slow relentlessness of the hydraulic press, Mark's jaw begins to drop. It is the reaction Bento is looking for.

"Wellity, wellity, well, this sheds a bit of light on what happened to you last night doesn't it?" 'This' just happened to be the funniest thing Bento has been a part of since he drew a dick on a dog with a vivid as a kid. Peak funny, comedy platinum. He can't hold it in any longer, and he belches out a peal of laughter, which sets Kevin off too. Before they know it, the pair of them are barking like a pair of harbour seals on a fish-finding drive.

"Fuck fuck fuck fuck fuck!" Mark says in abject horror.

"It's going viral bro!" Bento says through hard laughter, "five thousand views, in only four hours," wheezing.

"Fuck off."

"Well, what did you expect? There's no way that does not get filmed."

The monkey chitters in delight.

"Jesus!"

"Ha! He's not gonna help you, but maybe you could ask your mates at Radio Christ. See if they'll put in a word for you tomorrow when you do your interview. Ha ha ha!" Bento, doubled over, banging his hand on the bed. Howling.

"Fuck off cunt!"

It's absolute bedlam between Kevin and Bento, but at least Mark won't need to find a short descriptor for this episode, it already has a name.

"And look at the title!" Bento is struggling to get the words through the laughter. *Waster in Emu Suit Looks for Drugs in Own Vomit.*

Then Kevin settles, puts his arm on his brother's shoulder and, adopts a more responsible tone saying, "you've got an interview at a Christian broadcaster first thing in the morning, and your face is all over TikTok wasted on drugs. Not a good look."

"The cap obscures my face."

"Barely," Kevin says.

"Cool story, bro," Bento still laughing.

"How'd that even happen anyway?" Kevin asks, trying to get to the bottom of it.

It's a struggle to recall the events of the previous night, but Mark gives it a go, "well, I felt sick after I left you lot, and I do remember vomiting, but to be honest, that's pretty much all I can recall."

What had happened was this...

Struggling with nausea, Mark came up short of the Portaloos and he vomited under the light by the falafel stand bins. The first quarter of the MDMA he'd taken was affecting him. The rest of it, the second, much bigger bit, the bit that'd never been digested, was still wrapped in the Zigzag paper, and its sitting in the middle of the pool of vomit. Through flickering eyesight, he tries to salvage it, but the first bit of MDMA, the bit that was currently working was having a negative effect on his hand to eye co-ordination, and as much as he tried, Mark couldn't physically make his fingers pluck the Zigzag ball from the puddle. It didn't stop him from trying though. In fact, he kept at it enough that a small crowd assembled and filmed it from all angles.

"Well, I was pretty wasted."

"Everyone was wasted mate, no one else was fingering their own chunder."

The monkey chitters.

There follows a pause of about ten seconds, then Kevin pipes up, "hey, have you heard about that rain that's coming through? Tomorrow morning, you need to be careful on that scooter."

"Yep, supposed to be heavy, you better get up extra early doofus."

Mark's mind is alive again.

Right Shoulder – Fucking stupid cunt, allowing yourself to be in that that video.

Left Shoulder – Interview!

Thirteen hours and counting.

Right Shoulder – Maybe you should do yourself in?

Left Shoulder – Get a shower.

A pleasant shower. Warm, insistent. Mint Source shower gel about his nether regions, delivering upon his bollocks, arsehole, and the rim of his bellend an authentic menthol freshness. Content in his glow, he shuts off the shower and steps out of the cubicle, when suddenly his foot slips forward on the wet tiled floor. On a reflex his right hand reaches out and he grabs at the shower curtain, ripping the hooks at the top. The other arm flailing into the only mirror in the house, shattering it beyond use and carving a deep forearm laceration. The blood is quick, and Mark goes to stem it, before he does that, he wipes the water from his eyes, but the towel has been used to clean up a spot of monkey ejaculate. Now he has monkey spunk on his hands and face, his lips and nose. Some of it went in his mouth. He can taste it. It's disgusting, it has a weird salty taste and a cream like texture. It is all over his face and he bleeds as he struggles with monkey jiz. Trading towels and hoping for the best.

"Fucken monkey!" He shouts angrily, while his inner turmoil keeps on.

Right Shoulder – Liz would've done a better job. She'd have cleaned it, gently wrapped it in a soft bandage but she left you because you're a fucken loser. Cuck-boy.

Chapter 9

THE CHRIST PUNCHER

Monday, 18th November - 07:12

All is quiet in the Goodenough family residence, a two storey, painted white bach in weatherboard cladding by the beach. Jutting from the bush, this is the last house in the street. Its occupants, Mark Goodenough, Kevin Goodenough, Bento and his monkey, each out cold. They're sleeping the hedonist's sleep and imaginary stacks of the letter Z are piling up above them, each of the consonants dissipating like smoke into nothingness the higher they get.

NNNNNNNN
NNNNNNNN
NNNNNNNN

Mark's alarm is going off. It's one of those old clock radios. Mum's silver Sony. There's a large round snooze button built into the top of its plastic housing. It isn't a gentle alarm like the ones you get on your Samsung. Oh no, this has a staccato scream that can gnaw at a man's very soul.

NNNNNNNN
NNNNNNNN
NNNNNNNN

It's the second time it's gone off that morning. Dismissed at six by the base of his fist. Now he's moving, slowly at first, hauling himself forward into his pillow like a giant walrus temporarily roused from basking on a rock. The gash is the first thing he notices. The stinging of it is raw. A small, slug-like mucus-ball clings to where his nose meets his throat. It wants to be grunted out, but it remains out of reach. His head is vacant. His body is as rough as guts, and then a memory starts to emerge from the fog of his mind.

Four hours earlier, Mark seethes on the couch. Just him. He's entirely occupied by his phone and the blue beam of misery it casts down his right arm, and directly into the hippocampus. Yes, it was just as she'd told him in the Countdown. They'd been to Queenstown, and they wanted everyone to know about it. 'Gloating' is how some would describe it. Mark Goodenough, stalking the comments section of her latest Facebook story, scanning the wishes of the friends of friends as he comes down from his MDMA high.

"*Gawjuss hun. Mwaaa! :)*" Chloe Mitchum

"*Sole mates.*" Dan Ruthers

"*Massive improvement girl!!*" Tenile Soloeli

"*You go girl.*" Nicole Cleepers.

"*Handsome couple.*" Danny Fractions.

"*Must of bin a good trip.*" Gary Stackstreader.

"*Good to see you've cast of the dead wood. Yaaas Queen!*" Shenny Gipley.

"*Struggling to walk after a holiday like that sister? LOL*" Destiny Hansen. This one also featured a succession of aubergine emojis.

"*Congrats you two, always knew you'd get together sometime. Love you, Mum.*"

That last one had been liked by fifteen people. All of whom Mark knew. Turns out Gavin Gregson had popped the question. The cheesy prick had done it on a mountaintop with a photographer present.

Right Shoulder – A professional photographer at a spontaneous marriage proposal. Fucking Brilliant. You were too stupid to think of that.

She'd failed to mention the engagement when he'd seen her at the Countdown. Then again there'd always been things omitted with her.

Right Shoulder – I wonder if I'll get an invite

Left Shoulder – you're late!!

The shower isn't happening now, nor the shit, nor the shave. No combing. No ironing. Instead, Mark flattens his hair with his hands, throws on his least creased shirt, and steps into his only suit. No time for coffee. No breakfast, nothing. Rushing around in the half-light of his room, he gauges the intensity of the rain by its sound on the roof. Teeming. Heavy drops. He has no time to change into the waterproofs or for the detour up Glen Brook Road. He'll *have* to go past Liz and Gavin's.

As he approaches their place on O'Brien Road, Mark sees Gavin's black Raptor on the couple's steep driveway. And there, standing in the rain at the driver's side door, stopping to watch Mark on his little red scooter, straining up the hill, is his old mate Gavin Gregson. The Great Betrayer. He gives no acknowledgement, but Mark gives him the fingers anyway and carries on past the ends of Okoka and Te Whau Roads, through another major rain event.

Right Shoulder – Look at the state of you. Cucked. Wet. You're not going to get this job anyway, what's the fucken point?

Left Shoulder – Ignore that.

He rides past the Countdown, and swings right onto Wharf Road. The rain is coming down in sheets now. By the boatyard, Gavin Gregson's big black Raptor barrels dangerously by and Mark takes a drenching from the vehicle's outsized Maxxis tyres.

At the Mātiatia ferry building he looks like a drowned rat in a cheap suit, and he scurries aboard the boat and into the humidity of the main cabin, where exotic human body odours coalesce through the main cabin, Château des Feet, L'eau du Piss, and Parfum du Armpit. It is rank and Mark is uncomfortable in his wet clothing.

At no time as of yet that morning has Mark even thought about *Waster in Emu Suit Looks for Drugs in Own Vomit*. He remembers somewhere in the Motuihe channel.

Right Shoulder – Fifteen thousand views in sixteen hours, dickhead.

He arrives at the Christ Network with one minute to spare, the first impression is the colour of the place. Everything in the building is painted white, the desks, the chairs, the walls. Everything. Chaste and modest, clean and bright. There are two rows of four cubicles, where four young men and four young women are seated. They all wear white. Notwithstanding the fact that he is piss wet through, this is as close to Heaven as Mark Goodenough had ever been. What told him it wasn't Heaven, was the music. Someone called Josh Groban is singing a song called *You raised me up,* a sound which successfully dials in with the unidimensional aesthetic of the room's colour scheme.

"Like, Good Morning Sir, my name is erm, Gretchen, welcome to erm Radio Christ. Erm, like. How, erm, can I help you?"

During their interaction, Gretchen doesn't meet Mark's gaze once. Then, she sends him off to the long white leather couch by the window. Mark sits on it and the leather makes a loud bawwing noise as he does, exacerbated somewhat by the damp of his clothing.

Within a moment, the lean frame of, five-foot nine boomer and local media magnate, Roger Shilbottle emerges from his office.

"You didn't have to have a shower for the interview," Roger loves the gag, but then again, his smugness is legendary in the Auckland radio scene, pouring as it does from every cell of his being. All the time. Twenty-four-seven, three-six-five. A self-made multi-millionaire, with a seat next to Jesus in Heaven. The chosen one. He's always well-tailored, is Roger, but his most remarkable features are his rosy cheeks and forehead which measures about four rugby paddocks in length. This behemoth forehead is punctuated by two black eyebrows. He wears a grey moustache; it has a brushing of black running through it. His grip is firm at first, but the handshake withers, as quickly as Roger's eyes widen.

Right Shoulder – He's recognised you off TikTok, ya fucken tool.

Left Shoulder – It won't be that.

Together, the pair walk on over to the Radio Christ meeting rooms, where, sitting behind a long table, a thirty-something woman from the company's People and Culture department called Fiona Tuckery is waiting. Fiona has mouse brown hair, which is wild and makes her look like she's been electrocuted. She is boss-eyed too, one of her eyeballs is out shopping, and the other's coming back with the change. But that's not all. The poor woman has teeth like a witch doctor's necklace and two of them overbite her bottom lip.

Right Shoulder – Good job she works in radio.

"Have we met before?" She asks.

"No, I don't think so."

"It's just that you look so familiar." It is *Waster in Emu Suit Looks for Drugs in Own Vomit,* but Fiona is yet to make that connection, "maybe it's church, which church do you go to?"

"I go to lots of different churches." A nervous chuckle. "Wherever I lay my hat, you know?" He lies. Uncomfortable in the wet clothing that is tight upon his skin.

"But don't you live on Waiheke? Wouldn't you go to the one in Ostend?"

"Er, yeah, yeah, mainly."

"So, you'll know Reverend Tipene then."

Mark has no idea who Reverend Tipene is. "Yes, saw him in the Countdown yesterday."

"The Countdown?"

"Yeah, the Countdown, if you live on Waiheke, you always run into people you know in the Countdown."

"I thought you would've known him from church."

"Well, yeah, but you know I saw him in the Countdown, as well."

After that it's a case of *auto-interview* and going through the motions. Feigning the interest, hardening the sell. Playing up his skills and his contacts. On the face of it, it seems to be going well, except that is, for a weird tension in the room. Eye contact, minimal with Roger, impossible with Fiona whose wayward eyeballs only make matters worse. What also strikes Mark as weird is how the pair of them stifle a giggle when the subject of salary expectations comes up. That's a first in an interview. And the weirdness goes on.

"You saw sense then?" Roger says as talk turns to Mark's previous experience.

"Sense?"

"Well, says here that you worked at an Access Radio station. The one on Waiheke."

"Oh right," confused, "I mean I volunteered there as a kid."

Suddenly Roger's demeanour changed, "Pffft. It's unbelievable that they get *that* frequency for free. No one even listens to it. Should be ours. We do *real* good for real people."

Roger's diatribe doesn't stop at Access Radio, he has something to say about student radio station, 95bfm, and the city's Iwi stations too. In Roger's mind it's a waste of taxpayers' money giving away sought-after space on the frequency spectrum, especially when there are stations that are prepared to spend large with other people's tithing cash. God's work should be getting priority, and to get God's work done, Roger only needs one thing.

[Angelic singing]
And lo it is written that Roger Shilbottle will be the CEO and major shareholder of The Christ Network. Owners of the frequency 89.0FM in the Garden of Mount Eden. Auckland City.
[/Angelic singing]

As Mark leaves the interview room, a young woman with a crucifix around her neck approaches him from the bank of white desks. The woman's name is Chelsea. Her name badge says so. She is a reporter from the newsroom and wants to know whether Mark is keen to take part in an on-air debate about the dangers of drugs. In five minutes.

Right Shoulder – I told you it was a waste of time. Even she knows.

"No."

"Can I get a selfie then?"

"No."

On leaving the offices of *Radio Christ*, Mark ambles back up to Symonds Street and waits two minutes for a bus. Climbing aboard, the driver breaks into a chorus of *For the Love of Money*, the old O'Jay's number from the TV show *The Apprentice*.

Right Shoulder – He's taking the piss out of you.

Left Shoulder – He's not. He's just eccentric. A singing bus driver. They do exist.

In minutes, the bus is at the Britomart, right in the centre of the city, but by the time Mark crosses Quay Street, the ferry has already cast its mooring. The next boat isn't for another hour, so he sits on one of the public benches by the ticket booth, weighing up his options.

An obese man in black jogging bottoms and an *Ed Sheeran* T-shirt takes an over the shoulder selfie of him.

Of the two shoulders, the right side is the most efficacious of the voices, and Mark soon scuttles away to find the closest pub. Somewhere quiet, somewhere close. Somewhere that does a pint. A place where a chip is called a chip and not a potato wedge. At the top of the steps at the *QF Tavern*, the barman looks at Mark and chuckles.

"In for the pokies bro?"

"No, just a drink mate."

"You sure?" The barman says quizzically.

Right Shoulder – Now he's recognised you.

"Yeah man."

"Riiiight."

As the barman is pouring the pint, Mark slips off to the gents to wash his hands and face. It is then that he catches sight of himself in the mirror. It is the first time he's seen himself in a day or so, and as he does, the bell chimes. The penny drops. It becomes clear. All the weird shit. The sly snigger between Roger and Fiona when talk had turned to remuneration. The song of the bus driver. The barman and his quip about the pokies. Yes, now he knows.

The dollar sign contact lenses from Saturday night were still in his eyes.

Chapter 10

THE NEWS BULLETIN

Tuesday, 19th November – 12:10

The lunchtime news quietly goes about its business from the Samsung telly that's built into the kitchen joinery. As it does, Kevin and Bento sip coffee and finger their phones on the breakfast bar. The news bulletin is talking about the release from prison of neo-Nazi, henchman and leader of the New Zealand National Front, Caleb McGill who is at the end of a two stretch for ABH on a Muslim. The sound is low, but the closed caption subtitles at the bottom of the screen allow Mark to follow on. McGill faces the camera as Bento looks up and clocks it.

"Oooh, face like a bag of boiled bollocks that one. Woof! Child frightener."

They both laugh and Mark is in and out of attention. Frying bacon with his good hand, and casually watching TV. The word 'radio' being spoken on the news piques his attention properly. The image above the newsreader's Left Shoulder features a radio behind a no entry sign. He turns it up.

"Shhh."

Journalist - "Despite howls of derision from Bay of Plenty locals, Broadcasting Minister and Act Party MP Jamie Saddleback, today announced the dissolution of one of the country's fourteen government-funded community Access Radio stations."

"Radio Te Puke had served thirty thousand people in the Western Bay of Plenty for the last twenty-five years, giving a voice in the mediascape to ordinary residents, but that all came to a dead stop last night when the station, blighted by ill-discipline, broadcast its very last signal.

The report then cuts to vox-pops, a series of short interviews featuring many different people and lasting no more than five seconds each. As each talking head changes, Bento gives voice to the new one's most prominent facial attributes.

Vox pop 1 - "Aww, there were tears, yeah, I'm still a bit choked up now to be honest." A middle-aged woman in a giraffe onesie, fanning her eyeballs.

"Oi pyjamas, you've got a nose like a crushed éclair," says Bento.

Vox pop 2 - "Yeah, it'll be missed alright." A man with a mullet and a big slack jaw.

"Dickchin," says Bento.

Vox pop 3 - "I've been coming down to the station to do my ska show for over ten years now, I don't know what I'll do now, I'm gutted." A man with bulbous cheeks.

"Hey Cheeks! Get those golf balls out your mouth!!" Says Bento.

The piece then cuts to the Minister for Broadcasting, Jamie Saddleback standing behind a lectern, addressing a room.

"This prick. Again." Bento's tone becoming serious.

Minister Saddleback - "Access Radio has often been a hotbed for libellous comments and ill-thought-out content with very little penalty, and at the start of my tenure, I implemented measures aimed at bringing these broadcasters into line. Radio Te Puke has violated those measures, contravening on-air standards on more than five occasions over a twelve-month period, and it has cost them their status as Access broadcasters."

Journalist - "Saddleback implemented the five strikes and you're out policy in September of last year and Radio Te Puke is the second station to fall foul of the rule, after Radio Te Anau.

As the journalist speaks, a random shot of a broadcaster in a random studio fills the screen, then the New Zealand On Air offices in Ghuznee Street, Wellington. A ferry, a dog with headphones on, then a longshot of *The Beehive*. It cuts to a one-on-one interview with the Hon. Jamie Saddleback.

Saddleback - "This is a win for the ordinary New Zealand taxpayer. It's through these new measures, we've cleaned up the airwaves and we've saved the million dollars that were required to renew the station's frequency. Added to that, the three hundred thousand dollars in operational costs each year, a saving to the taxpayer of almost two million dollars."

Journalist - "Well what about those that say it's a valuable community resource?"

Saddleback - "Well, why aren't they tuning in to it then? Because I've looked at the numbers and no one's listening, meanwhile these stations cost millions of dollars every year while sitting on valuable frequencies that we should be selling off. And for what? So, two fifteen-year-old school children can share their recipe for crystal meth live on the radio during the school run?

"Look, it's no secret that I don't like Access Radio, I've always thought it was a waste of money and at a time of national austerity too. It's an affront to the taxpayer. I'm hopeful that going forward the measures I've implemented can save hardworking New Zealanders some of their hard-earned money."

An image of Oneroa Beach, Waiheke Island, then flashes up on the screen, and this is followed by a long shot of the Waiheke Island Radio station house.

"That's Oneroa," Bento says.

Journalist - "Meanwhile chair of the Association of Community and Access Broadcasters Mr Larry Minto said today he was appalled." The news report cuts to a man with a beard and glasses.

"Oh, I know him," Mark interjects, "he's from the radio station on the island."

"Shhhhhh!" Bento motions towards the TV and he, Kevin, Mark, and the monkey listen to Larry Minto lay out his opinion.

Larry Minto - "It's a disgrace, an affront to democracy. They've taken minority voices out of the Bay of Plenty and are collectively punishing a whole community for the actions of a few. It flies in the face of democracy. I'm just concerned it's the thin end of the wedge."

"I'll tell you what's an affront to democracy," Bento says, "that crooked cunt Saddleback. Him and his carpet bagging cronies, they fucken stole that election, everyone knows it, but no one wants to say anything."

"Oh, here we go."

"Nah man, they fucken did. They astroturfed it."

"They did what?"

"You know, astroturfed it, made out they were working for ordinary people, but it was all just corporate bullshit for corporate interests. Got rid of that smoking ban for Philip Morris didn't they, then he came for electric cars because the oil companies lobbied him for it, now it's this. Bullshit is what it is. The cunts used their bots to stir shit up too, didn't they? I mean, at least they legalised monkeys, but come on man, they were all over TikTok, and X spreading far-right bullshit and bogus solutions on the run up to that election."

"So? All politicians do that."

"Yeah well, it's dubious."

"You're oversimplifying it."

"Nah I'm not, I monitored it, the patterns were all there, man, I even set up my own bots to counteract them."

"Set up your own bots? Tony Stark now, eh?"

"Nah, man, there's a community of us."

"A community of bots?"

'A community of people who create bots for political reasons, just like them."

Kevin looks up from his phone to engage the pair, "you know there's a job going at Basil, Katz, Slipper, Foote, eh?"

"What? The law firm?"

"Yeah man, ninety grand a year too."

"Ninety? Really?" Mark's attention turns to the money. He's interested, forgetting how much he hates corporate New Zealand, forgetting why he left it to pursue a degree, to chase his radio dream. Forgetting the gruelling commute, forgetting about how he wants to follow in his dead father's footsteps. Factoring in the fact that he has the experience they seek. The four years of slog in his early twenties at another of the country's top-tier law firms, Mussell Dekker Biggs.

"Yeah."

"You should probably apply; you'd have a good chance."

Chapter 11

THE MEDICAL CENTRE

Wednesday, 20th November- 08:00

"Well, it's a 'no' from the Jesus lot," says Bento from the kitchen counter as he brandishes a letter with a logo on it.

"What?' Mark has just got up.

"Yeah man, they don't want you."

"What are you talking about?"

"They don't want you."

"Who?"

"Radio Christ, y'dickhead," and with that Bento thrusts an opened Radio Christ branded envelope towards Mark, "it's a rejection letter, isn't it?"

"Are you opening my mail now?" Mark says aghast.

"Yeah bro."

"You don't open someone else's mail."

"Well, I was first to the letter box, everyone knows that the person who brings the mail in from the post-box is the one who opens it."

"Nah."

"Yup."

"It's addressed to me."

"In a house *we* share."

"It's my mail fuck-knuckle. It's addressed to me. It's against the law to open someone else's mail."

"Nah."

"Yeah."

Bento is right. It is a rejection letter, and of all the rejection letters Mark

Goodenough ever got, this one, direct from the desk of Roger Shilbottle at Radio Christ is the quickest one he's ever got. From the moment Mark left Christ HQ, to the moment Bento was given the letter by the postman, there'd been a sub forty-six-hour turn-around time on it. Its contents, written large. The usual bullshit.

"Thanks for your interest, but..."

The rebuff comes as no surprise but the brutality in the promptness is noted and Mark, considers a similitude in the timing of this and of Gordon West's late-night emergency eject phone call on the boat, straight after *The Dead Air Incident* had happened. That's it now, the dream has a flat line. Humiliated at UNZ, unwelcome at Radiohub, and pegged as a drug fiend by the folks over at Radio Christ. All that remains in the radio sector is RNZ, two iwi stations, two Access stations and 95bFM. The latter is run by volunteers; the rest inhabited by job limpets. His mind is made up, back to IT it is. At least the money's good in IT.

🐶

The ride to out to Passage Rock is always a slog, especially if it's done on a scooter. Fourteen Ks from the Goodenough place. Mostly on a tar-sealed lane which meanders through the otherworldly landscape of the island's east-end. From the air, looks like videotape unspooled over a distressed green baize and from the ground it resembles the rolling green pastures of Teletubbyland. In amongst it, one of the island's best lookouts is at the layby just ahead of the pass on Orapiu Road, before the road disappears into the bush. Full spectrum out there. In the North out to Little Barrier, the sea around it dotted with smaller islands sprinkled up to Kawau further North. South to the Hunua Ranges. The City and Rangitoto in the middle, framed by the Waitākeres, where the distant television antennae sits at the highest point on the West Auckland ridge.

Mark isn't here for the view. He's been forced to stop. It's the arm. The vibration of the handlebar has made it worse. It smoulders and pulsates like the radioactive remnants of reactor number four at the Chernobyl power plant. The Elephant's Foot. The two painkillers he's taken too. Neither use nor ornament, either of them. He shakes his hand violently, trying to throw the pain away. With his good hand, he pulls out his phone to find two missed calls. One is from Bento's number; the other is from an Auckland number beginning with 357, probably the job at Basil, Katz, Slipper, Foote. No way of checking out here though, no signal.

Three hours later and Mark has been in the waiting room at the Gulf Medical Centre for twenty minutes. In the background, wafting from the speakers, the musical accompaniment has included the likes of Celene Dion, Ronan Keating and Boyz 2 Men. It is Radiohub's Boomer vehicle *Treat FM*, which, for Mark, holds all the treat appeal of a kidney stone with a decorative bow tied around it. Receptionist Abigail seems oblivious to it. Too busy fending off the barrage of calls that are coming through to her switchboard.

"Gulf Medical, please hold."

"Gulf Medical, please hold."

"Gulf Medical, please hold."

"Gulf Medical, please hold."

"Gulf Medical, please hold."

An abundance of fine living has caused an outbreak of gout on the island. It's rattled through the Palm Beach and Onetangi communities, carving a swathe of joint pain in its wake. As Abigail puts the last of her gout callers on hold, the door swings, and in hobbles Big Bill Tong.

"Ah howsit me breur. Keep seeing yer, don't I? Wha'choo in for?"

"I've done my arm in, had a fall in the shower, I put it through a mirror, reckon it's infected. You?"

"Gout," says Bill, before quickly singing the next four words, "*The disease of kings*" and laughing, "What happened with your clothes? They're all covered in grass?"

"Oh, it's from the mowing job I have at Passage Rock."

"Oh, you're doing that now are you?"

"Yeah."

"But you know there's a job going up at the station?"

"Our station?"

"Yeah."

"Waiheke Island Radio?"

"Yeah, you want to be applying for that. You might get it."

Chapter 12

THE INTERVIEW

Friday, 22nd November - 09:55

Mark walks into Waiheke Island Radio's tiny reception area. On the left side of the room there's a large plate glass window which looks out into a broadcast studio. At his right is a green couch with an oval-shaped coffee table in front of it. There's a white door on that wall too which opens to a toilet. On the opposite side of the room from the front door, a big brown reception desk offers a silver bell. Mark rings it.

Seconds pass before a young woman about his age pushes through the royal blue partition behind the reception desk. It's the resting bitch face girl from the picture in last month's paper. Even with the sour face, she's pretty. Slender, brown eyes, olive skin and shoulder-length black hair, the hair is checked at the nape of her neck by the band on her Sennheiser headphones. She has these denim dungarees on and a white ironed T-shirt with the words *Waiheke Island Radio* written in Impact Bold.

"Oh hi, erm, I'm here for a 10 o'clock appointment with Larry Minto."

"Mark Goodenough?" She asks as the resting bitch face melts away.

"Yeah, that's me."

"I'm sure I know you from somewhere, you look familiar to me," it was *Waster in Emu Suit Looks for Drugs in Own Vomit* again.

"Probably the Countdown."

"Yeah, that'll be it. Well, anyway, my name's Melody. We spoke on the phone." She offers him a hot drink and a seat.

Mark sits down on the couch and picks up a years-old copy of *Mojo* magazine from the stack on the table. Coldplay are on the cover. They're promoting their album *Emotional Cripple*. The publicity shots feature the four members of the band posing in self-propelled wheelchairs. Naturally, Chris Martin had gone the whole hog, by having an LED-lined feeding tube inserted through his nose for their tour. Early reviews noted that when the stadium lights were turned off and his LEDs were set to shuffle, it looks like there's a rave happening inside of him.

Before opening the *Mojo*, Mark's eyes are drawn to the pictures that are on the wall at the side of the plate glass window. New Zealand's roll call of the great and the good. Former Prime Ministers, Shelly Clarks, Baswinder Aherne, Don Key. Celebrity broadcasters, Paul Henry, Mike Hunt, and Hilary Barry. Mikey Havoc is there. All the big guns, all happily posing with the same bearded man, Chair of ACAB and Station Manager at *Waiheke Island Radio*, Larry Minto.

At 10 o'clock sharp, Larry Minto appears from behind the partition. Five foot eight, thick black glasses and a beard of grey. His hair is also grey, short and neat. He looks like a retired scooter boy. He wears light blue jeans with a black Lacoste polo, a grey blazer with a grey handkerchief in the breast pocket. It looks like Larry might have a neck twitch, because two seem to pop off before he says warmly.

"Mark Goodenough, I presume," he looks down at Mark's bandage, "eyeah, what happened with your arm?"

"Oh that? Slipped in the shower, put it through a mirror."

"Looks painful."

"It is."

Larry's office is a mess, spruced albeit by a can of lavender air freshener, emptied in a vain attempt at masking the room's must. A large poster of Larry's favourite alt-country band *Brother Brothers and the Brothers Brother*s is tacked to the wall behind the desk, below that a dusty credenza displays a collection of awards.

Mark had Googled Larry the previous day. He knows about the *World Radio* and *NZRA* gongs Larry won twelve years earlier for a docuseries charting his recovery from a horrific car accident. The show was called *Higher than the Sun* and it was a massive hit with radio stations throughout the Anglosphere.

As Larry settles into his swivel chair his tic pops off again. Then, he gets things underway. "Did you know, Mark, that *per* capita there's more radio stations in Auckland than there are anywhere else in the world?" a small pause, "Thirty-five FM stations, fifteen AM stations, and no one really knows how many low power FM stations there are. Add to that, internet radio, and podcasting and you start to get an idea of how saturated it really is."

Mark nods and the interview continues.

"Still paying off your student loan, eh?" Larry says, matter of fact, twenty minutes in.

"Yep."

"What's that? Thirty grand?"

"Yeah, around there."

"Gee ya won't want to be going back to *Mussell, Dekker, Biggs*, after spending large like that eh?"

Mark sniggers, "Nah."

There's a pause as Larry looks over at his laptop. Then he takes a deep intake of breath, tics and says, "So, er, I've heard you're a bit of a walkout guy eh? That true?"

Left Shoulder – FUCK!!

Right Shoulder – Wasting your time again, dickhead.

"It might be."

"Well, why'd ya do it then?"

"Look, er." Mark shakes his head, dejected, "it's just that I was working at Radiohub, part time, producing, I'd done all the training and that. Thing was though, my girlfriend, well, she'd just left me. She worked there too, so, you know, it was starting to get awkward. I mean, I'd seen her on the morning that I got there. She was working at The Sock FM."

"The Sock?" Tic.

"Yeah, The Sock FM 93.4. Skewed to the male 19-34 demo. Hard rock, alt rock. You know, Nirvana, Foo Fighters, Tool, Korn, Pearl Jam, Chilli Peppers, System of a Down. Yeah?"

"Ahhh, yeah yeah, I know it," then mocking, "'I'm so depressed Mummy won't lend me the keys to the Volvo' music."

Mark sniggers at Larry's put down and continues, "we'd been together for years. She left me for my oldest friend, mate. I mean, I wasn't in a good place, Mr Minto. It's not like I'd ordinarily walk out on a good job like that, is it?"

"How would I know? But so far from what I've heard, you've had two jobs in radio, and you've walked out on both of them. Doesn't look good, does it?"

"Oh man, look, I know it sounds bad, but you know, it's not as straightforward as all that, is it?"

"All I've got to go off is your CV and what people tell me."

"Well, I won't be doing it again."

"What? Walking out?"

"Yeah."

"Good, but just for the avoidance of ambiguity. You've walked out on shifts at both UNZMedia and also Radiohub eh?"

"Yeah."

"I've never heard of anyone else in radio ever having done such a thing. Never mind twice," eyebrows raised.

"Look Mr Minto, I think I had a panic attack." This isn't going well.

"It's, Larry. So, this was during the *Yesterday's News Tomorrow* show."

"Yeah."

"Duncan Farmer?"

"Yeah."

"That's a big show."

"Yeah. Called me a dickhead. On air."

"Ooh harsh."

"Yeah man, my mum was listening to it too. All I said was we should have a congestion charge in Auckland, and he went off."

"Mmmm, you wouldn't want to be called a dickhead on the radio eh?" Another tic. "I wouldn't worry about it. He called me a commie once. I'm a Communist because I work in Access Radio. Yeah, right."

"He called you a Commie? On Air?"

"Well, I work for the state, don't I? Access Radio. Government funded. The man's a plank of wood with nails for eyes."

"He threw a chicken sandwich at me, mayonnaise, stained my trousers. Look." And, while remaining in his seat, Mark shows Larry the stain on the hem of his right trouser leg. Reaching down for it, waving it about a few times. There's a pause as the pair do a reset and Larry pops off another of his neck tics.

"Walked out on that cricket game too, eh?"

Right Shoulder – Game over.

"Yeah," crestfallen.

"Probably weren't in the right headspace for that either, I expect?"

"Nah."

"You know I spoke to Gordon West at UNZ about you yesterday, he told me what happened during that broadcast. He said your manager went AWOL. It wasn't just you. Apparently, he was at a party. Should've been at work." Larry eyeballs Mark as he speaks, "not a good look for either of you guys." Then, (voluntarily this time) he shakes his head and taps his biro on the desk, before smiling. "Unbelievable," another pause, "I've heard it, you know."

"What?"

"The audio of the broadcast from your cricket game."

"You've heard it?" Mark says with alarm in his voice as his eyes widen.

"Yeah, there's audio of everything these days."

Left Shoulder – The Dead Air Incident.

"Well, where did you get it from?"

"Westie."

Left Shoulder – A stock image of a West Highland White Terrier.

"Westie?"

"Yeah. Gordon West. You know, your old boss's-boss. He told me he fired you himself. Said the line kept cutting out. I can't believe he sacked you over the phone. That's new."

Mark doesn't say anything. He is shitting bricks.

"I've known Westie for years," Larry continues, "I phoned him up to ask about you. He said you were alright at first. I'm not sure he likes you now though." Larry with his hands clasped together in his lap. "Hey er, I've got to ask. Why did the theme music from *The Benny Hill Show* start playing during that cricket audio? I mean, that was crack up, man. What was the deal with that?"

"It was the boss's ringtone, I think."

"But he was on the phone to you."

"Yeah, I think he had two phones."

"Two phones?" Larry says raising his eyebrows, "that's a bit sus eh?" Then he laughs shaking his head in apparent disbelief, "I'll bet you didn't get any shrink vouchers out of old Westie though?"

"Shrink vouchers?"

"Yeah, you know vouchers to see a shrink. They're supposed to give them to you as part of a parachute payment. You know, in case you kill yourself over it. They point to the shrink vouchers and say 'well, we tried to help'."

"No, I didn't get any of that."

With a tic, Larry then flicks his hand as if to wave the conversation away. It's time to move on to the next part of his pitch, staffing. The station has a Sales and Marketing Manager, her name is Melody Longs, and she is responsible for bringing in and looking after the station's sponsors. Quite coincidentally, Melody's stepsister is Larry's wife, Holly Minto who works part-time as the office administrator, and is wont to pop in and out of the station at random throughout the course of the week.

The vacancy Mark is going for is that of the station's Programme Director. The person who looks after everything that goes to air. Live and pre-recorded programmes on a wide variety of topics. Foreign language radio shows, religious ministry, shows for kids, shows on women's issues, and amongst other things shows by dissenting voices. It's all there. In fact, at Waiheke Island Radio, there's around fifty shows, most produced locally by the station's volunteers, the rest, licensed from either the BBC, NPR, or ABC.

"We're not judged by the size of our audience, Mark. We're judged by the breadth of the content we put out. See, most of our funding comes from *New Zealand On Air*. That's a government-funding agency. They fund us to broadcast as many unique voices as we can on the radio. It's a function of Democracy. For ordinary people to have direct access to traditional media. We have to tell people's stories, that's our remit." Larry has it off pat and Mark is already across it. He knows that every year the Government's media funding agency NZOA divvies a kitty of around ninety million bucks amongst New Zealand media projects like films, TV shows and digital media. Of that money, two hundred grand goes to each of the country's remaining thirteen Access Radio stations for operational costs. Traditionally, NZOA pays for the frequency too.

"Oh yeah and the frequency's up for renewal next year although our friend, Mr. Saddleback, has changed the rules a bit around that too. Yeah, this time, we need to contribute ten percent towards the frequency."

"Oh yeah, I saw that in the paper."

"Well, we're almost there with our fundraising now."

"When do you need to close this out?" Mark asks, sensing the interview is ending.

"Well, I've got to get it squared off as soon as possible. In an ideal world, I'd have someone starting next week so the outgoing PD can give them a rundown of the broadcasters and the job," tic pop.

"Next week? Are you serious?"

"Yep. What's your availability?"

"Immediate."

Chapter 13

THE NEW JOB

Tuesday, 26th November – 11:00

"You'll never guess who's been jumping the queue at the chippy," asks Melody Longs, the Sales and Marketing Manager at Waiheke Island Radio.

"Justin Timberlake?" Larry Minto, Station Manager shouts, peeking his head around his office door like a mole, in the game whack-a-mole.

"Nope."

"Hilary Barry?" The new Programme Director Mark Goodenough, suggests, from his new desk, upon which sits his new computer, his new in-trays, his new pens and pads of paper.

"No."

"Duncan Farmer?" Larry again.

"Getting warmer."

"Come on! Tell us," Mark.

"No, go on, have another guess,"

"Christino Ronaldo?"

"No. It was Mike Hunt."

"Mike Hunt?" Larry says feigning ignorance.

"Yeah, Mike Hunt. You know him," tutting, "Dickhead with the blazers," open palms, "Fulla off Radio Talk. Does the breakfast show."

"Is this the one who sounds like he's juggling balls in his mouth when he talks eh?"

"Yeah, that's him."

"Oh yeah, yeah, yeah."

"Quelle surprise," says Larry.

"What chippy was it?"

"I Believe I Can Fry."

"What a knob. I mean, who does he think *he* is? Phillip Schofield?" Mark says.

"No, that'd make the chippy the Queen," says Larry, correcting.

"No, it wouldn't, the chippy would be Westminster Abbey, the chips are the Queen." Melody corrects with authority.

"What was he ordering?"

"Thirty-dollar chips, eight potato fritters, nine fish, three fish-cakes, and four sausages. Twelve sachets of aioli, ten of ketchup too," Melody still laughing, "rocked up in a massive purple Jeep too. Parked it on the kerb, when there was parking at the garage next door. The dickhead. Apparently right, he's walked up to Jerry's boy Ranjit waving a $100 bill in the air, going 'you can serve me first, you know who I am.'"

"And did they?"

"Did they what?"

"Serve him first?"

"Well. Yeah. I mean. They had to. Money talks doesn't it. Besides, it *was* Mike Hunt after all," Melody dripping with sarcasm, "apparently, they had a selfie with him. It's stuck to the wall now, next to the one with Ed Sheeran, Miley Cyrus and Jessie Peach from *3News*."

There's movement at the partition separating the office from reception. It's Mark's midday appointment, yellow and black shell suit, the non-binary sausage sizzler, Wendy Metcalfe. They're flying to Perth in a day, but have agreed to take time out of their day to come up to the station to give Mark the lowdown on some of the broadcasters, and explain what his responsibilities would be in his new job.

Wendy walks ahead of Mark and their shell suit shushes with every step. Mark stands off, waiting while Wendy shares a quick hug with Melody. Just as Wendy is about to take the seat opposite Mark, he clocks their facial expression. Clearly, Wendy is performing a Terminator-vision scan of their old workstation. A furrow coming over their one-and-a-quarter eyebrows. They give a sneer at the missing Evanescence sticker that was unceremoniously peeled from the back of the monitor on Mark's first day.

"It's weird to be sitting on *this* side of the desk," says Wendy, who isn't happy. "I was always where you are."

It's weird for Mark too.

"You know, I'm sure I know you from somewhere, don't I?" It's *Waster in Emu Suit Looks for Drugs in Own Vomit* again.

"Outside the Countdown, you were on the sausage sizzle with Bill."

"Yes, that's right." A brief pause, "hope you know your way around a barbie, 'cos, you'll need to."

"Yeah, yeah, I do yeah," Mark chuckles, but Wendy isn't moved.

"I'll tell you what, here's a copy of the on-air schedule, I can like, go through a who's who if you want."

Wendy unfolds the schedule upon Mark's desk and then, with a red vivid pen, she circles the timeslot of each show as she talks about them. "So, like, you're looking after everything that goes to air. Music, podcasts, promos, adverts, like, most important though are the broadcasters. We've got, like, thirty regulars, most of them are great, but this place is a bit of a magnet for whack-jobs, and you know, we've definitely got our fair share of TERFS here too.

"Check your opinions at the door's what I say. I know I do. Like, nod along politely. Else you'll end with someone talking at you about Donald Trump or 9/11 or something. You don't want that. Trust me. You'll just get talked at for fifteen minutes straight.

"Now, The schedule's broken into zones, Health and Special Interest, from ten until three each day. That's shows like *Better Living* who talk about medical issues. It's a prerecord that one. It's actually pretty funny. Like, you know Ruben Roberts yeah? Acne?"

"No."

"Yeah well, he does a show on cars *Full Throttle*. Erm, Anderson Yogamum, he does a travel show, *Going Places*, it's called. We have a lady called Tui James, she comes up from the Marae to do a show on Saturdays.

"We've got another show aimed at blind people, it's called *A Blind of Difference*, goes out on Fridays. Scottish guy called Ken, lovely old fella, brings in a guide dog, Sheba's her name, she's a good dog, just sits under the desk and, like, goes to sleep. You'll have to help him settle in though. He needs to get his bearings because he can't see the desk." Wendy now tracking down the schedule on the pamphlet with the pen, "At three on weekdays we got the *Youth Zone*. That's shows like *Chart Attack* and the GLITFAB Crew on Fridays."

"GLITFAB?" Mark is looking at the acronym in the pamphlet.

"Stands for Gay, Lesbian, Intersex, Trans, Fluid, Asexual, Bi. It's essentially the old Rainbow Club from Waiheke High School, but like, they've got Darcey Knight now. You know Darcey, eh? The boxer? They're like, an Olympic champion."

"I know the name."

"Yeah, they're non-binary now, same as me. To be honest, that show can get quite..." Wendy stops to inspect their inner lexicon. It takes more than a couple of seconds, "...*raunchy*, in fact they got a complaint upheld by the Broadcasting Standards Authority. Dumb. I had to give them a warning."

"Now, *The Ethnic Zone* runs from six 'til eight. That's mainly foreign language shows. We've got Japanese, Korean, Chinese, French, Arab, Punjabi. Erm, there's a German show. Like, most of them come in as pre-records. I mean they're all pretty regular. *Punjabi Time* is probably the biggest show on the station, a guy called Kuldeep Chahal hosts that one, comes in on Friday evenings. He usually brings people with him. Yeah, he's quite professional. It's a big show that too. They get more than four thousand downloads every week."

"Also, we've got quite a few Spanish speaking shows, you know, for all the Argentines on the island, that's across the week. *Juan Night Stand's* one of them, that's Juan Martinez, he does this magazine-style show, a lot of soccer chat. It's on Thursday nights in Spanish. Ever met him? Bald, five-nine?"

"Not yet, no."

"Like, erm, sometimes it can get a bit loose with his guests. I've heard he's smoking pot on the deck, but like, to be fair, he's a lovely guy, changed my tyre once in Palm Beach. Very charismatic, he's got quite a big..." All of a sudden, the station goes quiet. Silent for more than five seconds. The pair of them pivot.

Left Shoulder – Dead air!

It kicks back in again after six seconds. Nothing more than a failed button push and a hint of minor panic, but both Wendy and Mark are tuned to the frequency where silence is intolerable and sound, however inane, is the solution.

"What was I saying?"

"*Juan Night Stand*, he's got a big..."

Just for a second, a look of pure terror passes between the pair of them until Wendy, red about the gills, regains their train of thought. "Er, his audience like," another hot flush, "it's pretty sizable. You know? On the podcast."

"On Saturday we've got the *FriendZone*, that's a collection of shows run by different social services. Gambling support, battered wives, budgeting, Citizens Advice Bureau, lost pets, that kind of thing. It's lovely because all the people from all the shows'll bring food and wine and they'll stay and socialise. Yeah, Saturdays are pretty lovely up here."

"Every night we have a music zone from eight 'til midnight, *The Nacho, Lalo and Pablo Techno Show* does what it says on Wednesday. I can't stand that 'doof doof doof' music, but they're lovely people. Like, watch them for weed too. On the balcony there. The man in the house over the back's been complaining about it too. Anyway, after that, we switch to BBC World Service. There's comedy on a Saturday morning and then it's wall to wall religion on Sunday."

"Jesus!" Mark, said reaching for a gag, Wendy doesn't laugh though, they just plough on.

"Now, you also have to produce the breakfast show every day too. Make sure you've always got someone rostered on, otherwise *you'll* have to do it. You need to give your host stuff to talk about. I always made these little featurettes; you know, This Day in History, Celebrity Birthdays, you can get that off Wikipedia. It's easy.

"Do a celebrity sightings feature. You can either make them up or ask Melody. She's always seeing famous people. I think she needs her eyes testing..."

Melody doesn't hear Wendy. She has her headphones on, she's listening to Ed Sheeran again.

"...yeah, look I mean if you have to invent it, do so. Listeners love it. Do celebrity birthdays too. Encourage listeners to email you with birthday shoutouts. Sometimes they send them in. If you don't have any, make them up. You want to be getting at least three interviews on every show, put more in if you want. We've got some regular guests, erm, people like Constable

Willie Hamilton from the Police, usually he comes in twice a month, Tuesdays. Firefighter Lasagne comes in monthly too, Fridays usually. Like, it's easy to set up, just like check the papers. There'll be press releases. Talk to the broadcasters. Like, there's always somebody with something to say. Spend no more than half an hour a day setting that up."

"And what happens between shows?"

"It goes to the computer. We're running *autoDJ*. Automated playlist."

"So will I be picking the songs for the *autoDJ* then?"

"Well, you can if you want. To be honest, I leave that to Larry. Reckons he knows what he's on about. He's into all that weird American guitar music."

"Oh yeah?"

"You know, Brother Brothers and the Brothers Brothers, Flattened Fish, Pavement, Clubbed Knuckle, Sonic Youth, The Band, Cucumber Attack, The Phoenix Foundation, Battered Bastard, Big Search, REM, Life as Lived By, The Beta Band, Biscuit Shoe, Antoine Diligent, George Nubbin, Fuqphlapps, Dick and Ethel Tit, that kind of stuff. It's a bit weird for my tastes, I'd prefer normal stuff, you know, P!nk, Evanescence, Adele, Ed Sheeran, Coldplay, Maria Carey, Miley Cyrus, Katy Perry, Spice Girls, Elton, Scissor Sisters, Queen, that kind of thing, normal stuff, you know, *quality.*

Right Shoulder – Musical Slop for Generation Spreadsheet.

"What else? Yeah, er, some people pay for airtime. It's not cheap, but it does get your sponsor's name out for a year. We run adverts for those customers too. Other than government announcements, those are the only adverts we're allowed to play, but you'll have to make most of them. We've got seven sponsored shows on the roster now. You know Bill Tong, yeah?"

"It was him who told me about this job."

"Well anyway, *his* show is one of the ones that's sponsored. You know, *Hammer Hands* the builders?"

"Yeah. I know a guy called Jesus who works there."

"My partner works for them, well, he did until last Friday. Anyway, they pay for his airtime; they expect him to read out a couple of announcements, but he sometimes forgets. You know it right? Hammer Hands?"

"Ahhh."

"Like, they've got that weird logo, like, it's got hammers marching in twos and wearing a top hat and monocle."

72

"Right."

"He plays that heavy metal music for Bogans, you know, AC/DC, Led Zeppelin, Motörhead, Cold Chisel, Dragon."

"Yeah, yeah, yeah."

"Oh, and erm, like, I should probably tell you about Sarin Murray. She's another that pays for the airtime, only she's on the Golden Package. It's worth quite a lot of money to the station, so be nice to her. Being honest though, she's a bit of a nightmare." As Wendy says this, they look left, purse their lips and sigh.

"Yeah?" Mark says sensing concern.

"Well, she runs a show called *The Red Pill*. Her and Denise Gee. Wednesday lunchtimes. When it started it kind of had an anti-big-pharma message. Now it's all conspiracy stuff. I wouldn't mind but they're supposed to be promoting her aromatherapy oils through it. Not sure what that's got to do with Donald Trump though," Wendy takes a sip of coffee before continuing, "and you've got to keep her sweet too, because outside of NZOA, she's the station's biggest source of income. Fifty thousand bucks it's worth, that show."

"*Really?*"

"Yeah, but the big thing with her is the complaint she caused. It was upheld by the Broadcasting Standards Authority."

"What for?"

"She said the N-word twelve times in a feature about hip hop. It was almost as if she was doing it on purpose."

"*Really?*"

"Like, she played *Pussy Crook* by Mystikal to illustrate her point. In the middle of, like, lunchtime it was. Do you know it?"

"The song?"

"Yeah."

"Nah, I don't know it."

"Neither did I. I do now though."

"And she's white?"

"Yeah, super white. Like, Remuera white," Wendy says. It's the first time they've cracked a smile since they walked through the door.

"But aren't they clamping down on complaints?"

"Yep, that's the new Broadcasting Minister, he hates Access Radio."

"Five strikes and you're out, right?"

"Yep, we've got another one against us too."

"Three?" Mark says aghast, "That wasn't mentioned in the interview."

"Yeah, he's had his head in the sand for ages on this one. It's one of the reasons I'm leaving."

"Well, what happened then?"

Casually, "I think I already told you the GLITFAB Crew had got one, like, but Derek Barnaby got one too. His show's called *Tipping Point.* I mean, like, he's not a bad person. It's just that he, like sometimes says some of the maddest stuff. Reckons he's promoting a 'masculist agenda,'" Wendy illustrates what Derek says he's promoting by using air-quotes, "whatever the fuck that is this week." I think he might be senile. Like, it's mind-boggling. He's always losing stuff, and he lives in that RV with his mate Barry. Goes around dressed like a priest, you know, wears one of those white dog collars. If you say 'Hello Father,' to him, he'll say 'Bless you my child back."

It's an energy for Derek Barnaby to say, "bless you, my child." It makes him feel good. A rare thing. Undisputedly, 'father' Derek Barnaby probably ranks as Waiheke Island's seventh most famous person. Famous for being on the front page of the New Zealand Herald. That day's bogeyman Derek had been the lead story on all UNZMedia and Radiohub news vehicles that day too. Even RNZ picked up on it. In the days that followed the incident, a camerawoman and a man with a microphone followed him around. It went viral on TikTok too. He got hate mail. Somebody sent him a finger. They all know him down at the Waiheke WINZ Office.

"You know he's not a priest, eh?" said Larry later that day, ticcing.

Chapter 14

THE SHEERAN CRITIQUE

Friday, 29th November – 19:00

Radio Countdown, bustin' loose with club-card song-bird Ed Sheeran and his number 'Happier'. If you go to the bottom of aisle four, you'll see why he's so much happier when you see the price of Tim Tams.

In an instant, the volume of the music coming through the public address system at the supermarket is hiked. One of the teenage Customer Services crew on the Self-Service aisle did it. The booze-approvers all love Ed Sheeran. Everybody loves Ed Sheeran. Everybody except Mark Goodenough. He hates him. The ubiquity of the man. Always everywhere, all at once. Forcing his gormless face into everyone's consciousness whether you like it or not. Shovelling his songs out the stable door, twice a day. Mark has better and more mundane things to do than humour Ed Sheeran, one such thing is pushing a green trundler made from recycled milk bottles around the Countdown on a Friday evening, and that's what he's doing when he runs into Melody Longs by the chop fridge at the top of aisle four.

Melody wears black jeans, navy blue training shoes and a lime green t-shirt with 'Fame' written in rainbow lettering. To Mark's eyes, she looks good. That said, he's not given much thought to Melody's personal life, but here in the Countdown, standing by the chop fridge and looking at the evidence contained in her trolley, he comes to the conclusion that she lives alone.

Exhibit A. One tub of Ben and Jerry's.

Exhibit B. A single bottle of Church Road Pinot Gris.

Exhibit C. A small pack of crackers with solitary triangle of brie.

"You know who I saw coming out of the Coinsave today," she says.

Mark sniggers, saying "go on."

"Missy Elliot."

"Missy Elliot? The rapper?"

"The hip hop colossus." Pause, "she had a Fruju. A grapefruit one."

"No."

"It was definitely her. I'd know her anywhere. I'll put it in an email, you can put it in your Celebrity Sightings bit."

"Great, yeah, do that."

"I didn't realise you had a girlfriend," Melody is looking directly at the box of condoms which is sharing the basket with a French loaf and a bunch of seven bananas.

"Oh, no, no, no! those aren't mine. No, no no, they're for my flatmate, well, they're for his monkey."

Raising an eyebrow, "Your flatmate's monkey?"

"Yeah."

"You live with a monkey?"

"At the moment."

"At the moment?"

"It's moving out soon."

"Where to?"

"Dunno, we'll probably just get it put down."

"Put down?"

"Yeah."

"We?"

"Well, me."

"You wouldn't." Melody Longs' love of animals is legendary. She's always had a cat; she's got two of them now. When she was a kid, she had a dog called Sam and now she's an adult she volunteers at WISCA's cat rescue centre.

"But it's in season."

"And?"

"It does a lot of wan..." Mark checks himself, this is a work colleague after all. And a woman, "erm, I mean it likes to relieve itself. A lot."

"What? It's pissing in your house?"

"No, not pissing, but it's stained my mum's couch."

"Oh, you live with your mum now?"

"No."

"So, it's not *her* monkey then?"

"No."

"So, whose monkey did you say it was again?"

"My flatmate's."

"But isn't it illegal to keep a monkey as a pet in New Zealand?"

"He reckons they've changed the law on it now. Apparently, it was one of the first 100 things they did in 100 days. Kept it quiet though."

"Bullshit."

Mark sniggering, "No, it's true, the Act Party put it through, it was another one of their coalition dealbreakers."

"But it's cruel."

"Well, that's the monkey lobby for you, isn't it? Throw enough money at a libertarian lawmaker and eventually they'll change the law for you."

"No, but it's cruel, monkeys should be in their natural environment plain and simple."

"But it seems happy."

"Please, that monkey is frustrated, anyone can see that, they'd just have to look in your shopping trolley to come to that conclusion."

"What do you mean?"

"Well, that's what the condoms are for, isn't it?"

"The monkey?"

"Yeah."

"Well, they're not for me are they, I only use extra-large condoms..."

Left Shoulder – What the fuck are you doing!!

The voice on Mark Goodenough's Left Shoulder is acutely aware, as the words are coming out of his mouth that he is committing a form of low-level sexual harassment. It happens in slow motion for him.

"...those monkey Johnnie's are much too small for a man like me."

"A man of like you?" Melody says with a look of disgust on her face.

Right Shoulder – Pass round that sex register.

It was meant to be an off the cuff quip, a silly joke. It's bad one. A really bad one. A man joke. A joke you don't crack around a woman. A joke you don't crack if you've been through puberty.

Left Shoulder – Maybe it was a stroke.

Right Shoulder – Maybe she thinks you're a nonce.

"It's called Bubbles."

"What?

"The monkey"

"Bubbles?" Melody's face is still contorting with indignation. Her forehead creased, a contemptuous scowl, the resting bitch face dialled up to eleven, "and you'll have it put down if you can't find it a new home? Oh my God, do you know how that sounds?"

"I'm not having it put down, I was just joking."

"Get better material, Mark." She shakes her head, "Pfft, that's about as funny as a burning orphanage."

Melody has been down on men for the best part of a year. She doesn't need much encouragement. Ghosted by an American lover called Gene, who'd headed off back to Detroit some two days before Christmas. No goodbye, no forwarding address, no explanation. It traumatised her. She tried to track him down, terrified he'd been in an accident. She didn't get anywhere with that though. And then came the Dear John letter on the 28th day of July. Flicking her off like she was nothing. It made her feel worthless. She'd been a nervous wreck ever since.

"But he's in season."

"Bubbles? More's the reason it should be living with its own kind, Mark, the poor thing is frustrated. He's self-soothing isn't he. Even an idiot could see that."

"Well, it's not for family viewing, I'll tell you that." He's trying to defuse it.

"Well, you shouldn't have a monkey as a pet Mark. Its animal cruelty." Melody is not amused.

"It's not mine. Jesus, I wish I'd not told you about it now."

A silence falls between the two of them, it is on the edge of being awkward,

Right Shoulder – She thinks you're nuts. You ARE nuts.

"This music's a bit shit, eh?"

Ordinarily Melody Longs enjoys the output of *Radio Countdown* and when they play Ed Sheeran, she's all for it. Especially this song, *Happier*. It speaks to her. Talks about her and Gene. It is deeply personal to her. If only Gene cared as much about her as Ed Sheeran cared about the woman in the song.

"What? You don't like Ed Sheeran?"

"Not really no."

"But how can you not like Ed Sheeran Mark? I can't believe you don't like Ed Sheeran. I mean, you're weird you are, first you're talking about your frustrated monkey, next you're talking about how big your dick is, now you're bagging off Ed Sheeran."

"Look, I wasn't trying to offend you, and you know, I can respect that he's done a lot for charity. It's just not my bag."

"Well, he's lovely, I saw him at Mount Smart. It was the best concert I've ever been, and *I* saw Coldplay's *Emotional Cripple* show."

Right Shoulder – Musical slop for generation spreadsheet.

"He's too nice though."

"Too nice? Too nice? Have you heard yourself? How can you be 'too nice'?"

"Well, he's nice all the time. No one can be that nice without some of it being fake. I'm asking where the line is? What's happy, what's not. When is he irritated. When is he angry? Never, he's just always happy. Like a robot."

"How dare you? Ed Sheeran is not a robot and I won't have that said about him. Nobody can be *too* nice. It's impossible." The pair lock eyes as she says it. She doesn't like him. It's plain as day. Where there might be a sparkle, there is none,

"Come on, please just *listen* those lyrics. She's left him, but he's happy, she's happy with someone else?"

"And?"

"Well, I mean it's hardly 'normal' is it?"

"What?"

"Putting someone else's happiness before your own? It's unhealthy is what it is. What kind of message is that to be telling people? They should be happy that they're not good enough?"

"I think it's sweet. I'd be happy if my ex-boyfriend was happy that I was happy that I'd left him. Anyway, what would you know about sweetness, you want to put Bubbles down."

"Well, I haven't come to a firm decision about that." Mark says grinning.

Chapter 15

THE FOUR BAR FIRE

Monday, December 2nd – 09:00

Melody is soaked and she barges through the partition steaming mad looking for a fight. She doesn't say anything for a moment, instead choosing to shiver with rage.

"Fucken James Corden, the fat Pommy fuck driving in his Range Rover. I'd recognise that fat prick anywhere. The fat self-centred wanker didn't even notice me. Fucken bastard's driven through a puddle in his fat fucken car and it's splashed it all over me."

Without saying anything, Mark gets up from his desk, goes over to the utility cupboard and returns with a four-bar electric fire and a Delonghi oil fin heater. Then, he corrals them into the space that separates their desks and drapes her cardigan off the side of his chair to dry. As it does, it raises an invisible steam which scents the room lightly with her Anaïs Anaïs perfume.

"Wanna coffee?"

"Y'making?"

"Yeah."

"OK."

As Mark walks over to the kitchenette, Melody's eyesight twitches into Terminator-vision. Green tint, LCD font. Simultaneously she is calculating the angles of his cheekbone and his jawbone, while displaying the findings in small, continuously fluctuating numbers in the corner of her peripheral vision. The results of these readings relate to how attractive she is finding him. Out of 100, they are hovering around 50, yesterday they would have read 30, maybe even 20.

By one minute to ten, Melody looks happier. She is sitting at the table in the kitchenette. Sitting opposite, Mark waits with biscuit for Larry to call the weekly meeting to order. Unknown Mortal Orchestra are closing out their number *Can't Keep Checking My Phone* ahead of the pips on the hour. Larry is prompt again. Taking his seat and rattling through the agenda and gunning a seven-hundred and fifty millilitre black coffee from a *Battered Bastard* mug.

"Righto," he says, ticcing twice, "just a little bit of housekeeping and a small reminder, I'm off tomorrow, back Monday. I'll be in Gisborne for my uncle's tangi. It's in the wops, and I don't know what the signal is like out there, so, if you need me, maybe hold on to it if you can until Monday. I mean, it's not like the station's just going to burn down is it?"

"Don't worry Larry, we'll keep it together," Melody says.

"Righto. Next, we have a couple of months 'til the frequency renewal, and there's still a bit of money that needs raising," tic.

"How much?" Mark asks.

"Well, it's down to thirty now."

"Thirty *grand*? Oh." Mark aghast.

Left Shoulder – First the complaints, now this? What's next?

"Don't worry about that Mark," tic, "we'll get there. I'm not worried at all. I've got two grants to come, one from *Creative NZ*, the other from *The Broadcast Council*, that'll bring us to within ten grand."

"So, I guess we might need to keep Sarin Murray sweet, then eh? Might end up needing her money after all." Melody says.

Larry inhales through his teeth, "Mmmm, yes that is a possibility. Actually, talking of her, have we heard from *her* lately?"

"Well, she's not been in since *I* started." says Mark.

"Wasn't she supposed to have been in Christchurch?" Melody, half asking herself.

"I'm not sure about that one. There's something a bit off with her, you know what I mean?"

"Yeah, I do, but we still need her money so," Melody adds, trailing off, "keep her sweet and keep the fundraising going."

"Maybe we should do another Chalk Fest." Larry says, remembering last year's successful fundraiser. People loved it, chalking art onto a square of concrete in front of the Artworks theatre to make a bigger artwork which is then photographed from above with a drone, the subsequent art sold off as a charity calendar. All welcome. A nice idea… "but… we need to be thinking bigger," Larry says pinching his chin with his thumb and his forefinger, thinking hard.

Melody is also pondering it when Mark says, "what about the Oneroa Santa Parade, couldn't we just do that? Pretty sure I read they'd pulled it this year. Couldn't we just pull that together? You know, as a station? There's enough of us."

"Wow, that's a great idea, Mark," says Larry, suddenly enthused. "Reckon it's possible Mel? We'd be saving Christmas for the children of Waiheke Island, that's got to be a winner."

"Well, the only day I could conceivably do it would be the weekend after next, but that's pretty short-notice. We'd need to get a council permit, get the road closed. You'd have to do that part Larry. I can get the message out and we'll need floats, of course they'll need painting, we'll need a grotto, all that. I mean if we pool the station's resources we could, I guess."

"I could easily put some promos together to promote it on air. Get them playing throughout the day. We'll need posters for it too, by this arvo ideally, but we have to move on it. Real fast." Mark says.

"It's definitely doable eh?" Larry adds.

"I'll call Bryony at the *Gulf News* now, see if we can get some publicity on it from that end," Melody says.

"Shall we do it then?" says Mark.

"I'm in."

"So am I," Larry is pointing with his biro again, motioning towards Mark. "Oh, and one other thing, Mark, you need to keep your workspace a wee bit cleaner eh. You're gonna short your keyboard out with all those pie crumbs." As Larry says this, Melody shuffles forward in her seat, happy it's being broached.

"Oh, also Derek Barnaby wants one. Says he forgot to fill in the form for a new promo before your deadline. He says he wants to know if he can still have one. He wants you to make it funny. He says he likes that one you did for Ruben Roberts."

"Ken Oath wants one also," adds Melody before doing a full handbrake turn. "Hey er, Larry, are we still having the Christmas barbecue at your place?"

"Oh, yeah, yeah, yeah, I forgot about that, yep, look I've talked to Holly about it over the weekend. It's definitely on, weather permitting. I'll send out the invites before I head off tomorrow."

Part Two

Chapter 16

THE SHADRACK SLANDER

Wednesday, December 4th – 11:50

The settlement of Surfdale is the closest thing to a suburban community you'll get on Waiheke Island. Stilted homes, by the hundred, clinging to a series of rolling hills, each sweeping down to meet the sea at Te Huruhi Bay below, and there, close to the school, at the corner of Alison and Kennedy Roads, a little brook runs idly under the road.

If you look closely, there in the bushes live a family of eight ducks. Mother Duck, Father Duck, and their six babies hatched just the day before. Tiny little fluff balls, small enough to fit in the palm of a toddler's hand. It's the happiest Mother Duck has ever been, and you can see it in her smile. Only the dolphins look happier.

As Mother Duck and Father Duck lumber back from a day at the pond, their babies follow them closely. Bobbling about like pollen spheres dancing over the ground onto the shale close to the pavement.

"Wish you'd built that nest closer to the pond, eh? It's like we're living in the wops here." Father Duck says in a full Kiwi accent.

"It was your idea." Mother duck replies.

"It wasn't."

"Yeah, it was."

"No, it wasn't."

"Yeah, it was."

"No, it wasn't."

"Yeah, it was."

"No, it wasn't"

"Fucken was."

"Fuck you."

Of course, the human ear isn't capable of comprehending the nuances of the ornithological dispute, whether it's in a Kiwi accent or not. We'd perceive a grunting and a quacking. Momentarily this would get louder, then there'd be a flap of feathers, and then everything would calm down.

"Whoa! Wait, wait, wait." says Father Duck. "Stop here for a minute, ooh, the ground's lovely and warm here. Let's sit down."

"Oh yes this is nice. Stand still, kids." Mother Duck says.

"Oh, yeah, that. Is. Lovely. *Sweet* As."

"Choice…"

Suddenly: rubber, terror, weight, heat, metal, pressure, feathers, blood, beak, noise. A red Porsche Cayenne GTS 957, four-wheel-drive SUV with sport suspension and aerodynamic body kit has just driven over the family of ducks rendering a pathetic sight. Father Duck flapping his remaining wing hopelessly as his life drains away. In front of him, the love of his life, Mother Duck, glued to the asphalt by her disembowelled intestines. The last thing Father Duck ever sees is his six offspring reduced to six little spots of road carpet dotting the tarmac in yellow.

Inside the Cayenne, its driver, the former catwalk model Sarin Murray is utterly oblivious to the carnage she's just caused. She's too busy singing along to The Robbie Williams number *Strong*. Sarin is in her late forties and twenty years have passed since her last photo-shoot. She retired to Remuera not long after, trophy wife to a property kingpin. It was she who got the house in the divorce. For now, though, she's turning the *Cayenne* into Hamilton Road without indicating.

Some two hundred metres on, Sarin brings the Cayenne to a stop and leans on her horn thrice. In minutes, a short overweight woman with a patch over her left eye bounds towards the waiting vehicle. Denise Gee it is, Sarin's sidekick. Bloated cheeks, dorsal hump and eyes like coal on a snowman. Ginger hair, formed in the vogue of a bowl cut. She is wearing a baggy blue gingham shirt and a stonewashed denim dungaree.

Within ten minutes, Sarin and Denise Gee are trotting up the paved path and into reception at Waiheke Island Radio. A text message comes into

Sarin's mobile phone. She stops under the awning by the door to read the message as Denise goes on ahead. The message contains one word 'TODAY' is what it says.

Whenever she walks into the station, Sarin Murray always makes a point of looking through the window in reception and over at Derek Barnaby as he hosts *Tipping Point* live to the island. She waves and blows him kisses. Derek loves the attention and reciprocates ironically albeit muted for Barry's sake. Barry doesn't need to know about Sarin and Derek's post-show liaisons by the Mudbrick winery, about the private road where Sarin leaves the Cayenne's engine running so she can feel Derek's dick vibrate as she rides it.

Sarin loves Derek Barnaby's dick. It's the biggest dick she's ever seen. It's the kind of dick they measure in weight rather than length. A whopper with veins on its veins. A monster. Sarin likes to get dressed up for it. Wants to look affluent for it. It works. She looks fine. Striking. Caked on base, hard red Botox lips, black hair tied up in a bun. Tall and slender. Shades of a Robert Palmer video. Austere, striking, rich.

Better than you.

Better than all your friends.

Better than Mark, who is in the middle of an email to the New Zealand Association of Gaelic Speakers trying to persuade one of them to start doing a radio show, better than Melody, who is getting to her feet to greet her biggest fish.

"Kia ora, Sarin."

"Hi, how are you?"

"Yeah fi..." suddenly she stops in her tracks, "who's this?" she is pointing at Mark, arm fully extended, as if she's just spotted a roach on the carpet.

"Ah, this is Mark, he's our new Wendy." Mark doesn't like being referred to as the '*New*' anyone, but he lets it slide because he likes Melody, and he can sense her trepidation.

"But I liked Wendy."

"They went to Australia."

"They? You mean 'she'."

Mark cuts into the conversation, "Hi Sarin, my name's Mark Goodenough. I'm the new PD here. I've heard a lot about you. I've been listening to your show. I love it, really excited to have you back on board."

Sarin seems conflicted. It's as if she doesn't like Mark's first comment but loves his second one. She looks a little off-guard.

"Erm, yes, and what, did, you, erm, like about it?" Slowly replying, the tempo akin to that of David Attenborough describing animal droppings at dusk. Gently inspecting shit with a pencil. Pushing it around in the red dirt.

"Well, you don't take any bullshit, and you call a spade a spade, and you're clever enough to know where the line is without crossing it." Of course, Mark knows all about Sarin's upheld *Broadcasting Standards* complaint, but he wants to see if she'll broach it first.

"Ooh," she said, delighted, "but there was that one time."

"Yes?"

"Oh, you know, political correctness gone mad," she giggles, "Can't say anything without offending someone these days."

"So, what have you got on your show today, Sarin?" Interjects Melody, keen to keep her and her money sweet.

"Well, I've been let down by Councillor Brad Shadrack. The coward. I'll probably mention that. Scared of the media."

In actual fact, Councillor Shadrack's mother had passed on just two days earlier and he is taking a day out to grieve the loss. He'd tried to inform Sarin, but she'd not bothered to check her messages. "Well, it's nice to meet you, Sarin, if there's anything you need from me, please just yell."

One hour later.

"Sarin you've just called Councillor Shadrack a paedophile live on air," Mark is outraged. "We could lose our jobs because of stunts like this."

"I mean, please? Don't you know who I am? You could lose your job if *I* stopped paying your wages," Sarin has just slipped a lisp into the way she is speaking. In her mind, this conveys the authority befitting that of a top-tier private education. To Mark, it sounds like she is having some sort of stroke.

Melody says nothing, well aware that the station needs the fifty grand Sarin pays as a gold-band sponsor. She's still ropeable about it though, and she grips the side of her desk, knuckles white, biting her bottom teeth on her top lip. Derek Barnaby hears it too and, being an old school lefty, doesn't like it one bit. Like Melody though, he is also compromised, relishing the fuck he's expecting in the back of Sarin's *Cayenne*, and so he keeps it shut.

"Anyway," continued Sarin, "Wendy said this is a place of free speech, so I'll say what I want about who I want."

"Not if it's false you won't."

"What if it's true?"

"If it's true, then where's your evidence?"

"Pfft. It'll come out in the wash."

"You don't know that, but for now, you've just defamed him." Mark is vexed. "When you started, you signed a document saying you understood the rules and guidelines in relation to libel laws."

"Oh please, who reads that shit?"

"Well, if you *had* read it, then maybe you'd be thinking twice about calling someone a paedophile on live radio."

"Of course he's a fucking paedo," Sarin says, indignant, "look at the state of him".

"But you outed him too."

"Everybody knows he's a fruit, just listen to the way he talks."

"What's that got to do with anything?"

"Oh," Sarin says rolling her eyes, "I don't know why I'm talking to you about this. You're beneath me. Where's Larry?"

"He's at a funeral."

"It's just that I'd rather talk to the organ-grinder than I would his monkey," and with that she walks out through the partition, into reception and leaves the building, Denise Gee close behind. As they go, Mark and Melody look at each other in astonishment.

"We need to tell Larry about this?" says Melody.

Right Shoulder – You don't have to, he never told you about the first three complaints in the interview.

"I'm not sure I want to disrupt his family's grieving with a matter like this."

"Your call."

"I know."

"Jeez but you can see why they named her after a toxic nerve agent, eh?"

Chapter 17

THE FALLOUT

Monday, December 9th – 09:02

The following Monday morning, Mark has his headphones on at his desk. He is listening to the *Between Two Beers* podcast when Larry comes barrelling through the partition looking angry. "Why am I being summoned to Wellington Mark?" He is hobbling over to Mark's desk, brandishing an open envelope with the *New Zealand On Air* logo printed in its top left corner. "This Friday Mark," he reaches Mark's desk, and he leans on it with both hands pressed on the top as he looks down at Mark, "This Friday! I have to go to Wellington to talk about the 'the on-going breaches of the Broadcasting Standards Act by the broadcasters at Waiheke Island Radio. Mark. I've only been away for a few days."

"Larry, Larry, look, I've been trying to call you, but it just goes through to voicemail. I needed to talk to you about this, Larry. I couldn't just leave a confidential message in your mailbox like that. I mean you never know who's listening these days, do you?" Mark motions with his eyes towards the envelope, "it's about Sarin Murray, yeah?"

"Yeah, it's about Sarin Murray," indignant, "who else is it gonna be about?"

"She called Councillor Shadrack a paedophile on the air. We've had complaints again, Larry."

"Complaints? You don't say."

"Look, I'm sorry, Larry."

"It's the timing, Mark. It couldn't be worse. It might affect our funding now," tic.

"Larry, I told Sarin myself as soon as she came off the air. Short of not letting her go on the air. What could I do?"

"Maybe we need to get a ten second delay."

"Might not need one the way things are going."

Chapter 18

THE NZOA MEETING

Friday, 13th December - 09:05

At half-past nine the taxi arrives outside the Rydges hotel lobby, and in no time, it's whisked Larry through the Wellington CBD and delivered him up to the Ghuznee Street office for his meeting with his paymasters at NZOA. At reception, two other people are waiting. There is no music, just silence. Larry sits in a plastic chair, shuffling from his left cheek to his right, all the while self-conscious about the noise his legs are making as they rock up and down. His suit is uncomfortable, much tighter than it was when he last wore it. The trouser fabric clings to his thighs like sausage skin around minced pork. He's ultra-aware of the neck tic too. It's dramatically increased in frequency this week.

A familiar face appears, it's Nazreen Rahman. Larry has known Nazreen for a while. She was on the board when he was given the job ten years earlier. Nazreen is sympathetic to Access Radio; she loves the ideal. It was through Access that she's come to assimilate to Kiwi life after fleeing Afghanistan with her young family twenty years earlier. Now, she switches her time between practising PR, advocating for women's rights and her NZOA commitments.

"Hi Larry." She says with a warm smile, "How are you?"

"Yeah good."

"Holly and the boys?"

"Good, good."

Even with Nazreen's warm smile, Larry senses that she's in business mode. It's there in the tone of her voice and in her body language. She's hugged him in the past, not on this occasion. She then leads him along the grey and blue tiled carpet and into the boardroom. A familiar space, different today though, ominous.

In the fifteen months since Larry had last been in this room, the board's makeup has changed substantially. Now, the faces of three strangers sit in expectation from behind the large rectangular table. At the far right is the ex-CEO of Radiohub and former National Party candidate for Wellington Central, Lambartus Butler. To Lambartus's left, outspoken libertarian media commentator, Beverley Watson. Dr Hamish Cameron, QSM, is present too, moving onto the board after stepping down from UNZMedia in the wake of *The Dead Air Incident* a couple of months earlier. Aside from Nazreen, the only other face Larry recognises is that of Hone Webster, the former Māori Party MP, turned South Auckland pastor.

Hone is chairing today's meeting, and he calls it to order. "Well, thanks for coming down at short notice, Larry. It's very much appreciated. Now, as you know there have been some changes to the way we are dealing with on-air complaints in the Access sector, and we need to address the on-air activity of a handful of your broadcasters."

"Sure."

"So, the station has had three complaints upheld by the *BSA* over the course of the last ten months alone, and the reason we are here today is that one of your broadcasters defamed a local politician last week, so effectively you'll have four upheld complaints now.

"As you'll be aware we've been working closely with the *BSA* on disciplinary matters, implementing the five strikes and you're out policy. This is five upheld complaints in a twelve-month period as the threshold for the removal of an Access station's funding."

"Yes, I'm aware of it," says Larry sheepishly with a tic.

"Look Larry, this case is complicated by the fact that your frequency is up for renewal soon, and as you know we at NZOA are responsible for supplying the majority of that funding. I'm sure you can imagine, this poses a substantial risk for us." Hone takes a deep intake of breath before continuing. "Now, before we try to figure out what we're going to do, let's have a look at the complaints, Dr Cameron."

Dr Cameron shuffles his papers, before pushing the frame of his glasses back up his nose. "Well, the first one came from a show called *The Red Pill*, in which the host Sarin Murray. Repeatedly used the N-word during a show about rap music. Now I believe that she was quite new to the station when that happened."

"Yeah, it was her second show."

"So, you could put it down to inexperience?" Nazreen asks.

"I guess."

"But she has proved herself to be more than a little provocative since then, hasn't she Larry?" Lambartus says pointedly, "I mean, she's contravened BSA Standard 4 here. It's blatant discrimination and denigration. She is the reason we're here really. She's the one who defamed the councillor last week isn't she, Larry?"

"She is, and in the spirit of full disclosure, we had another complaint about her, which wasn't upheld."

"Yes." Beverley says, her tone sceptical. "She played *Ding Dong the Witch is Dead* in the background whilst reporting on the passing of a well-respected community activist."

"Pffft, so how come the woman's still on the air, Larry?" Lambartus spits.

"Well, we've been fundraising for our contribution to the renewal of the frequency, and she is our only broadcaster on the Gold Band Package."

"And how much is that worth to the station?" Hone enquires.

"Fifty thousand bucks," tic.

"Ahh, the plot thickens," Beverley says.

"Larry, she's bringing you down." Hone says, open-palmed.

Larry doesn't say anything, he just sighs. "Ok, let's hear the next complaint."

"Well, that came from a show called *Tipping Point*, which is hosted by a guy called Derek Barnaby. During his show, which I note goes out immediately before Sarin Murray's show, he incited violence towards DOC workers spreading Ten-Eighty."

"Derek Barnaby? I've heard that name before," Dr Cameron, remembering. "Isn't he the funeral-picketer?"

"A funeral-picketer?" Beverley says in amazement. "Y...you've got a funeral-picketer on your roster?"

"Well, some people use that phrase, yes, but I don't think he's, you know, a Westboro Baptist Church type of funeral-picketer."

"What? He's not one of the 'bad' funeral-picketers?" Beverley, indignant.

"Well, I don't know. That's not really for me to say."

"But you've got a funeral-picketer on your books. I think that tells us all we need to know about his sanity and his suitability to be given a platform in the media."

It's a fair reflection. There aren't many word-pairings that can illicit quite as much controversy as when 'funeral' is hyphenated with 'picketer' but that was the slug line that'd screamed from the front page of the *Herald* the morning after Derek Barnaby got battered by fifteen fifteen-year-olds at a tangi in Manurewa.

'Dog-Collar Derek' the tabloids also called him. There were photos too, in one, Derek was dining on a luncheon of punches after being swarmed by a mob of children. He told everyone the article was a 'hit piece'. He was livid at what he said was 'total misrepresentation'. To be fair, he may as well have been holding up a placard saying 'Fags Doom Nations' as the coffin was lowered into the grave, if you went off what the *Herald* had said.

This had all happened midway through Derek's second nervous breakdown. Back then, he'd scour the newspaper for young deaths. He was looking for funerals of what he thought were suicides. When he thought he'd found one, he'd turn up at the service dressed as a priest and try to dissuade grieving siblings from going the same way. Derek was blunt though, and on more than one occasion became embroiled in a heated exchange with grief-stricken whānau.

"Look," Hone said, "I think we've gone off on a bit of a tangent here, this whole funeral-picketing thing really has nothing to do with this BSA complaint."

"No, but it certainly raises a red flag, wouldn't you agree?"

"Bev, there are hundreds of shows up and down the country, and we all know that Access Radio can attract passionate people," Nazreen counters.

"You mean nutters?"

"I don't think we should be denigrating the broadcasters like that, Beverley." Nazreen snaps back.

"Well, maybe not, but he can't be playing with a full deck if he's out on a picket line in front of a Chapel of Rest, can he?"

"I don't think it was like that," says Larry.

"Well, what was it like?" Beverley is getting annoyed.

"I don't know. I wasn't there."

Beverley sighs, "It's crazy really, the amount of money this country spends on giving these voices a platform, and we're giving it over to people who protest at funerals, what's the world coming to?"

"Look, let's stick to the agenda," Hone.

"It's relevant though, isn't it, Larry" Lambartus says.

"Yes, but we know what happened now, so let's move on," Nazreen.

"So, what was the upshot of the BSA complaint, what did you do?" Hone says.

"Well, I have had a long chat with Derek. He made an on-air apology and also I issued a statement disassociating what he had said from the station."

"Did it work, Larry?" Lambartus says.

"Well, he has been avoiding the really controversial stuff lately."

"Mmm, okay," Hone says, with a deep air of scepticism. "What about this third complaint?"

"Okay. Complaint number three." Dr Cameron, pauses. "There's a show here called the GLITFAB Crew. This is a show aimed at the rainbow community. It runs at five o'clock in the Youth Zone on Tuesday afternoons. The complaint centres on an episode where a panel of five compared the merits of twelve prophylactic penises, with the hosts road-testing these, erm, devices."

"What, on-air?" Lambartus blurts out in astonishment.

"Well, they didn't actually, erm, you know, try them out there and then, but they did talk about how it had affected them when they had used them."

Beverley gasps and giggles, before uttering, "And this is at five o'clock in the afternoon you say?"

"Yeah," Dr Cameron says.

"On a Tuesday?" Beverley continued. "Imagine you'd just picked the kids up from ballet class and that came on."

"How old are the kids?" Lambartus asks.

"Four and seven?"

"Mmm, yes and the segment was called *A Dozen Dildos at Dinnertime*." Dr Cameron adds blushing.

"*A Dozen Dildos at Dinnertime*, was it Larry?" Lambartus asks in a patronising voice.

"You know if it were Turkish, they might call it *A Dozen Dildos at Donertime.*" Nazreen jokes.

Everyone laughs for a moment. Lambartus pretends to laugh, but in fact, he only gets that joke the following Wednesday, when driving his Mercedes down Transmission Gully. It isn't that Lambartus Butler doesn't do humour, he just thinks that by laughing, you are making a concession to someone, and he doesn't give anyone anything for nothing. It's like respect, you have to earn it. Besides, he didn't really like that Nazreen, he didn't like that 'rag' she wore on her face. It isn't 'Kiwi'.

"And how many complaints have we had about this one, Larry?" Lambartus asks.

"Loads," replies Hone.

"Here let's have a listen." Bev says, playing the offending clip over the AV system.

The audio lasts for just under five minutes and is constantly punctuated by the cackle of Darcey Knight. It's a dirty laugh, the kind of laugh you'd never want to hear coming from your Nana. When it's finished, another quiet descends upon the gathering.

"Well, the way I see it, either the station has to go, or, its manager has to go." Lambartus says, breaking the silence.

"I doubt it's that cut and dried." Nazreen is clearly agitated now.

"Look." Dr Cameron says. "No one here wants to see the station shut down."

"Speak for yourself." Beverley says indignantly.

"If I may," Hone, shooting Beverley a look, "the way things are going, Larry, that's where you're headed. I propose that the board meets in January for our normal meeting to see if there has been any improvement. If there has been, then we will consider our options."

"What if we could have her pre-record the show and go through each episode, edit out the bits that might touch the cloth, that way we keep her money."

"Do you think she'll go for that?"

"I don't know. To be honest I don't know her all that well, I mean, she kind of breezes into the station and then out again. She did say she wanted her show to be live when we brought her on. It's in the contract."

"Do you think it'd be worth sending up a fact-finding delegation? I mean, it's such a big decision to be pulling the funding at this late stage. I think we need to have all our ducks in a row before we make any such decision. Livelihoods are at stake here."

"I think you're right, Nazreen. We need two pairs of eyes on it. Would you be prepared to go up next Friday? You could turn it into a long weekend." Dr Cameron says.

"Yes, I can do that."

"Who else wants to go?"

Lambartus raises his hand "I'll go too."

"But, we've got the Santa Parade on Saturday."

"You're organising it this year aren't you, Larry?"

 "Yeah."

"That'll be interesting."

"Well, that's probably good timing. It'll help us get a gauge on your community engagement." Nazreen remarks.

"Look, Larry, I think as a precaution we'll need to commence plans for the frequency to go to auction in case there's another infraction. We can always veto it if nothing comes up between then and now." Dr Cameron.

"And er, Larry, I'm going to need a report, tell me why the public should be paying for that frequency. By Wednesday thanks, and I think it's fair to say that if there are any more infractions, that's the end of the station, isn't it, Larry?" Lambartus says holding Larry's gaze like he wants to fuck him up.

"Yes, Lambartus, we've already ascertained that." Nazreen interjects.

"I agree with Lambartus. I don't see any other way forward in these circumstances," Beverley says. "It'd certainly save the country a lot of money."

"It would bring a lot of money in too," says Dr Cameron, "that frequency is one of the most sought-after frequencies on the Auckland spectrum."

"Why's that?" says Beverley.

"Well, there are an enormous amount of imported Japanese cars in this country, and most of those cars only pick up stations between 88FM to 89.9FM, because of the way the frequency spectrum is set out in Japan. So, you get a lot of people listening because that's all their radio can pick up. Believe me, Radiohub and UNZMedia have wanted to get their hands on that frequency for years, it's probably worth about eight million bucks on the open market."

"Are you serious?" Beverley says, before continuing, "We're letting eight million bucks slip through our fingers, so we can give a platform to a funeral-picketer, a firebrand and a bunch of perverts. You've got to be joking. It's a disgrace. You could build a hospital for that. I'm sorry, Larry, but as far as I'm concerned, you're already gone. I won't be voting to renew your frequency. I've heard enough."

"Let's get the report in and let me and Lambartus submit the report from our fact-finding mission before we start making decisions like that." Nazreen cautions.

"Sure," says Beverley sarcastically.

"Let's be under no illusion Larry, you're hanging by a thread here, one more upheld complaint and it's over. And also, I want you to let the Association of Community and Access Broadcasters know what is happening, they might have to get you to step down from being their chair there eh?" Hone cautions.

"Who owns the premises, Larry?" Lambartus asks after a brief pause.

"The council, we have a twenty-five-year lease with them on that property. It's also up for renewal, but we only pay a nominal amount to rent it."

"Unbelievable that Larry," says Lambartus, "more wasted money. You know you'll have to let them know that you'll likely be vacating the premises soon, in fact, do that first thing on Monday morning and I want you to CC me in on it."

"Copy me in on that too please Larry," Beverley says, "ooh, and er, Larry, have you checked the weather forecast for next weekend? Looks like there might a cyclone coming through, let's hope it isn't a washout, wouldn't want to get too carried away with things, eh?"

"And Larry, just, erm, as a concerned colleague, I, I must address this tic you have, probably need to get that under control, eh? I could put you on to a good neurologist," Lambartus adds thoughtfully.

Chapter 19

THE NIGHT BEFORE THE PARTY

Friday, 13th December - 19:10

Maybe it has something to do with her name, but Holly Minto loves Christmas music. In fact, she loves it so much she has a Spotify playlist of a hundred Christmas classics which she plays on shuffle throughout December and on until the twelfth night. They're all there. The staples. Lennon and McCartney, Mariah Carey, The Pogues, Kirsty McColl, Slade, Wham!, Bing Crosby, and Band Aid. For now, suede-headed Scottish songstress Annie Lennox is butchering the festive classic, *Winter Wonderland* into a motion of fireside synth, slap bass, and scoot toot-tootin' scat.

As the song draws to a close, Larry limps through the ranch slider, and winces at the song. He drops his travel bag and tics twice before Holly greets him with a lip-peck and hug.

"How was your meeting?"

"Terrible, the station might be finished," Larry says, downcast.

"What?" Holly, throwing her tea towel over her Left Shoulder and taking a seat next to Larry at the kitchen table. "Because of what Sarin said?"

"Well, it's not just that, Hol, Sarin's was the fourth complaint we've had this year. It's touch and go whether they'll even release the rest of the money for the frequency renewal at this late stage now."

"Oh shit."

"They're sending up a couple of board members for the Oneroa Santa Parade. They want to get a feel for the station, see how we function in the community outside of what we broadcast. They need to figure out whether the community values us or not."

"They can't do that. That station is central to this community."

"Well, yeah. You and I know that, but there's people on that board who're looking at it with money in mind."

"So, what happens after that?"

"They'll make their decision"

"Fucking ACT Party."

"Yeah and I think we need to cancel the party, I mean, what are we even celebrating anyway?' Tic.

"We can't cancel the party at such short notice, Larry. I've been organising this for weeks now, never mind the cost of it."

"How much have we spent then?"

"Eight hundred bucks. And anyway, there's not enough room in our freezer for all that meat."

"Just give it away. They've got a food bank freezer at the sustainability centre. I'll just take it there."

"Listen to me, Larry Minto. I'm not going to stand idly by while you give up on your broadcasters. I'm not having it. You need to bloody well harden up and take a bloody concrete pill. We're having that party, by hook or by bloody-well crook."

"Easy for you to say," tic.

"Larry, you can do this. You came back after the accident. They said you wouldn't walk again, but you did, and you did it on your own, this time you've got a whole community behind you."

"You know Sarin'll be there? How am I supposed to look her in the eye now?"

"You don't, just leave that bitch to me."

"You better not be getting in any cat fight. We still need her money."

Chapter 20

THE MINTO CHRISTMAS PARTY

Saturday 14th December

You can't really call Otakawhe a village. There's not enough dwellings for a designation like that. It's just a small collection of wooden houses snaking down a dirt track road and stopping short of a shale stone beach where the land runs out at the bottom of the island. When an Otakawheanite is at home, the nearest shop is a half hour drive away, that's a one-hour round-trip, just to buy some milk from the Onetangi garage, or a crate of piss from the bottle shop next door.

All up, there's about 50 Otakawheanites, and Larry Minto with his 3000-metre square section near the end of Nepean Road, is one of them. At the rear of Larry's section, there's a neatly mowed bowl-shaped lawn, it is punctuated by a steel framed swimming pool, a firepit and a trampoline for his boys. Larry mows his grass diligently, except that is, for the bit underneath the trampoline, where the grass grows wild and long. His three-bedroom house is near the front of the section, and on the other side of the deck, there's a granny flat. Due to the slope of the land, the house is on stilts, while below it, at the front of the property there's a large flat space. It is also neatly mowed and offers ample room for seven parked cars.

Larry is diligent about his mowing for one simple reason. Dog shit. Enormous dollops of it, direct from the arse of the family's oversized dog, Chunk. Thirty-five in dog years, and weighing in at 85KG, Chunk bears the black and white markings of a Friesian cow. He is a pedigree Newfoundland that never had his knackers snipped, and as a consequence is a frisky boy. Ordinarily, Chunk is a good dog, excitable and good. A gentle giant and good with kids, unless of course he's not eaten for a day, in which case he'll go for the throat.

Chunk has an excellent command of the English language, unfortunately for him though, his limited vocal cords and his inability to hold a pen in his paw, render an inability to express himself effectively to any human. In addition to his understanding of language, this is a dog with the reasoning skills of prime Sherlock Holmes, and like Holmes, he has a photographic memory, remembering the names of everyone he'd ever met, the way they smelled and whether they were nice or not.

At around two o'clock that Saturday afternoon, Chunk, lain sideways on a flank, is snoring like a bandsaw. Basking, sheltered in the shade of the table on the deck. The sense of smell is what wakes him. It's a unique odour, this one, a bouquet of ammonia on a light offshore breeze. Chunk recognises it immediately. It is the bouquet of Barry Twelvedogs' body odour. The dog calculates the distance at roughly a quarter mile. Sweet clay cat-litter. The engine sound is familiar too. Diesel. It fits the pattern. All the variables are in place. That smell, the noise of that RV, the firepit being on and the whole house being tidy. By his powers of deduction, Chunk correctly ascertains that there's going to be a party and Chunk loves parties. All that meat. All those smells. The tail starts to wag.

Within two minutes the Barnaby RV is parking on Larry's front section. Chunk, excited, displays his zeal, throwing himself headlong into the camper van's drivers-side door as Derek is opening it. The dog, wiggling his backside, wagging his tail, barking and pawing at the vehicle's white paintwork. Playfully Chunk bites down on Derek's arm, licking and slobbering. Turning his attention to Twelvedogs, Chunk gives it more of the same. He calms. Relieving the anxiety with a quick nibble on his rump's pruritus sores, then, he escorts Barnaby and Twelvedogs to the deck where Holly is waiting.

"Hello Father," she says.

"Bless you my child," says Derek.

"Hi Barry."

"MMMM g'day, Holly," Twelvedogs says through his electrolarynx.

"Where's Larry?" Says Derek.

"In the kitchen prepping the turducken."

"MMMM turd what?" At the best of times, Barry Twelvedogs sounds like a robot. He has done so since his real larynx was removed back in 2012. The laryngectomy had been forced on him after he got throat cancer from the million plus durries he'd nailed in the preceding thirty years. He'd started at ten. He is philosophical about it, reckoning it makes him sound cleverer, on account of Stephen Hawking having a similar accent.

"Turducken. It's a chicken in a duck in a turkey."

"MMMM sounds yummy," replies Twelvedogs.

"I can't get the temperature right on the fire pit though. Might have to cook it in my normal oven."

"When will it be ready?" asks Derek Barnaby.

"God knows. He's not even put it in yet. Mind you, the way *he's* going, *I'll* be the one who ends up finishing it."

"Come again," Derek says.

"He's been knocking them back since ten this morning." Holly cautions, drink-motioning with her right hand.

"Oh, leave the man alone, Holly. It's Christmas," Derek says jovially.

Twenty minutes later, Sarin Murray's red Porsche Cayenne GTS 957 parks on a slant next to the Barnaby RV. As it comes to a halt, the song *Born this Way* by Lady Gaga booms from the car's stereo, and momentarily becomes the dominant sound on the property, drowning out Holly's Christmas selection in the process. Travelling with Sarin in the Cayenne is her eye-patched sidekick, Denise Gee, whose left-side forearm rests on the open window and resembles a large fillet of fresh salmon on a fishmonger's slab.

"Sarin's here," sings Holly from the deck, "looks like she's brought the fat one off *Kath and Kim* with her too."

"Denise?"

"I think so yeah."

"Oh right," says Larry as a tic pops off. He is resting his hands as he leans forward on the windowsill that overlooks the front of his property, watching on as Sarin steps down from the vehicle. She is carrying a twenty-five-dollar bottle of pinot gris in her left hand. Her Chanel clutch, vivid in red in the other. Denise's contribution, (also vivid in red) is a two-hundred-and-fifty-gram packet of Bluebird Ready Salted potato chips and a face like a bag of tacks. As the pair of them walk towards the front steps, Sarin notices Larry who is standing behind the window above. She waves, shouting.

"Hi, Larry!"

"Please, God, let her stand in some dog shit," Larry says under his breath as he grits his teeth, fakes a smile and waves *hello* through the front window.

"Now, now, Larry," Holly says, looking on from the ranch slider.

"Eww, get it off me. Get it off *me!* I'm allergic."

Chunk has blindsided Denise Gee out on the deck with a king hit, licking her liberally and delivering a film of saliva upon her arm which is so viscous it will still be felt on her skin an hour after it dries.

"Chunk, heel!" Holly shouts in despair, but the dog ignores her, instead turning his attention to Sarin, barging into *her* with his enormous bulk, and blatantly sniffing at her private parts.

Obviously inappropriate, obviously crass, but it's not like the dog is trying to offend. He just sniffs things. It's what he does. He's a sniffer. It could be the cat's arsehole or the kid's lunchbox. It's all the same to Chunkie. He's sniffing it.

Unaware, unamused, and just a little embarrassed, Sarin lashes out at Chunk with her clutch, dragging the bag's metal detail across the open pruritus sores on his hind quarters. As the bag hits, a small mushroom cloud of remedy flakes puffs up into the air, discernible in the sunshine.

"Ooww!" snaps Chunk. Of course, to the human ear this is just the sound of a dog yelping.

Holly is incensed but she can't let on. She's promised Larry she'll play nice, so she turns her ire on the dog instead. Scolding it and pointing with her index finger towards the kitchen.

"*You, box, now!*"

Chunk, registering Holly's rage, retreats to his bed next to the fridge, confused about why he is being shouted at. In his box he settles, and he self-soothes by slowly licking the shaft of his big red penis for the next fifteen minutes, quivering himself to sleep.

"Let's get you two a drink, shall we?" says Holly.

As Holly goes back into the kitchen to pour Sarin and Denise a drink, the pair walk to the area of the lawn where Barnaby and Twelvedogs are sitting,

"Hello Father," Sarin purrs, glancing at the bulge of the juicer in Derek's trousers. Even without the size of his cock, Sarin has Derek pegged as a handsome man. The short grey hair. The Ray-Bans. The black shirt, and the black jeans. He reminds her of a (pre-cancer) Steve Jobs / Tom Cruise / Ron Jeremy hybrid and the priest thing makes her wet. He was only fifty-three too.

"Bless you my child," says Derek with a little less enthusiasm than usual. It is the first time the pair have seen each other since their fuck in the Cayenne after *The Shadrack Slander*. Sarin senses the reserve from Derek and, as usual, fails to acknowledge Twelvedogs.

"Ew gross," Sarin suddenly says, pouting through her botox-bloated lips. She gestures toward one of Chunk's deposits. It is nestled on the grass next to the pool. Larry missed it when he'd gone on turd patrol that morning.

🐾

Again, Chunk is the first to notice another of the guests arriving. Melody is thirty seconds away in her silver Mazda. The dog drifted off to sleep after his wank, but the sound of Melody's loose fan belt echoing down the valley stirs him. And even though he is technically still asleep, his tail begins to move slowly from left to right. Then, his eyes start to open, and he lurches into consciousness, wobbling up from his box next to the fridge. As soon as he catches sight of her car, he's off. Hurtling across the deck, down the wooden steps and across the front lawn.

As Holly climbs out of the car, Chunk lurches at her, barking and licking and turning in circles. Assuming the position, he gives her leg a quick hump before being pushed away. Melody doesn't mind the attention. She knows the dog loves her for more than sexual reasons. She's house-sat, baby-sat and dog-sat for the Mintos on many an occasion.

Melody has a basket of breads, and she crosses the lawn with Chunk following closely, smelling at it. She greets Holly on the deck and walks on over to the kitchen where Larry is hiding with his turducken. She places the breadbasket down on the countertop.

"You okay, Larry?"

"I'm fine, Melody, fine," he doesn't mean to snap at her. It just comes out like that, but he doesn't apologise either.

"Oh, right, erm, okay, I'm sorry. I didn't mean to intrude or anything."

"Look, Melody, I'm probably just a little tired from the trip down to Wellington. It must be jet lag or something."

"But you can't get jet lag on that flight, Larr, sure you're not sick or something? It wasn't bad news, was it?"

"No, no don't worry. I'm alright," Larry says, avoiding the part of the question about bad news.

"Oh, okay," Melody replies, reading the room.

"Look, I'll just get this food prepped and I'll be along in a bit."

After a couple of hours, the grounds of the Minto home are chocka-block with people from the station. Mark Goodenough has rocked up with Bento and Bubbles. Neville Southall and Peter Reid are there. As are Ruben Roberts, Anderson Yogamum, Kuldeep Chahal to name but a few. Blind Ken Oath is there too, and as usual, he has his seeing-eye dog at his side. A black lab, Sheba is a sober dog, disciplined and calm. Calm as she is, there's edge about her, as Chunk, lolloping over, is about to find out.

"Fucken stay away, cunt!" says Sheba, growling in a harsh Scottish accent, similar to that of Begbie from *Trainspotting*, "I'll fucken glass ye, af ya come any closer ye ken?"

"What?" says Chunk in his Kiwi accent, shocked at the aggression, "but I live here, this is my house. I'll go where I want. Anyway, I'm bigger than you are."

"I don't care how big ya'r. I'd fucken do ye," continues Sheba.

"But, but."

"Aye, that's right, fucken walk away, ya fanny."

Sheba had never been the kind of dog to suffer fools gladly, and as Chunk lumbers away, she continues to wait at her master's feet, listening to him chatting to Mark by the granny flat door. "You know that promo you said you'd make for my show? You made it yet?" Ken asks in his rich Glaswegian lilt.

"Well, I've written the script, and I've sourced a sound effect of a dog barking."

"Sound effect? What do you want one of those for, can we no just have a recording of Sheba barking hersel'?"

"You want me to record Sheba barking?"

"Aye."

"Barks on command, does she?"

"She does if you blow on this," Ken says, thrusting a dog whistle towards Mark.

Like any reasonable person Mark immediately presses the whistle to his lips and gives an enthusiastic blow of about five seconds on it. It triggers both dogs, but between the two of them, their reactions present very differently. Sheba still at Ken's feet lets out a short series of mid-level barks. The kind you might get if someone is at the front door. Out on the back lawn, however, Chunk, suddenly agitated, begins to walk in circles, tail clamped between his legs, barking and growling. In a heartbeat Bento's monkey skips over the table and onto the dog's back, riding it, as if it was a miniature shire horse at a half penny rodeo, for the five seconds that this happens, the monkey mimics the dog, barking and chittering with amusement.

Boy, are people loving it. After a couple of circuits of the garden, Bubbles deftly jumps off the dog's back and back to the feet of Bento who gives him a banana. The dog is still angry. The amusement of the guests turns to alarm. Then, Holly trots across the garden, manhandles the dog by his collar and again she shouts her canine disciplinary mantra, "You, box, now!"

This is a mammal with an IQ of 162, and here he is running around in circles and barking at nothing. A monkey had been riding on his back too. A fucking monkey! It doesn't look good, and one would never guess this dog had invented an automatic dog-food dispensary. The mechanics of it and everything, all figured out in his gargantuan mind. But then again, how's anyone supposed to express themself before the Intellectual Property Office if they're just a domestic pet.

"Jesus!" Laughs Mark nervously, "wasn't expecting that."

"Me neither, but you see how Sheba reacted, that's what you'd want eh?" Ken says.

"Yeah."

"You can borrow it, record her next time we're up at the station?"

"Don't *you* need it?"

"Ah've got plenty."

About twenty minutes later, another vehicle pulls into the driveway. A red Nissan Leaf. Chunk doesn't notice it. He is in sensory overload with all the voices, smells and food. Bento notices though, registering the driver's makeup, earrings and the beard from a distance of no more than ten metres. Then under his breath, through gritted teeth, like a child trying not to be noticed, he turns to Mark saying, "Mark, Mark. look, look, over there," he points while trying to be discreet, "look," there is an urgency in his voice. "It's that tranny from the petrol station, remember, I told you about her. The 'cycle path'?"

"Oh man," Mark says laughing, "calm down, it's only Darcey Knight. They do a show at the station,"

"Oh, you know her?"

"Know them," Mark corrects.

"What? all of 'em?"

"Yeah, I know them all, but in this case, I mean 'them' you know as in 'they/them'. Non-binary."

"Oh right. Yeah, OK." Bento says looking confused.

The monkey looks at him, scratching it's chin.

Darcey is the first to get out of the Leaf. Today they're showing out in a fabulous black velvet dress. It is complimented by a grey fur shawl, sheer black stockings and a pair of rainbow Dr. Martens. Just the one eyebrow today. Albany Westfield's out next. Divine, with polo neck jumper in lime and yellow pencil skirt. Hunter S. Plaza has a license to thrill in a black bow tie and white tuxedo. Last out the Leaf is Lynn Mall in pink with an ill fitted 80s pom-pom. Perhaps more remarkable than the collective fashion choices of the GLITFAB Crew is the amount by which the Leaf's suspension lifts as Lynn Mall gets out of it.

"Woah," laughs Bento "look at the size of that," Mark doesn't take him on. Then Bento turns his attention to Darcey saying, "you don't think she'll fuck me up do you.

"They."

"*What*?" Bento says, confused.

"You don't think, *they'll* fuck you up."

"Well, will it, will it fuck me up?"

"They! And no, they're not going to fight you here at a Christmas party about a perceived slight at the petrol station six weeks ago. They've probably forgotten about it.

"Hope so. I mean just look at the size of those muscles and if the fat friend gets involved, I'm going home in an ambulance. So are you."

A wisp of the smell of sausage meat travels on the breeze and Chunk follows it, lumbering from over by the pool and approaching the chatting circle where Melody Longs, Mark Goodenough, Bento, Holly, Lynn Mall and Big Bill Tong are conversing. Bill is a soft touch. He's already thrown a nugget of steak-fat and a quarter pork sausage at the dog that night.

"You know there's supposed to be a cyclone coming through next weekend. Hope it doesn't affect the parade," Bill warns.

"Cyclone?" Melody asks, "Please God no! Please don't make it rain on my parade."

"Yeah, Cyclone Frank, it's meant to be a bad one. You'll be buggered if you live all the way out here."

"Shit, that's all I need."

"We'll keep an eye on it eh?" Mark says, trying to quell Melody's anxiety

"Not to change the subject but does anyone know if it's bad luck to run a rabbit over?" Lynn Mall says.

"Four years of bad carrots," Bento replies as he passes a banana to the monkey.

The monkey chitters, before slamming the banana.

"Why?"

"Well, I'm pretty sure Darcey hit one on the way over. We stopped to see if it was okay, but it ran into a bush."

"Did you damage the car?"

"I don't think so."

"Count yourself lucky."

"You know, the roads have been really bad for roadkill this year," Mark says.

"Oh my God, I know, I almost hit a Weka by the eco-village the other day," says Holly.

"Yeah, there's a dead pukeko by Talking Tree Hill," Bill offers, tossing the remainder of his pork and fennel sausage at Chunk who has ambled over to sniff the monkey. The dog sucks the sausage into his face in one seamless motion.

"Seen the mess on Alison Road?" Melody asks.

"Five ducklings. Mom and Pop," says Bento like he's reading a football score.

"I heard Stevie from the Rec Centre did it, distracted by someone trying to warn him not to drive over them."

"Nah man that's bullshit, Stevie drives a Nissan Lafesta, that was an SUV that ran over those ducks, you can tell by the tyre tracks going through the feathers," Mark says with a hint of authority.

"That would've happened later, after they'd been mashed into the road," Bento, who else?

"Anyway," Melody retorts, shooting daggers towards Sarin's Cayenne, "our roads just aren't built for cars that big."

"Yeah, that's what Larry says too," says Holly.

"What? The roads aren't built for SUVs?"

"Yeah."

"Actually, talking of Larry, is everything alright with him? He doesn't seem himself."

"He's got a lot on his mind. To be honest I wish we'd have had this party last week." There's a slight weariness in Holly's voice.

"But it rained last week."

Chapter 21

THE ADMISSION

Saturday, 14th December – 18:45

By a quarter to seven, the turducken *still* isn't done. Instead, it's cooking in a marinade of worry and strife. By this point, the success of the party is neither here nor there as far as Larry is concerned. He has other things bugging him, and since he's completely hammered, he is going to get them off his chest. He limps from the kitchen, out to the deck, before struggling up on the table. He stands, and, using a silver fork, taps the side of his beer glass thrice to call the assembled to attention.

With everyone silently watching on, he clears his throat and starts airing the station's dirty laundry in public, using the dialect of the drunken slur with tics.

"Our stashon is thirty years old next year, an whatra a jurney we've bin on. From a hummul beginnin out in Rocky Bay to now having over fiffy broadcasters," Larry ticcing, emotional, choking up. "We've given a voice to people, some of whom, most would just ignored. We've brought a community together, heck, we *are* a community and I'm poud of every one of yous. Thish coming year was always gonnabe be a tranormsmative year at this station, and Mappy to say we've got our new PD Mark who's brought a fresh sound to the station of late. Look Arhll be hon-net with yuh. Arv got good news and bad news. I'll start with the good news. I found out yesterday that we have now raised the money to cover our ten percent of the cost of securing the frequency, but I'm afray theres bad news. As some of you know, Avbhunin Wellinton's week. I had a meeting with *New Zealand On Air*. Dreason for this was because we've had so many complaints upheld by the

BSA and I'm afraid to tell you, that as a result of those complaints we are now in real danger of the station being wound up."

As Larry slurs away, only Derek notices that Sarin, who looks excited, pulls her phone from her red Chanel clutch. She spends a moment fingering it, smirking as Larry continues, "so whass-gunna 'appen now is New Zealand On Air are sendin up two of board members to the island on a fact-finding mission this weeken. In fact they'll be here for the Santa Parade on the weeken. So if you see 'em be nice. Look, the station is on probation now. If we want to save it, we're going to have to pull everything we have together, and we can't have any more breaches of the rules. No swearing, no calling people out, no incitement, nothing."

Right on cue, the timer for the turducken goes off and Larry, visibly shaken, steps down from on high to try to salvage the evening with novelty meats.

Chapter 22

THE TEXT

Saturday, 14th December – 19:10

Chunk is the only one to notice the smell of meat coming from Barry Twelvedogs' jacket. It's a pocket full of sausages he's squirreling away in a foil carry bag to take home with him. Barry is still in the naughty corner, set apart from the rest of the gathering with Sarin, Denise, and Derek. Neither has said much since Larry's drunken announcement, except of course for Denise, who's mentioned her allergies several times.

Sarin speaks up. Her superiority lisp is back, "I mean what's with his tic? Jesus, I'd have that looked at if I were him."

"Fair go, Sarin, leave him alone." Derek abruptly says.

"Pffft," Sarin pauses, she means what she is about to say, "makes him look like even more of a cripple."

Outside of their sexual congress in the back of her Cayenne, Derek doesn't know Sarin. He has the measure of her now though. This is one stuck-up-bitch. She could easily turn on him too, but the two-hundred-and-fifty-gram boerewors between Derek's legs grants him a modicum of leverage.

"You didn't have to come, Sarin," Derek says, fed up. "In fact, you've done nothing but whinge ever since you got here."

Sarin looks affronted and without saying anything, she motions to Denise and the pair stand up to go to the bathroom, Sarin leaving her phone behind on the seat, unlocked. Derek looks down at the phone as its screen dims, but, before it goes fully dark, a message comes through, re-lighting its face with a ding. It catches Derek's attention, and he picks it up and reads the message.

Great job love, keep turning the screw JD XX

Derek can't help himself. He taps the phone to open the message. It's a reply to a message Sarin sent.

It worked!! The cripple just announced the station is as good as finished!! LOL S XX

Thinking quickly, Derek grabs his own phone and takes photos of the messages, then marks them as unread and places the phone back on the seat.

When Sarin returns from the bathroom, she doesn't bother sitting down. Instead, she scoops her mobile and her clutch, saying. "We're going now, I'll see you on Wednesday, Derek." She pauses and turning to Barry, she points at his gut saying, "oh, before I forget, I've been meaning to say this for ages, but you know, Barry, that Liverpool shirt you always wear stinks. It's too small for you too. I mean, it's disgusting, everyone can see your gut and your pubic hairs sticking out the top of your trousers. You look like a fucking hillbilly, and you stink of BO. Oh, and there's a grease stain on your jacket pocket where you've been hiding those sausages. Come on, Denise, let's go."

Chapter 23

THE HUNCHBACK OF ONEROA

Monday, 16th December – 09:10

Monday Morning's edition of Island Breakfast is running, and Anderson Yogamum is at the helm. Fijian by birth, local by choice, he's rostered on Mondays and always has a few of his own scripted featurettes. Easy and effective. Music News at seven-fifteen, Box Office Top Ten at quarter-past-eight, and now, over a bed of *Oxygene Part Four* by Jean Michel Jarre, Anderson is up to Leo in his weekly horoscope feature.

On the other side of the building, Larry cocks his ear. Never one to admit it, but, being born in late July, he always pauses for Anderson's horoscopes, seeing what the future might hold for those born around the same time of year as him. It is the first time Larry has paused in more than an hour, immersed as he is, in the report he is writing for New Zealand On Air. Extrapolating excuses from his frontal lobe, before depositing them into Microsoft Word. Bent double over his keyboard like a Twenty-First Century Quasimodo.

As Larry listens, he gazes out of the window to where Melody is standing at the post-box by the path. In her left hand there are around five or six envelopes, normal for a Monday. In her right, she holds a flyer which she avidly scrutinises with a scrunched-up face. Moments later, enraged, she is in Larry's office pressing the same flyer into his hand.

"Look at this," she spits.

Larry scans the slug line at the top of the pamphlet before saying, "Jesus," slowly drawing out the word so as to better illustrate his disappointment in humanity, and then he tuts before continuing.

"Where d'ya get that?"

"Post-box."

"Here?"

"Yeah."

"Our post-box?"

"Yeah."

"Really?"

"Yeah."

"But who's gonna do that?" Larry is aghast.

"I dunno."

"D'ya reckon it was a kid?"

"Might've been, I mean, the spelling's pretty child-like."

"Look, give it to me. I'll mention it to Constable Willie tomorrow," and then, he puts the piece of paper down, face up in his in-tray.

Forty-five minutes later, Anderson brings Island Breakfast to a close. Drawing the curtain with *The Captain* by The Phoenix Foundation, it is on the first chorus when Larry pushes send on the email to Bruce Bennett at the council. As they've requested in his meeting with the NZOA Board he copies in Beverley Watson and Lambartus Butler and then he moves on to his next appointment. The weekly meeting. Always around the kitchen table and always accompanied by a plate of biscuits and a pot of coffee.

"Look, I need to start with an apology. I really shouldn't have said what I said on Saturday. It was the booze. I'm mortified."

"Do we need to start looking for new jobs, Larry?" Melody says.

"No, not yet."

"Yet?" Mark is aghast.

"Look, it's not all bad. It's still in our hands. They did set a provisional auction date for the frequency though, so we can't have any more complaints."

"They've set an auction day? When's that?"

"Valentine's Day."

"But, Larry, if our frequency ends up going to auction, we can't possibly win." Melody says dejected. "It'll go for millions. Radiohub or UNZ will end up buying it."

"Nothing is set in stone yet. This is just a worst-case scenario. No more complaints though eh?" Larry says forcefully, as he points with his pen in the direction of Mark, "If we do that, we'll be OK. If we don't, we're toast."

"OK, what else? So, I think I mentioned this on Saturday too, but they want to send a fact-finding delegation up on Friday, for the Santa Parade and because of this, I can't be Santa, so we'll have to get someone else to do it."

"Mark'll do it."

"I won't

"Oh, come on."

"No way."

"It'll be fun."

"No chance."

"Come on."

"Get Bill?"

"Nah, he can't do it."

"Why not?"

"Well for a start, they've not got his size Santa suit on the island," says Melody.

"Not to mention the restraining order." Larry adds under his breath, coughing.

"But, but."

"Come on, you have to, you'd be brilliant at it."

"I'm not fat enough though."

"Come on, Holly'll make you a fat suit." Larry offers.

"I don't know."

"Oh, *come on*. We need you."

Mark tuts. Then begrudgingly says, "Alright, I'll do it."

"'Maybe you could get the monkey to come? We could dress him as an elf," Larry says.

"I can ask."

"No, I don't want the monkey there, from what you're saying it's behaviour might not be appropriate for family event. And anyway, I won't be party to any monkey business, it, it's cruel."

"Fair enough."

"Okay, no monkey. Gotta say, I'm a bit worried about that storm that's coming in though, we'll have to have a wet weather plan for it."

"Oh, Cyclone Frank apparently that might only be coming through on Sunday now, maybe even Monday, we might be ok." Mark says.

Larry, keen to get through the agenda. "Okay, that's decided then, no monkey and Mark, you'll be our Santa. Righto, so I've got to finish this report for New Zealand On Air, so I'll be flat tack on that over the next couple of days. What else?" Larry tapping the words written on the agenda as he addresses each associated subject. "Look, we'll need to get hold of Sarin, Derek and every one of the GLITFAB Crew, they can't do their shows live anymore. They're gonna have to do them as pre-records from now on. Mark, I'll need you to contact all of them ASAP. Tread carefully with Sarin though, I don't want it getting to Wednesday and her saying she's been ambushed."

Chapter 24

THE CHMP

Monday, 16th December - 11:50

At ten to noon, Larry stands at the kettle for his third coffee of the morning. He always watches it boil, but this time his attention is taken by a red Nissan Leaf parking out front. He recognises the car, the blue Waiheke Island Radio sticker on its back bumper and the four-character number plate reading CHMP. It's the GLITFAB Crew, and non-binary kingpin Darcey Knight is at the wheel. Larry continues to watch as Darcey and their four passengers trot up the path towards the radio station in the following order. Korean drag queen, and trans activist, Sylvia Park (She/Her), recently engaged couple Lynn Mall (They/Them) and Hunter S. Plaza (He/Him), and Albany Westfield (She/Her). While Darcey wasn't a founding member of the GLITFAB Crew, they most definitely had the highest profile, and this was because they were as hard as fuck. It hadn't always been this way.

As a child Darcey Knight was bullied mercilessly at school. Born a boy, but not sure why and naturally different from all the other pupils. By the age of eleven Darcey took up boxing. They excelled at it and quickly passed through the ranks. Fuckin' up straights for shits and giggles. By the age of nineteen, Darcey was so good at boxing, they were standing on top of the podium with a gold medal draped round their neck at the Istanbul Olympics. The first Kiwi in over a century to become an Olympic boxing champion. A national treasure.

The New Zealand tabloid press had always been cruel though, and they christened Darcey a 'misfit' due to their unpredictability in their interviews. When Darcey went on *Walt Hooper's Kiwi Sports Afternoon* on a Sunday, and outed themself as non-binary, it went off. For a lot of Walt's live stream crowd, it was *really* confusing. Here was this hard cunt but they exuded femininity. A fighting machine with luxuriant hair, elegant earrings, make-up that would've taken hours to apply. They looked good, but the common man's boner-killer would've been the muscles. The muscles and the beard. There's also the fact that if you thought it through to its logical conclusion, you'd never get near the remote if you shacked up with them.

"G'day, boss," Darcey says. Today, their hair is tied up in a bun. Red lipstick. Black nose hair extensions. Darcey has shaved their left eyebrow off a week earlier. Seeing whether it worked as a look. Double denim stonewash. Jacket and jeans. Cowboy boots which make a clopping sound on the wooden floor of the kitchenette.

"Hi, Larry, you OK, hun?" Sylvia says with some concern.

"Yeah, I'm OK, look erm. Look, I'm sorry about the speech I gave on Saturday. Pretty embarrassing. I was hammered, I'd not eaten much, drank too much."

"Well, Larry, and I think I can say this for all of us that it'll be a bit tamer from now on, Larr. And honestly, all jokes aside, we're all really sorry about *A Dozen Dildos at Dinnertime*. We'd no idea. We shouldn't have done that. We just got carried away. We're all guttered, Larry. Sorry," says Darcey, before continuing, "grope hug, grope hug, come on bring it in." Larry is in his element in that embrace, and the group hold onto it for about seven seconds or so.

When they break the huddle, Larry takes the room again, "thanks for agreeing to pre-record the show at such short notice folks. Listen, we'll get through this. We've been through worse. Oh also, we have the Santa Parade coming up on Saturday, now assuming the weather holds up are any of you available to help out?"

"Or hanson-deck, Larry."

"Cool, I'll send you an email. There's loads needs doing."

"Don't worry, Larry, whatever you need."

"So, er, what are you going to be talking about in your show today?' Larry asked.

"Well, darling, we've got a five-minute segment on cock rings, and we've done some vox-pops on butt-plugs" Albany Westfield almost singing it, and throwing out jazz hands simultaneously.

"*You've got a what?!*" Replies Larry, spitting out his coffee in alarm. "You haven't!"

"No just kidding, Larr!"

Everyone laughs. Larry comes around saying, "Ah, look, you weren't the worst culprits."

"Really."

"No, not by a long way."

"Oh well, we all know who that is, don't we?" Darcey interrupts, irritated. "Hardly rocking-science is it? I mean, everyone knows who it is. Aunty Vax, Sarin Murray, she's the only one who's always trying to rustle people's feathers."

"I can't talk too much about it," Larry says, pretending to be neutral. Not wishing to correct someone who could dry their back with his spine.

"She's a fucking menthol case if you ask me. Fucken TERF, nazi scum."

"Erm, look, I can't really be talking about this. I could get into a lot of trouble for it," Larry says.

"Wait, Larry, now that they mention nazis, have you seen this?" Sylvia Park is pulling one of these new racist flyers from her pocket and pushing it towards him.

"Ahhh, pfftt, not another one. It's the third one today." Larry says as he shakes his head.

🐶

All up, a hundred copies of that new racist flyer were printed. Two had been placed on windscreens at Christchurch Airport the previous day. Four had been placed on windscreens at Auckland Airport. Twenty were dispatched in the Auckland CBD and thirty were put through letterboxes, and on cars on the island. It's a piece of A4 paper, folded in half and styled like a tabloid newspaper. KEEP NEW ZEALAND WHITE it says on the front, and in it there are racist tropes about Māori, Asians and black people.

Chapter 25

THE STENCH

Tuesday, 17th December – 05:00

It's five in the morning and Larry can't sleep. He never got off in the first place. Between eleven and one, for the second consecutive day, he spent two hours reassuring his youngest son, Oscar that the bogeyman does not in fact live under the bed. This, despite the youngster having been told otherwise by a 'man with spots' at the party on Saturday. The dog's apnoea is the second reason, the grunting sound it makes as it snores, loud enough to wake him albeit from another room. The third reason is the radio station. All these worries and concerns and stresses and strains, the lack of sleep, it's all accumulating in the amygdala part of his brain and he climbs from his pit, he makes a flask of coffee, and he leaves for work to go and finish his report.

It's a forty-minute drive from his place, across the island and on to the township of Oneroa, all before sunrise. As he drives, he listens to the tail end of Radio New Zealand *Nights*. He gets to his desk, he's at it straight away, and for the next two hours, he is buried. Solid graft until the sound of a diesel engine piques his attention. He looks out of the window. It's a Nissan Civilian motorhome and it is reversing into one of the gravel parking spots out front of the station.

Derek Barnaby and Barry Twelvedogs climb out. Barnaby seems annoyed at Twelvedogs and is motioning towards a rip that runs down the right seam of his black trousers. As usual, he is wearing his white-clerical-dog-collar and holding a red hardback book close to his chest. Twelvedogs looks like he stinks. He has his dirty Liverpool football shirt on again. The pair trudge into the station, and knock on Larry's office door, which has been open all along.

"Morning, Father, morning Barry," Larry says curtly. He's been bereft of his usual joviality for over a week now.

"Bless you my child," says Derek Barnaby.

"MMMM Morning Boss," says Twelvedogs with an electronic buzz.

"What's happened to your trousers?"

"Oh that? This bloody idiot..." he says, motioning towards Twelvedogs, "... he's only gone and damaged the panelling in my campervan toilet."

"MMMM it was an accident," protests Barry.

"Yeah well, it's ruined my good trousers, hasn't it, I love these trousers too. I got them from Rembrandt."

"So, what's wrong with the panelling then?" says Larry.

"Oh, it's come away from the wall."

"You could always use our sewing kit."

"MMMM What? For the wall?"

"No, for the trousers."

"Nah, she'll be alright. I'll fix them in the van later. I've got a sewing kit in there. Hey er, Larry, look I know we touched on it on Saturday, but I just wanna let you know how sorry we are about this whole mess. We didn't think it'd turn out like this. We were just, you know, testing the limits, prodding the bear. Speaking truth to power."

"See where the truth got us, Derek?" Larry says, deflated, "look, at least you've agreed to doing the show as a pre-record. Thanks for that but I'm afraid this is how it'll have to be from now on. We just can't risk any more complaints."

"Yeah, that's fine." Derek says looking down at the floor like a child outside the headmaster's office. Then he continued, "Actually, there is something I think you'd be interested in seeing Larry."

"Oh yeah, what's that?"

Derek turns to Barry saying, "Can you leave us alone for a second Dogsy?"

"MMMM oh? Okay," Barry has a slow wit and hasn't yet twigged to Derek's affair with Sarin. Derek wants it to stay that way. Duly, as Derek steps into the room to sit down on Larry's office couch, Barry scuttles off to the green three-seater in reception, oblivious to the body odour he is taking with him. Now, Derek is free to continue, saying, "look Larry, remember that speech you gave on Saturday?"

"I do."

"See Sarin?"

"What of it?"

"Something's going on Larry."

"What do you mean, 'something's going on.'?"

"She smiled, Larry." Derek leaning in now, "Larry, she smiled when you got up onto the table and told everyone the station was almost finished."

"I mentioned *that*?"

"Well, yeah amongst other things. Everyone heard it. You called for silence with a fork and a glass."

"I did?"

"Are you not listening, Larry?" It's not often that Larry is the one to play the fool in a conversation between him and Derek Barnaby, but this is the role he inhabits now, "Right. When you said the station might get defunded, she started smiling."

Larry looks like a stunned mullet.

"She was the only one there happy about it, Larry. I saw it with my own eyes. Clear as day. Gets worse though, 'cos after that, she left her phone open on the seat next to mine. Anyway, this message comes through. It's pretty sus. I took a picture of it on my phone," as Derek speaks, he pulls his phone from his pocket and thrusts it into Larry's face.

Great job... keep turning the screw... LOL... JD XXX

"Well, what does that even mean anyway Derek?" Larry says, irritated.

"Look, there's another one, Larry, see, *this* message is a reply to an earlier message. I've got a picture of that one too, look."

It worked!! The cripple just announced the station is as good as finished!! LOL S XX

Larry can only stare at the image for a moment in silence. He can't speak due to the ball of rage that's spinning inside of him, when he does speak this is what he says, "And I'm the cripple here right? Derek man, what are you trying to say here?" he snaps.

"I'm saying she's doing it on purpose. I think she'd been trying to get us in trouble with New Zealand On Air, Larry. Remember that Ten-Eighty piece I got in trouble with?"

"Yeah."

"She egged me on for that. Gave me a blowjob in the toilet after I'd done it. It was in the toilet, just there," he says pointing at the wall. "It was a good one too but I'm not sure…"

"Whoa! She gave you a blowjob?"

"Yeah."

"In that toilet there?"

"Yeah."

"Why didn't you do it in your RV?"

"Toilet's closer. Larry, she dragged me in there."

"Have you any idea how disgusting that is?" Larry is incredulous.

"Come on Larry, harden up, it's only a blowjob," Derek says matter of fact.

"It's right next to my workstation, Derek," pointing, "that's a thin wall."

"Sorry, Boss."

"It'd have been between your shows too, eh?"

"Yeah."

"Around lunchtime, right?"

"Yeah."

"But I'd have been *eating*." The word 'eating' being drawn out slowly to illustrate the disgust. "I can't believe I, with my tuna sandwich, was separated from *you* getting your dick sucked by a thin wall. That's appalling."

"It's not an easy thing to turn down for a man of my age?"

"Should've done it in the RV. Anyway, we're getting off topic. I think we're going to need to bring Mark in on this whole Sarin Murray situation. He is the station's Programme Director. It's his wheelhouse, this." Then, Larry turns towards the closed door and bellows "*Mark*!!" through it.

⊌

"So, in summary, Sarin Murray might be involved in a conspiracy to destroy our station. She's using sex to manipulate Derek here, and it turns out that she's been the architect of three of the four BSA strikes."

"Now sports!" Derek says, delighting at his own gag.

"I think we need to find out who this JD is," Mark says, "we've got to get as much information as possible. We want to be getting her phone."

"How're we supposed to do that?"

Derek pipes up, "Remember once, there was this buzzing in Studio One. Wendy said it was a mobile phone thing. Wouldn't let anyone in there with a phone for three weeks. Why don't you just tell her that there's a problem with the gear and that phones aren't allowed."

"That's not a bad idea, shame you'd only have the phone for a few minutes."

"Not unless you cloned it," Mark says.

"The phone?"

"Yeah."

"You can do that?"

"Bento can."

"The monkey man!" Larry says with a tic.

"Yeah."

"You know he told my kids our house is haunted."

"Ha!"

"It's not funny. He told them that it's an old house and that there'd been a murder in it, in the nineties. A dissident Chinese poet called Gu Cheng, apparently. Killed his wife with an axe, while they were both away in exile. Chopped her up, hung himself in the bush."

"Well, is it?" Mark says laughing.

"Is it what?"

"Haunted."

"No! That house is in Rocky Bay. It's on Fairview Road. Anyway, they've been having these nightmares about it ever since. Kept me up last night, that and the dog's snoring.'"

"Oh man, you can't take him anywhere."

"Can he really do it? Clone a phone? Your mate?"

"Yeah, he did it for my brother when his screen broke."

"How long does it take?"

"What?"

"Cloning a phone."

"Dunno, five minutes? Probably depends on how much data's on it."

Larry is sceptical, and he snickers through his nose before saying, "You know, even if you do get her phone, you still won't have the PIN."

"Oh, Bento can get through them too."

"Yeah?"

"Is there no end to this man's talent? Reckon, he could come up tomorrow?"

"I can ask."

"Is any of this even legal?"

"Maybe not. Who knows?"

"D'ya care?"

Just then there's a knock at Larry's office door.

"Come in," says Larry towards it.

Chapter 26

THE SPELLING

Tuesday, 17th December - 09:25

"Allo, allo, allo," says Constable Willie Hamilton QSM as he opens the door and pops his head around it, "did someone call the Police?" His voice is deep and honeyed and once a fortnight, listeners are treated to its sound as he delivers his segment on crime and crime prevention during Remington Dill's *Tuesday Island Breakfast.* As usual, Willie is dressed in full uniform.

As soon as he hears Willie's dulcet tones, Larry looks over at Derek and Mark, hoping that the surprise copper hasn't just heard them conspiring to commit a crime, "Willie!! Just the man!" Larry, thinking on his feet, "have you seen these racist flyers doing the rounds? I've got four of them now."

"Keep New Zealand White?"

"Yup."

"Brains of a rocking horse, eh?"

"That's the one."

"Have you seen the spelling?"

Larry just laughs.

"...diabolical. Have you seen it? 'Must of bin' come on. Do better"

"Speaks to the intellect, my dear Willie. You onto anyone?"

"I think so. Can't really hang about here and talk about it though, I'm running late." With that Willie slips into the on-air studio, where Remington Dill is in the hot seat.

Even for one so young, Remington Dill is a pro, and he'll precede Willie's segment with a self-made musical intro that's set to the fanfare from the film *Rocky*. Over the top of the music, Remi had spliced in the sound of a riot ripped straight from *YouTube*. It is gritty and it has dogs barking in it and sirens too, shouting low in the mix. Remi does his introductions over the tail end of the bed and then fades it below their chat.

"Now Willie, have you seen these racist flyers? I've heard from a lot of people on the island who've found them. What's with that?"

"Yeah, that's right, Remi. I've seen them. They started showing up on Sunday night. Larry just gave me this one here." As he says it, Willie rustles the paper into the microphone like a pro, "About twenty have been reported now. Pretty indiscriminate really."

"So have you got any leads on this one, Constable Willie?"

"Well, as it happens, we do." Willie replies smugly.

"Go on then."

"Well, the leader of the New Zealand National Front, Caleb McGill is on the island visiting his uncle in Palm Beach, so that's a red flag. Now, the same leaflet started showing up on car windscreens at the airport in Christchurch, then some were reported at Auckland Airport, several were picked up in Auckland City and the rest have been here on the island."

"Go on."

"Guess where Mr McGill lives, and for a bonus point guess how he got here?"

"Christchurch? Came by plane?"

"You got it. I mean, come on, Mr McGill, it's not even police work with specimens like you. It's as easy as following footprints in the snow. They don't even try, Remi. It's an insult to us as police officers."

"So will you arrest him?"

"Well, when we know for sure it is him, then yeah we'll have a chat, but we need to be able to prove it first, so keep on the lookout folks."

Chapter 27

THE LOGICAL SONG

Tuesday, 17th December - 11:45

"So, I take it you've not been able to raise Sarin yet?" Larry says from his desk with Mark opposite as *The Logical Song* by Supertramp plays in the background.

"Nah, no answer every time."

"Did you leave a message?"

"I've left a few."

"Did you tell her we want her to go to pre-records in those messages?"

"Yeah."

"And she's ignored you?"

"Yeah."

Tic, "Well, we're gonna have to assume she's ignoring your calls for a reason."

"Yep."

"You know, I reckon she'll be in to do her show as usual tomorrow. We should prepare for that. We've got to get that phone, it's the only way we can get to the bottom of this."

"You know, I've gotta say, Larry, I think Derek Barnaby might be on to something. We can just tell her that there's a buzzing sound coming off the speaker when a mobile phone goes near it. I'll put a notice up on the door. What's she going to do? And as a back up I'll re-programme the desk, play one of her earlier shows. She'll never know."

"Make sure she hands you that phone. If she doesn't then don't let her into the studio."

"OK, boss."

"And Bento's coming up to clone it is he?"

"Yeah."

"That's confirmed?"

"Yeah."

"And he knows what time?"

Chapter 28

THE NAZI

Wednesday, 18th December - 11:50

Just five minutes to go until Sarin's show is due to air and there's still no sign of her. The trap is primed. Bento sits on the couch in Larry's office. In front of him his is cloning kit. A mobile phone connected to a laptop via an orange USB cable and a spare phone sits beside that. As the pair wait, Mark is in the kitchen snaffling a biscuit from a plate in the centre of the table. As his teeth move through its custard crème centre, the bell in reception dings.

"I'll get it," Mark shouts, walking over to the partition. He pushes through it and as he does, he immediately recognises the visitor saying, "I know you."

The visitor is a man called Caleb McGill. He is known for being the leader of the neo-Nazi group, the New Zealand National Front. Caleb was recently released from prison. Mark recognises his face from TV a few weeks earlier when his release had been reported on the news. Bento was right, Caleb is indeed a child frightener. The face, a mash of boils, and a nose reminiscent of a mollusc. Shelled and dominant, resting on his face like a sleeping dick. His eyeballs consistent with the rest of his face's topography, unusually close together and bulbous as all Hell, clamping at his nose's bridge like two thumbs clasped around a zit. Ugly but cut. His arms are like tree trunks. He could dominate many a man.

"I'm here to see Sarin Murray." He grunts, eyeing Mark up and down like he wants to dominate him.

"Really?"

"Yeah, said I should meet her here at quarter to twelve, I'm a bit late though."

"You've been in touch with her?"

"Yeah, spoke to her yesterday."

Mark pauses, before saying, "Right, well, before you get any ideas, mate, I've got a couple of gays in the pre-record, a gypsy in the booth, the boss is half Jewish half Māori, my colleague's also a Māori, and a man in an electric wheelchair will be along any minute."

The comment disarms Caleb. And a sudden air of reason seems to radiate through his face, he softens, "oh no, no, no mate, mate. I don't want any trouble. I'm just here to talk about globalism."

🐶

Outside, Sarin's red Cayenne is parking in the gravel and even with his limp, Larry seems to levitate away from what he is doing gliding over to the door. Up the path he goes, out into the carpark, and then tapping on Sarin's car window he says, "Why's New Zealand's top Nazi sitting my reception area Sarin?"

"You dare ambush me," Sarin spits as she opens the car door, "don't you know who I am?"

"Listen Sarin, I'll not stand idly by while you invite people like that into my radio station."

"Oh, he's not a nazi," Sarin says, laughing as she gathers the Chanel clutch from the passenger seat of the car, "I met him at an anti-globalisation rally in Christchurch last week. He wants to come on the show and talk about the one-world government," she continues, smirking a smirk that would be on the other side of her face if she only knew that Mark had reprogrammed the desk, and that today's episode of *The Red Pill* would be a harmless pre-record from six weeks ago about Ten-Eighty.

"Oh, by the way, Sarin, there's something wrong with our fold back."

"The what?"

"Yeah, the fold back. You know when you get that buzzing sound sometimes when your phone is too close to a speaker?"

"Right."

"Well, you can't take your phone in there, we can't have the speakers blowing."

"Okay, whatever."

As Sarin is about to enter the studio, she hands her phone to Mark as a petulant teenager might. Caleb follows suit.

Chapter 29

THE CLONE ROSES

Wednesday, 18th December - 12:49

Throughout the duration of her half-hour show, and whilst under the misapprehension that she is broadcasting live to air, both phones are cloned to new devices. It takes a little longer than normal because it's chock full of data. After it's finished cloning, Bento boots it. Pressing the button on the left side panel.

"Do you get your broadcasters to fill out their information when they join the station?"

"Yeah, there's a declaration to abide by our rules, they have to sign it."

"Has it got their date of birth on it?"

"Yeah."

"Can you pull her file please?" Bento is unusually business-like.

"Mark's got them, what do you need that for?"

"PIN number."

"Yeah, good luck with that mate," Larry says sceptically.

"Twenty-third of September Nineteen Eighty," says Mark.

Duly, Bento taps in the numbers 230980 into the iPhone in his hand, "yes!" Larry looks on in amazement and tics as the phone seems to move past the lock screen.

"Always works, bet yours is your birthday too."

It is.

After a few seconds of elation, nothing happens. Twenty seconds more go by, but the phone is stuck halfway between the lock screen and the home screen.

"Come on!" Bento urges the phone through gritted teeth, willing it to do something, anything. A minute passes before he starts to concede, "Fuck! It's frozen."

"Let's have a look at it," Mark says sceptically, adding "reboot it," duly the phone is restarted and once it boots back up, he taps in the same six-digit code. The same thing happens again.

"Mate, I think we've got the passcode, but I don't think it's been cloned right. It should've gone in straight away. You can keep trying but you'll get the same response."

Chapter 30

THE FIRE

Thursday, 19th December - 09:25

Larry is first the first one to arrive at the radio station the following day, pitching up at ten past nine, Mark arrives five minutes later, and at twenty-five-past, Melody pulls in the mail at the bottom of the garden path and scans the two envelopes in her hand. Both are addressed to Larry. One of them has the logo of the Auckland law firm Mussell Decker Biggs in the top left corner. The other is housed in brown and has 'bill' written all over it. As usual, Melody strolls back in, hands the mail to Larry and goes back to her desk where she places a call of a personal nature.

"Oh, hi, Gretchen," she hesitates, "erm, look I know you're probably busy, but I just wanted to see how you were, erm. I, I saw the fire on the news this morning. Well, I just don't know what to say. Give me a call, if you need to get away. I've still got that spare room here on Waiheke and I'll cook if you want," again Melody pauses, "anyway er, let me know that you're alright, I'm worried about you." And with that the call is terminated.

"What? What's this about a fire?" Larry asks, doing a slower, more considered whack-a-mole around his office door, the letter from Mussell Dekker Biggs unopened on his desk.

"It was on the news last night. There was a fire at Radio Christ."

"Jesus, Radio Christ?"

"Yeah."

"Anyone hurt?"

"I dunno. Says on X it's arson. I mean, who'd want to burn Radio Christ down?"

"Well, he's not without his enemies, you know."

"Who?"

"Shilbottle."

"Really?"

"Pfft, yeah," Larry says incredulously, "drives a Bentley, preaches about sacrifice. Not a good look."

"He didn't drive one of those when I worked there."

"He does now."

Chapter 31

THE COUNCIL

Thursday, 19th December - 9:30

It's half nine and Larry is about to get to the Mussell Dekker Biggs envelope. He considers it in his hands as his desk-phone rings again.

BREET BREET

BREET BREET

"Excuse me," he says to Melody, before reaching across the desk and picking up the receiver.

"Larry Minto."

"G'day mate it's me, Bruce, from the council."

"G'day, mate."

"Sorry I missed the party, mate. I was over on the mainland."

"No worries."

"Got your email. The one about the building," there's a pause here, "Larry, what are you trying to say, mate? You've got that lease for as long as you want it. All you need to do is keep things ticking over."

"There's more to it than that, Bruce."

"Well, are you giving notice or what?"

"Not exactly."

"What've you sent this email for then?"

"The board at NZOA told me to."

"That's your bosses, right?"

"Yeah."

"I noticed you'd copied them in. I don't know what's it got to do with them. They've no involvement in our arrangement."

"Bruce, the truth is, we're one more complaint away from being wound up."

Bruce, going up an octave, "oath?"

"Yeah, oath."

"Jesus, Larry, I didn't realise. Is this common knowledge?"

Sheepishly, Larry says, "I might've mentioned it at the Christmas party."

"Oh, Larry, but you know what is weird. I had this fella call me, wanting to view your stations property."

"What?"

"I had this phone call from a fella wanting to view your station's property."

"The station property, what?" Larry is completely confused now, "But how could he have known about that?"

"Well, it's not come from me."

"Duh!"

"Thing is, you're going to have to facilitate the request. Show him around, humour him, Larry, I mean, I'm on your side but if it gets out that I've in any way blocked anyone from viewing that property, I'll be for the high jump, especially if you've given some kind of notice on the place."

"Well, I don't want to get you in any trouble."

"Mate, there's plenty of people on the local board who'll be happy to see that building sold. It's worth millions on location alone. And you know what'll happen then, they'll just bowl the place over. Another faceless McMansion."

"Yeah, don't I know it. So, er, when's he wanting to view it then?"

"Tomorrow morning."

"*Tomorrow!*" Larry is aghast, "*you sure?*"

"Yep."

"What time?"

"Ten."

"*Ten?* But that's when the delegation from NZOA is arriving."

"What? They're coming up too?"

"Yeah, they're sending a delegation up, I'm telling you mate, I'm shovelling shit up a hill against a downward wind."

When the call is terminated, Larry moves on to his next task. The mail.

He knows who Mussell Decker Biggs are but has no idea why they would write to him. That's until he reads the three words in bold at the top of the page.

Chapter 32

LETTER BEFORE ACTION

At nine thirty-five on the morning of the seventeenth of December, Constable Willie Hamilton appeared on a radio show entitled *Island Breakfast* on *Waiheke Island Radio*. That edition of the show was hosted by a young man called Remington Dill.

Mr Dill asked Constable Hamilton whether police had any leads on a case where racially sensitive flyers had been distributed about several Waiheke Island post boxes.

Constable Hamilton confirmed that there was a suspect, and that the suspect was my client, Mr Caleb McGill. Mr McGill refutes all knowledge of any criminal acts and will pursue legal action through the courts. He will also be lodging a formal complaint with the Broadcasting Standards Authority.

Chapter 33

THE SECOND COUNSEL

Thursday, 19th December - 10:40

It's panic stations inside the manager's office at Waiheke Island Radio. Outside, Holly is walking up the path toward the station's front door, the crimson Santa Claus outfit visible through the dry cleaners' bag that's draped over her forearm. In her right hand she carries a yellow Pak 'N Save eco-bag, in which there's a Santa Claus wig, beard, and sundry accessories. Her first port of call is Larry's office.

"What's up now?" She says with gentle exasperation as she leans on the open door's frame.

"Read this," Larry, red in the face, tic deteriorating. It has two parts to it now, does Larry's tic. Neck-jerks-back. Right-arm-twitch-front

He thrusts Letter Before Action from Mussell Decker Biggs in Holly's general direction with another right-arm-twitch-front. Holly walks into the room and takes the letter, then sitting down, she proceeds to read it. This takes about sixty seconds, "you know they don't necessarily have a case here. This is probably just a scare tactic, some kind of strategy," she says.

Larry doesn't reply. He just sits there shitting bricks. It has been Code Brown ever since that letter came in from NZOA ten days earlier.

"Larry, there's not much anyone's gonna do this side of Christmas. You need to be switching off. Have a break from it. Keep it quiet 'til the New Year."

"Reckon?"

"Yeah, keep it quiet, you don't want to be ruining anyone's holiday."

"Guess not."

"You know you never told me what happened with Sarin's phone, did you get what you needed?"

"The cloning?" Tics.

"Yeah."

"It corrupted."

"The clone? Oh no."

"It always was a long shot, Hol."

"There must be something else we can try."

"Beats me."

"Ask that idiot friend of Mark's, the one with the monkey. See if he's got any more tricks up his sleeve?"

Chapter 34

THE DOCTORS OF DISTINCTION

Thursday, 19th December - 13:45

Thursday afternoon, one 'til two and the show *Better Living* is playing on the station. It's in its fourth year now and has a song with original lyrics for its promo. It's one of Mark's new ones. It tells listeners everything they need to know about the show. What it is called, what it is about, and when it is broadcast. Loosely, it goes to the tune of *The Girl from Ipanema* by Astrid Gilberto and Stan Getz:

Memories of ailments and treatments.
Visions of rashes and cures.
Gout has always been a popular subject.
Boils and bunions and sores.
One o'clock, Tuesday lunchtime,
Tune in for health and more.
Better Living's here to help you.
Tune in for healthy talk.

As well as having a great promo, *Better Living* is prerecorded on a Tuesday night, and broadcast two days later. In post-production, the show's producer, Jane, nullifies objectionable cusswords by reversing them. A game for the hosts, is seeing how many cusswords they can get Jane to reverse for each half hour of talk time they have. Pretty childish but people love it.

The show is also notable for the length of the pause between Neville Southall's opening word on each show (which is always "now") and the next word he'll say. "Now," The auld boy lingers for a personal best, seven seconds, before getting into it. "...David from Surfdale's touching cloth. Says on Facebook he's getting a strong abdominal pain when he's stressed out, says he can't control his own bowels."

"Nasty," says Reidy on mic two.

"Female sufferers say it's worse than childbirth."

"Nothing's worse than childbirth."

"You'd know more than them yeah? Even though you've never experienced either."

"I might."

"Anyway, Dave's saying here it comes on very quickly. He's saying he's worried he's got cancer. What do you reckon?"

"And this is David in Surfdale right? Which one?"

"Doesn't say. It just says Dave in Surfdale."

"But there's loads of Daves in Surfdale, I know at least five Daves in Surfdale. Maybe they could form a club. The Dave Club. They could do football or bowling. Hacky sack."

"Riiiight."

"Clearly, the *tnuc* needs to have it looked at, doesn't he?" Says Reidy, suddenly straight "But, you know, to *me,* at first glance, that sounds like IBS-XL, the most irritable of bowel syndromes. I wouldn't go planning any funerals just yet. And it's not as uncommon as you'd think, you know. I've had loads of these *desra yttihs* cases in my surgery in the last few years. It's all the *etihs nekcuf* people are eating. All that processed *knaw,* giblets, lips and *selohesra.* Bottom shelf *tihs.*" Intake of breath.

"I had a patient in just last week, said he'd been having IBS-XL attacks. Said he'd go from not needing a *tihs* at all, to feeling like a victim in the film 'Alien'. Said it felt like a creature had gestated in his lower intestine, had a quick rummage through his digestive tract and was now about to kill him on the tiles in the bathroom."

"Yeah? That's a lot of detail."

"Yeah, it is Nev, *nekcuf* oath brother. I'm tellin' ya, I've seen a rise in these cases too. People are *gnittihs* themselves every *erehwydoolb.* It's brought on by stress, fear, and anxiety, it is."

"God help us if there's a war then eh?"

"Eh?"

"Yeah, you know, a real one with fighting and conscription and that. It'd stink. We'll be *dekcuf*. Royally *dekcuf*," Reidy sounds deflated. "We'd have no chance. It'd be the end of the realm." It's always like this with that show. Smutty but factual. Toilet but good. The pair didn't give a fuck whether you like it or not. That's your problem. Not theirs. Thankfully it isn't a problem for Mark, who has listened to it in his headphones, checking for loose swears, finding none.

🐶

Ruben Roberts is live in the studio hosting *Full Throttle* and Mark is in the audio-booth recording Ken Oath's promo when the bell in reception gives a ding. Melody answers it.

"Is he in?" Bento pushes through the partition and takes a seat at Mark's desk. He has the monkey with him. It is holding his hand before it let's go and skips onto Mark's desk where it starts picking pie crumbs out of the keyboard and eating them.

"Mark?"

"Yeah."

"He's just gone in the audio booth. I think he's recording a voiceover."

"Reckon he'll be long?"

"Probably not."

"Do you mind if I wait here then?"

Melody shrugs her shoulders and says, "is it called Bubbles?"

"Yeah."

"Like Michael Jackson's one, eh? You know it's cruel to keep a monkey. Should be in the wild."

"He's a happy monkey. I look after him. And anyway it's legal now"

"Pfft, I can't believe they legalised monkey ownership. This is supposed to be a progressive country."

"Well, I'm glad they did. I mean, he'd still be in a cage at the cigarette testing facility if he wasn't with me."

Melody shrugs her shoulders and continues with her work. As usual, Bento is fidgeting, and he reaches out for the first thing that catches his attention. It is Ken Oath's dog whistle which sits on Mark's desk. Of course he's going to blow it.

"Doesn't work," Bento remarks with disappointment.

All of the dogs within a one-hundred-yard radius would tell you otherwise. It is in excellent working order, and a ripple of barking is rolling along the main strip, all the way down to Blackpool.

"It's a dog whistle," Melody says, looking up again, "it's not for you to hear. It's for dogs. Clue is in the name, Sherlock."

Bento blows on it once more, a long enthusiastic burst that goes on for at least ten seconds. As he does, Ruben Roberts in the main On-Air studio, back-announces the track that just finished.

"Well, that was Tool there with the track *Schism...*" he says.

Unbeknownst to any human, the sound of Ken Oath's dog whistle is travelling again. This time it's travelling into the On-Air studio, through the room and into the main microphone. It travels up the transmitter, and by way of the fact that it is broadcast live on air, it isn't just the local dogs barking now, it's every dog within ten metres of every device listening. The strays at WISCA are going ballistic, Lloyd's having kittens, there's a fullblown riot underway at the Erua Road doggy daycare and all the dogs at Short-Shorts Dogsitter are staging a rooftop protest.

The sound isn't just being broadcast either. It's being recorded too, inadvertently committed to playback after one of the microphones in the audio booth captures the sound as Mark records Ken Oath's promo. Dogs will hear the whistle in the background every time the promo airs now. As Bento stops blowing, Mark emerges from the audio booth.

"Did he say 'Tool'?" Bento says.

"What?" Mark replies looking confused.

"Tool. Is that what he just said?"

"Who?"

"That DJ in there. Fat fella with the glasses and the bumfluff goatee."

"Oh, right, yeah, yeah he would've, yeah."

"Tool?"

"Yeah, man, it's a band."

"Really, but why would you name your band after a spanner?"

"Who says they named it after a spanner?"

"Ahhh."

"They might've named it after a spirit-level."

"No, definitely a spanner. Got your message."

"Well?" Mark looks at Bento expectantly, "is there anything else we can try?"

"There might be."

"Yeah?"

"Yeah."

"You know, you don't actually need a person's phone to get information on them."

"Really?"

"You only need the number."

"You can get her texts without the handset?"

"No, but sometimes you can get to the voicemails."

"Oath?"

"Yeah, bro."

"Go on then, how?"

"First, you hide your number. Then, after you've done that, phone her. Two seconds later I phone her. *Your call* is the primary call on the line. *My call* goes through to her voicemail. The voicemail has a backdoor, and no one ever updates their PIN. So, it's always at a factory default of four stars on the keypad. Assuming the PIN is four stars, you'd have access to the messages in her mailbox."

"What happens if she answers?"

"Put the phone down."

"Where'd ya learn that?"

"The Levison inquiry."

"What?'

"Yeah, man, there was an inquiry into people having their privacy invaded by crooked journalists in the UK. This is how they did it."

"Oath?"

"Yeah, they hacked a murdered child's voicemail for a story."

"Seriously?"

"Yeah, and because the message had been marked as 'listened to' it was 'saved' in her inbox. The girl's parents thought she was still alive. She was dead though."

"Those fucking lowlifes."

"All bastards."

"And we're just as bad."

"I wouldn't put it like that, we're doing it for the right reasons. Anyway, we'll try it now, listen to her messages, see if there's anything there. Do you have anything to record it with?"

In less than two minutes of Bento entering the building, the game is back on again. He, Mark, Melody, and Larry are all huddled together in Larry's office listening to Sarin's only saved message.

"Message Number One..."

"Write it down." Bento says.

"**From** 021 557 668 was left yesterday at 4:27 P.M."

"Hey, erm, can you give me a call, it's me, Jay."

"Think it's the same J? You know, JD from the text message," asked Melody.

"Who knows?"

"Check his mailbox too, do the same thing, but for that number that you just wrote down." Bento lit, "you can't fuck around, go for the jugular."

When they do, they find seven saved messages.

"Right, now listen. See what you can learn from this," Bento says, "have an open mind. Write the numbers down."

Message number one from an unknown number was left at 10:20a.m. on Monday 16 December: "Hey, Mate, it's me, Jared, I'm looking for two tickets, four gardeners and eight little fellas."

Message number two from an unknown number was left at 11:32a.m. on Monday 16 December: "It's me. Greenlight. Call Bruce and tell him it has to be ten on Friday morning."

"I know that voice," says Melody.

Message number three from 027 554 3433 was left at 4:30p.m. on Monday 17 December: "It's me, I've heard you're taking that raghead to Waiheke, do you think that's a good idea? Call me." This is a woman's voice.

"That's Sarin's voice, that bitch. Told you she was up to something," Melody says.

Message number four from an unknown number was left yesterday at 3:20 p.m. "Whaddup, dude, it's Kavanagh, five little ones and a gardener, three tickets. Usual place, mate."

Message number five from, 021 574 639 was left yesterday at 11:23p.m. "It's done."

Message number six from 021 433 777 was left today at 10:47a.m. "It's me Chiggy. Two gardeners, four cheeky lads, and a ticket. Usual place. Usual time."

Message number seven from 022 165 6677, was left today at 12:33p.m. "Hi, Jay, it's me, Mr Singh, just confirming I can meet you in Auckland on Monday. I'll come over and see it then. Thanks for your time yesterday."

"He's selling drugs," Larry says.

"What?"

"He's selling drugs. Those are code words, 'tickets' is cocaine, 'little fellas' is MDMA, and 'gardener' is pot."

"Little secret there, eh?" Bento asks.

"Actually, I've got a bone to pick with you," Larry is serious.

"Yeah?"

"Did you tell my son our house is haunted by the ghost of Gu Cheng?"

"Me?"

"Yeah you."

"What do you mean?" Bento defensive.

"My son said that at our party, you told him our house was haunted."

"Aaah right, yeah," Bento with the memory flooding back. "Yeah, nah, you're right I do remember that, yeah. Yeah, I did tell him that yeah…" Matter of fact.

"Well, what did you do that for? He's only six." Larry only slightly playing.

"Oh, was just a bit of fun. I was only joking."

"Well, he thinks it's real."

"No, no, it's not real."

"Well, I know that don't I?"

"Er, yeah, I suppose you do."

"I've had sleepless nights because of you."

Chapter 35

THE MAKEUP

Thursday, 19th December - 16:25

"Oh," Melody pauses for effect, "you know who I saw today?" as usual, she's enthusiastic, calling from her desk. Right now, *Lazy Universe* by Phoebe Rings is playing off the *autoDJ* in the background.

"Go on."

"Richie McCaw."

"Nah."

"Yeah, he was coming out of the Countdown with milk and a French Loaf. It was definitely him. Hundred percent. And then, I saw him again driving a BMW SUV towards me on the road to the Onetangi Sports Park. He had a dog on his lap, a big one. An Alsatian. The dog's head was sticking out the driver's side window. For a second, I thought the dog was driving the car.

"And this is a German Shepherd you say?"

"Adult German Shep. AGS."

"It won't have been him. He wouldn't do that. There's no way Richie McCaw would let his dog drive the car, not in this media climate."

"He'd let it drive a rental."

"Yeah, I suppose he might do that."

"Listen, I'm one hundred percent sure I saw Ritchie McCaw. He reminds me of a seagull, a wise one."

"I like it, I'll put in the Celebrity Sightings Feature on Friday's Breakfast Show."

"You will?"

"Yeah, why not. What's this?" Mark says changing the subject, fingering a small stick of what looks like white lipstick. It is the size of a cigarette lighter.

"Greasepaint. It's for your eyebrows, makes them look snowy, don't waste it though, leave it 'til Saturday. We just want to make sure the suit fits today."

Melody is nothing if she isn't thorough. Now that she knows Cyclone Frank isn't going to rain on her parade, every detail of it will be right, especially the Santa.

"'Bit nervous, eh."

"Oh, no one'll even know it's you. Besides, there's only two parts to the job, the parade and the grotto. Big Bill Tong's gonna tow you on the parade. All you've got to do is ride the sleigh and throw lollies to kids. Shout stuff out. 'Merry Christmas' 'Ho ho ho', that kind of thing. It'll be fun."

"It'll be hot."

"Yes, and I've pencilled in a water break for you. After that, at half past one, you'll go to the grotto for photos with the kids."

"And this entails?"

"You just have to have a little chat with each child, give them a bit of Santa's time. Ask them what school they go to. Say their teacher sent you a letter saying how good they'd been. Make them feel special. Then you make them smile for a photo."

"Just like that?"

"Just like that."

"Easy for you to say."

"Look, there's a video on YouTube called *The Seven-Step Process to being Santa Claus*. I'll link you in on it. Shows you what you need to do. I'll send another one too. Shows how you put the suit on. Sounds like the 'getting dressed in the right order' part is probably harder than the 'talking to kids' part."

"*You say*. I'm shitting it."

"Have you not worked with kids before?"

"No."

"So, you don't have any kids yourself then?"

"Nope," Mark winces.

"Well, what about nieces and nephews? Have you got any of them?"

"My brother's got kids. They live in Wellington. I never see them."

"You've a brother?"

"Yeah Kevin, he's a couple of years older than me. My Dad died a few years ago and after that, Mum moved to Perth to marry an Ozzie fella called Merv. I mean he's alright. He's a nice guy. I like him, but honestly, it's weird seeing Mum with someone else. It's like she knows it and we avoid each other out of awkwardness. And I mean, he's hardly a substitute for Dad. How could he be? He never tried. I'm glad he didn't. I never see them. So, it's just me really, me and Bento and the monkey in the family. At least it's free."

"Gee you're lucky not having to pay rent. Still, I've been lucky with my landlord. She's just happy to keep it ticking over. I used to share it, but not anymore. Hey, have you met Larry's wife, Holly?"

"Larry's wife?"

"Yeah Holly. I'm related to her, not quite as loosely as you're related to Merv, but yeah, we're related, she's my stepsister. *My* dad married *her* mum, Bluebell. See, my parents split up after my twin died." As Melody mentions her twin, her voice cracks. The two sisters had been dealt very different cards in life. Melody, healthy and full of energy. Cadence, a quadriplegic. A deaf mute, confined to a positioning wheelchair. Cadence had a condition called CDKL5 deficiency disorder, she couldn't move and was reliant on a feeding tube for nutrition. What Cadence loved though, she loved with the light in her eyes. She loved Melody more than anything. And Mum. She loved Theresa too. Theresa was her soft toy, a baby doll. Cadence kept Theresa tucked under her clenched right hand. Melody used to wash Theresa for her sister when they were little because Cadence used to get vomit on it, but Theresa belonged to Melody now, and had for almost twenty years.

"Hardly ever see Dad now 'cos of Bluebell," Melody never really saw eye to eye with Bluebell. She realises she's directing the grief of losing her sister and having her family torn apart onto her, but it always kicks off when they're together.

Chapter 36

THE OLD FRIEND

Thursday, 19th December - 21:04

Fretting about tomorrow, Larry can't rest, he worries about the Nazi, the station, the voicemail and tomorrow's visit. Watching telly isn't any use. Taking Chunk for a walk, equally ineffective. Facebook isn't of any use, nor TikTok, nor X. None of it. Fed up, he turns off his phone. He's feeling a little bit bloated from the six cans of beer he's ploughed since getting home from work. The rice in the curry he'd had, soaking it all up. Holly has a remedy.

"Larry, if you're looking for something to do, we really need to tidy that granny flat. Looks like a pigsty in there. People are going to need to use that room this Christmas, if you want to invite extra people. Oh, and you know 'old mate' from the radio station?"

"Who?"

"The Funeral Picketer."

"Derek?"

"Yeah, him."

"Yeah."

"What the hell have you invited him for? And without asking me too."

"I feel bad for him. He's been living in a campervan with Barry Twelvedogs for months. His mum died this year too. And his brother took his own life back in the nineties. Fair go, it's Christmas. At least his heart's in the right place."

"*But his mate stinks of cat piss,* and anyway is there even enough room for a campervan like that on our lawn? They might have to park by the beach at the bottom of the road."

"She'll be right, Hol. All Christmases *should* be memorable. The best ones are."

Like Larry's office at the station, there are parts of that granny flat that haven't had a dusting in years and the main room has that heavy dander feel about it. A stale-smell, the kind that makes the eyeball want rubbing. A silver patch of matted cat fur at the end of the bed. Soon Larry is on a roll, setting about the room to cicadas and 95bFM. The Professor (Thursday Xtra). Hard rock and hard house. Music to work by. Larry opens the ranch slider, introducing the warm night air to the room. He strips back the bed, moves the boxes to the deck and hoovers the carpet. Within an hour the room is tidy.

At the back of the room, three large packing boxes have never been unpacked. Larry sets about them, and it's a trip down memory lane alright. CDs, notebooks, clothes. Boy, are there a lot of clothes. Larry had always been a sharp dresser. It's what he was known for in his Dunedin days, studying dentistry, that and being a caner. A card-carrying hedonistic flag-bearer.

Every garment he pulls from the box has its own story to tell. The hash burns on his Russian army jacket, the red wine stain on his white Adidas polo, the oil stain on his green Hugo Boss jacket. It's the same Hugo Boss jacket he'd been wearing on the night of his accident. He hasn't seen that jacket in years. He almost died in it.

It has a bulge in the right breast pocket. Bulbous. Like a balloon. As soon as he feels it, he knows what it is. A long-lost friend in a bag of trapped air. Quickly he opens the coat and fishes his fingers into the pocket. In a heartbeat, Larry remembers every detail from the night of his crash. Instantly, transported back to the mangled car, the dark and the pain.

The leg.

The leg.

THE LEG!

The red and yellow light of the McDonald's sign at the motorway services in Mercer. Why was he on the Waikato Expressway that night? Being in Melville buying Quaaludes from Jaco on Thursday. He might've had one. He's never been able to remember.

Quaaludes were big with American drug abusers in the late 20th Century, but they'd never really taken off in New Zealand. They'd taken off with Larry though, coming through a South African connection with an angle on Mandies and Quack. Now, 15 years after his last one, the drug has been raised to almost mythical status by the film *The Wolf of Wall Street*. They'd be worth a small fortune now.

As the Ziploc bag opens, a breeze of fifteen-year-old Quaalude-infused air is released back into the wild. The smell has a chemical tang. Larry likes it. He sits on the edge of the bed, looking at the bag the way a child looks at a kitten. It's like being reacquainted with a love thought lost, the love he'd had the ride of his life with. He takes one of the Quaaludes out of the bag and gives it the once over to see how fit it is. He moves it between his thumb and forefinger. What a time to find a bag of euphoria-inducing tranquilizers. The perfect time to check out. And then, before he does anything rash, he reminds himself that the delegation from New Zealand On Air is due on the island in the morning, and it's probably best not to indulge in a night of self-induced cerebral palsy.

Chapter 37

THE LATE-NIGHT PHONE CALL

Thursday, 19th December - 22:30

As Larry processes internal conflict over the Quaaludes, Sarin Murray sits alone in the lounge of her Church Road home. She is occupied by a repeat of *Friends* and a half Toblerone. Her phone buzzes on the arm of her couch. It's an incoming text message which says.

Listened to your show yesterday. What happened to the Nazi?

Sarin phones the texter back straight away. She gets the first words in and laughs. She has a laugh like a heron's bill snap and exhibits vocal fry at the end of her sentences. Sometimes, if she is trying to sound authoritative, she intentionally inserts a lisp into her *th*iblants. She makes a point of doing this when she thinks she is being superior about something or someone.

"Well, it wasn't like he was going to go on the thstation and shout 'Heil Hitler' was he?"

"He didn't shout anything," then a brief pause for a sniff. "All I heard was your mate, cyclops harping on about native animals and pesticides."

"Denise?"

"Yeah."

"She wasn't there yesterday."

"She was on the radio yesterday."

"When were you listening?"

"Usual time. That's half an hour of my life I'll never get back."

"But the Nazi was on for the whole of the show."

"He wasn't."

"He was. He called Asian people 'lice' you didn't hear that?"

"No."

"Well, it happened."

"Not on the radio it didn't. You know what they've done don't you? Those commie dole-bludgers, pulled a switcheroo on you haven't they? They'll've got skittish when Jack Boot rocked up. Yah, Sarin, they've played a pre-recorded show instead of letting you go out live."

"They wouldn't."

"They have."

"Bastards."

"Don't sweat it, Sarin. I'm coming over tomorrow. Let's see what I can do about getting that last complaint eh?"

Part Three

Chapter 38

THE RETURN OF JAY DICKS

Friday, 20th December - 08:15

Starflyte is running the eight a.m. Auckland Mātiatia passage today. She is just off North Head and carrying diverse human cargo of anti-commuters: tradies; a group of jet-lagged, guitar-strapped, Argentine hippies; the supermarket workers; the woman from lab tests; and James from the shop by the garage in Ostend. Amongst them, staring off into the distance of the North Shore beaches, is the lean frame of JD. Otherwise known as the former Network Programme Director at UNZMedia and Mark's former boss, Jay Dicks.

Jay Dicks'd had a make-over since *The Dead Air Incident*. A rebirth of sorts. He's aping the look that cage-fighting Irish badass, Conor McGregor had a decade ago. The suit, the beard, the swagger, the lot. All down pat. He looks rock hard. Handy. Skilled in battery. Unfortunately for Jay Dicks, the opposite is true. The man's as soft as an auld quilt. Never even been in a proper fight. He's so soft that rumours of stress-related irritable bowel syndrome still swirl the media industry whenever talk turns his way. Jay Dicks though is cunning. A citizen of the *Post Truth World*. If he *looks* hard, and he projects hard, he *is* hard. Game over.

A month old tattoo of a Mexican sugar-skull decorates a bit of the lower left flank of Jay's neck. It makes him look even harder than what he did before he got it. It peeks from under his collar, checking like a cockroach hiding under a fridge. Jay Dicks is easily the hardest looking dude on the boat. Suited and booted. Dark grey jacket, half-mast trousers. Black tie on a green paisley shirt. The only things missing are the cane, the top hat and the monocle.

Since being fired from UNZMedia, Jay has been reduced to just the one phone, the same Samsung Galaxy S10 he was given for a ringing endorsement on *Rance Gander's Dream Drive Five 'til Nine* about a year earlier. The screen has a crack in it now. Jay hurled it across the room immediately after being sacked by Gordon West on the night of *The Dead Air Incident*. *The Benny Hill Theme* is ringing out from it in full, rasping from his breast pocket. Two renditions of the fun-time classic lost under the hum of the boat's massive engines. Even if Jay Dicks could've heard his phone ringing, he wouldn't have answered it. That wasn't part of his plan.

Today, the plan is to meet his old schoolmate, property developer Garrett Wentworth at Mātiatia. Garrett lives on one of Kennedy Point Marina's biggest yachts. Garrett got lucky in life. His parents were a part of the nouveau riche scaffolding set. For all the pretence though, and there was lots, Garret Wentworth was as rough as a bear's arse, with a mouth as dirty as an open sewer. He's agreed to drive Jay around for the day, since Jay is bringing a wodge of cocaine with him.

🐶

"What time's your appointment cunt?" Garrett asks, left hand releasing the handbrake to move the Range Rover out of the Drop-Offs Only parking space.

"Ten."

"That's not for another hour yet. Shall we get breakfast?"

"OK, yeah, why not?"

"So, er, Dicksy? What's this business you've got with the radio station?"

"Oh, it's one complaint away from being defunded, and if it is, the frequency goes to auction."

There is a pause wherein the penny is dropping into the Garrett's basket, he then mischievously says, "Ah, fucken cunt. I see, and *you're* going to be bidding on it aren't you?"

"I mean, please? Don't you know who I am?" Jay says laughing,

"Oh, you dirty fucken capitalist pig you," Garrett, joining in with the laughs.

"I've a client waiting in the wings to lease it to."

"You're clipping the ticket, eh? You dirty auld fat-cat. How dare you." Garrett's laugh gets louder and then it slows, and he says, "This is the building next to the library, eh? The one by the Artworks theatre?"

"I dunno, mate, never been there before."

"Yeah, man, I think it is, the view up there'll be fucken primo. Bet it's worth a bomb. That's if it's the building I think it is. Pretty sure it's a council building."

Garrett is right about both of those things. It is just a house. An old bach, painted in a dark grey colour and with a red tiled roof. It is situated up on the side of Oneroa Bay, high above the beach, just thirty seconds away from the Oneroa strip by foot. A world-class view, it looks back across the beach and the headland. The council own it and they gift it to the community for a radio station via something called a 'peppercorn lease,' One dollar a year.

"Can I come in with you?"

"If you want."

"Wait." Garrett says, confused, "if you're working the frequency, why d'ya need to go to the station?"

"I'm using it as a showroom. I'm bringing my client back here next week showing him what a radio station might be like, you know in the flesh. I wanna check it out for myself first though. See if I can spook 'em a bit in the process. The stupid cunts think I'm a property developer."

"You sly fucken bastard," sniggers, "you're off the chain."

"Yep," Jay says with a cackle.

"So, er, if I may, how much is that going to bring in?"

"Three quarters of a million a year for fifteen years."

"Yeah, but even if it does come up, you won't be able to outbid UNZMedia and Radiohub? You can't."

"A little birdie tells me I might not need to worry about that."

"Birdie eh?" A pause. "Who's your client?"

"Some raghead. Wants a station that broadcasts in some fucking darkie language. I'm going the whole hog for the cunt, wooing him. I've booked him an Airbnb so he can make a weekend out of it. Soft cunt's coming on his own."

Garrett laughs and adds sarcastically, "you corrupt, racist, insider-trading colonialist-bastard. How dare you?" he pauses for breath and says, "You can't talk like that anymore, calling a darkie a raghead. You'll get us all cancelled."

"There's another reason."

"Go on."

"You know how I lost my job at UNZ?"

"The cricket?"

"Yeah, that's the one," he pauses "well the cunt that did it, works there now, I can't wait to see that fucken muppet's face when he sees me."

Chapter 39

THE BLACKPOOL ROCK

Friday, 20th December - 09:48

Up at the radio station, the host of *A Blind Bit of Difference*, sight-impaired Scot, Kenneth Oath is here for his weekly show. A slight man of five foot seven, short grey hair, and always with the sunglasses. There's always been a wee bit of overlap between Kenneth taking the microphone and Anderson Yogamum relinquishing it.

Ken likes to get his guide-dog Sheba relaxed for a minute or so before he can get going, and Mark's is there helping him, orienting his fingers against the control desk. To help accommodate with Ken's switch, Anderson always plays a long song to close out Island Breakfast. Today it's the extended version of *Bittersweet Symphony* by Upholland High School old boys, Verve.

"So, what have you got on the show this week, Ken?" Mark says.

Ken carries a basket. It has about fifty sticks of Blackpool Rock in it.

"Rock."

"Rock?"

"Rock. You eat it," more specifically, British children eat it after visiting a North-West English seaside town, Blackpool. Rock, white tubes of hardboiled sugar with a red stripe corkscrewing down from the top to the bottom. Each stick of this Blackpool Rock is probably about the size of an Olympic standard relay baton. Longer than a drumstick, girthier than a hosepipe, hard as a truncheon. Before it became unfashionable, Northern English kids could suck on a stick of Blackpool Rock for days on end. This is why English people all have bad teeth. "Kids love it, eh,"

"What?"

"Rock. Blackpool Rock. The Blind Association are sellin thaim aff tae raise money for our deaf *an* blind brothers. ten dollars a pop. If you sell some, you could hold the money until next week eh?"

"Yeah, Ken all good. No worries at all."

"They're trying to raise awareness about the red striped canes. See, canes what got a red stripe running down them, well, their also fae deaf people, you ken, blind *and* deaf?"

"Is that so?"

"Aye it is. I leave about ten on the shelf will I? Put 'em in mugs. Maybe you'd be kind enough to tell people about it?"

Chapter 40

THE COCAINE FIENDS

Friday, 20th December - 09:57

Two hundred metres away from the radio station, as the crow flies, Jay Dicks and Garrett Wentworth have just finished their breakfast and are sitting in the latter's *Evoque*. Garrett's 'Rangey' is one of many luxury SUVs on the island for the summer. These Teutonic summer runners of the holiday-home-set are a noticeable factor on Waiheke roads at this time of year. Barrel across the white lines, they do. Locals call it Range Rover Season. Millennials call it Jeepmass, either way, locals want them the fuck back to Remuera.

"What were you looking for?" Jay asks from the passenger seat.

"Can you do five tickets?"

"Probably do ten if you want."

"Really?"

"Yeah man."

"Okay, fuck it, why not? You got any little fellas?"

"Yeah, loads."

"Can you do thirty?"

"Yeah."

"Got any gardener?"

"Nah, not right now. I might be able to get you an ounce if you can get to the ferry terminal in Auckland later today."

"Yeah nah, let me get the ten tickets and the thirty little fellas for the time being, I'll call you later about the gardening."

"Wanna quick bump?"

"Fuck yeah."

As always, Jay goes first, brings the spoon of coke up to his left nostril and hits it.

"Now, let's head to the radio station, shall we?"

"Shove it up 'em Dicksy, bunch of snowflake lefty faggots."

"Have you ever even listened to that station?" Jay, keyed in from his hit, "*I have*, it's all spastics grunting down the microphone, dykes banging on about periods, and Chinese cunts mobilising the sleeper cells. Fucken bullshit that our tax dollars are paying for that."

"Nah, fuck that though," Garrett says after his hit, sniffing, totally wired, "they need to be playing more fucking Phil Collins, if I'm paying for the cunt."

Chapter 41

THE CHAUFFEUR

Friday, 20th December - 10:01

This week's edition of *A Blind Bit of Difference* starts with *Superstition* by Stevie Wonder. Mark turns it up before strapping on his seatbelt, clicking the keys through the ignition and pulling out from the carpark. Moving on to Kororā Road and out of the junction, Mark goes right, down the hill on Ocean View Road, and on toward the ferry terminal. It's Larry's car. A battered auld Volvo with a blue *Waiheke Island Radio* sticker weathered on the black back-bumper.

Jay and Garrett have just rocked up to reception.

"You're late." Larry says curtly. The tic has two-stages.

"Yah, there was a queue at the gelato place," Jay says sniffing, the condescension palpable.

"Oh. Right. Good. Next time let me know if you're going to be late."

"Yah, sure, whatever. Are you Gary?"

"No, I'm not."

"I'm looking for the station manager, Gary."

"It's Larry," tic.

"Oh, right. Jay Dicks," no offer of a handshake, "I'm interested in this building. I've heard it might be coming up next year."

"What? Who told you that?"

"I've spoken to Bruce from the Council."

"What?" Larry is aghast.

"Yeah, and I'll be coming back on Monday with an associate. I want you to make sure it's open, yah?" Jay Dicks is talking to Larry Minto in the same way he'd talk to someone who was intellectually disabled. "And I'd like it tidy too. I mean, look at the dust here." he runs his finger across Mark's desk, "pie crumbs."

Melody is sitting at her desk saying nothing. She's watches everything though. Watches and listens.

Over the next few minutes, Larry fulfils his obligations to the Waiheke Council, guiding Jay and Garrett around the station. Hobbling over to the kitchen, limping though the office, and the pre-record studio. Ticcing and limping. Ticcing and limping. The little voice-over booth. He shows them the back garden, the server rack, the bathroom, and the barbeque deck, but, since Kenneth Oath is on the air, Larry stops short of taking Jay and Garrett into the On-Air studio.

Down at Mātiatia Ferry Terminal, Mark stands by the coffee shack. He holds up a piece of A4 paper, on which the words 'NEW ZEALAND ON AIR' are written in block capitals. He is approached by a lady in a black hijab and an overweight bald man with a grey and ginger soul patch.

"Hi, I'm Nazreen Rahman and this is Lambartus Butler, you must be Mark."

"Yep, here let me give you a hand with those bags."

Going off body language, Lambartus seems keen to get down to business, but Nazreen is already in holiday mode. Dawdling and stopping to take a photo from the pier. Posting it to Insta.

"Oh, I love José Feliciano," remarks Nazreen as she climbs into the back seat of the Volvo, "Is this the station that we're listening to now?"

"Yeah, this is a show for and about the visually impaired. It's called *A Blind Bit of Difference*, it's hosted by one of our keenest broadcasters. A guy called Kenneth Oath, he's sight impaired, lovely fella."

Chapter 42

#BLINDRADIOHOSTTRIGGERED–AFTERGUIDEDOGHURTBYHIPSTER

Friday, 20th December - 10:11

Larry Minto stands with his back to the door of the on-air studio, talking to Jay Dicks and Garrett Wentworth whilst holding in another tic. The urge has been off the charts since the pair arrived.

Behind the glass, Ken Oath reaches for the faders on the broadcast console. Guide dog, Sheba sleeps on the floor by the door. Suddenly the resolve for Larry to hold his tic in, busts and he lets one pop in three-movements.

Neck-jerks-back

Right-arm-twitch-front

Finish-in-the-fingers

Unfortunately for Larry, the 'finish-in-the-fingers' part of the tic knocks the basket-load of Blackpool Rock off the shelf by the door and twenty of them are bouncing across the polished wood floor by the studio door. Immediately, Larry bends over to pick up a stick. He slips on another stick, arse going over tit with it, cracking down on his bad side. Simultaneously, with Larry scrambling, Jay Dicks and Garrett Wentworth make a sudden move on the on-air studio door.

On the other side of the glass, in the on-air studio, Ken Oath has not yet realised anything is wrong because he is wearing headphones, and also because he is visually impaired. He is fading down the yuletide jazz number *Feliz Navidad* by José Feliciano and since he is about to speak about Blackpool Rock, he has activated his main On-Air microphone, in preparation for that.

Suddenly, Sheba's head cocks.

Listeners hear a whooshing sound followed by the thud of a sliding door hitting a rubber stopper on a wall, indistinct voices, and a dog yelping out in pain. It is guide-dog, Sheba. Jay Dicks has just trodden on her tail whilst in the process of trespassing in the on-air studio. Sheba's yelp gives way to a series of aggressive barks, that become angrier with each second.

If there was a chip in a radio set that could translate what a dog is saying when it barks, it would have amounted to this.

"Come oan, fucken square go fanny. I'll bite ye in th' fucken pus anytime yi'll waant fud. Aye ah wull cunt," naturally the accent is Glaswegian. Rearing up now. Offensive in the stance, saliva bubble inflating against the animal's pink jowls.

On the other side of the sliding door, Larry slips again on a second stick of Blackpool Rock. He struggles to get up off his bad side, and onto his feet. Melody dashes to help him. "Get the fuck out of there!" Larry shouts towards Dicks and Wentworth in the on-air.

It's the first time Melody has ever heard Larry swear.

"FUCK! A dog! Shit! Get it away from me. Get it away from me," for as long as he could remember, Jay Dicks has had a crippling fear of man's best friend. Ragged as a kid by a seven-pug-pack. A scar on a chin to prove it. Dogs can sense fear. The more they sense fear, the more they're inclined to attack. When Dicksy's about, dogs'll try to boss him from the get-go. They hate him. He hates them.

Halfway up Ocean View Road in the battered blue Volvo that is transporting the New Zealand On Air board members, Nazreen Rahman and Lambartus Butler, all have just clearly heard the word 'fuck' three times on a mid-morning radio show about blindness. Like a *Transformer (a robot in disguise)*, Nazreen morphs out of holiday-mode and firmly back into her business persona. An expression of pure terror washes over Mark's face. Lambartus Butler smirks. No one expects to hear top-shelf diction on a mid-morning radio show about the visually impaired. It is awkward in that car now.

"Who's there?" says Ken loudly into the microphone. He is startled, moving like a boxer, bobbing his head from side to side. Listening for a response. The dog is growling now, loud enough to be heard via the microphone.

"Keep your dog on a fucking lead man," Jay Dicks says, fronting towards a blind pensioner.

"Yeah, stupid fucken mut," chimes Garrett spinelessly.

"Leave ma dug alone or I'll have it set aboot ye ya wee cunt. An then I'll be comin' in fae aftas fanny. Get tae fuck while a host ma radio show, cunt," the dog is still growling. Snarling. Packed and ready to go.

"Yeah, whatever, old man. That dog comes near me again, I'll kick it in the cunt."

On the road, at 40 kilometres per hour, close to the entrance to the Top Carpark, Mark grips the steering wheel for all it is worth, his knuckles white from the pressure he's exerting on it. In the back, Nazreen lets out an audible gasp as Butler belches out a bark of a laugh.

"What the fuck're ya doing?"

"What does it look like?"

"I don't know, I cannae see."

"What are you? Blind or something?"

"Och aye ah fuckin' am ye wee cunt, dae ye want tae make somethin' ay it?" Ken Oath is using his Brigton fighting brogue now, addressing a part of the room that neither Dicks nor Wentworth are standing in. Jay Dicks a real-life puss-puss. He's never been a tough guy. Now, the combination of Sheba's snarling and Ken's fighting talk is stressing Jay, causing something inside of his stomach to bubble off and drop. Could it be that the rumours about his stress related IBS are true?

Larry, finally up on his feet, asserts himself, crossing the threshold to firmly manhandle Dicks and Wentworth out of the studio, but stopping to check on the broadcaster.

"You OK Ken?"

"Aye, the fuck was that?"

"You're still on-air Ken."

"Oooh shit, so I am." Ken reaches out to the console, feeling out to regain his bearings on the desk. He's out of whack though. His heart rate is up, the dog is nuzzling him repeatedly. He's going to need a few seconds help to recalibrate.

🐶

As Larry stays to assist Ken Oath in the On-Air, Jay Dicks and Garrett Wentworth conclude their business in reception. Doing it quickly.

"I need a shit, bro, I'll make my own way back to the ferry," Jay says as he dabs up Garrett.

"I'll get going then. You show that shitter who's boss, brother," the pair exchange a pound hug.

"Can do."

🐶

In the studio, Larry dashes to the desk, pushes play on the same José Feliciano song that'd just played and switches off the main microphone. Then he helps Ken re-orientate, saying, "give me a minute, mate." With that done, he skips off after Dicks and Wentworth.

He is too slow. There is no sign of Jay, while Garrett is climbing into his Range Rover. Any idea he has about apprehending Garrett Wentworth is stymied when he sees his Volvo parking in the gravel out front.

Chapter 43

THE DEBRIEF

Friday, 20th December - 10:18

As Nazreen Rahman and Lambartus Butler step out of the Volvo, neither are amused. This was supposed to have been a fact-finding mission. A little bit of a jaunt. In the five-minute drive up the hill though, the delegation has already heard sixteen examples of extreme language, one threat of violence, one instance of animal abuse, and someone has just made ableist comments against a blind Scottish pensioner. This, on a radio station they are about to audit for on-air profanity, amongst other things. Now, they're at the station which stinks of shit, while a stack of racist leaflets is clearly visible on Larry Minto's desk. Nazreen is ropeable as fuck. She wants answers.

"Can I get you a coffee?" Melody offers.

"No, I want some air freshener. Let's open this back door," Nazreen says, visibly angry, stalking the office area like an enraged mother rousing a dope-smoking teen. She has everyone's attention.

Jay Dicks exploits the commotion by quietly exiting the bathroom in reception unnoticed. He doesn't bother flushing, he just slopes off through the front door, trotting on down and left to the library and hailing a taxi at the bus stop.

"Larry, we need to talk," Nazreen says. And talk they do. Over the course of the next two hours, Larry lays it all out. Reminding her and Lambartus about the money that is at stake, the text message, and Sarin's affair with

Derek Barnaby.

"Yeah, there's something else too," tic.

"Oh, what now."

"The leader of the New Zealand National Front is suing the station for breach of privacy. I received a letter from his lawyer yesterday."

"Why?" says Nazreen.

"A policeman accused him of distributing these," Larry points at the racist leaflets, "live on air."

"Oh no. You couldn't make this up," Nazreen says.

"Well, that'll be complaint number five, and there'll probably be a sixth one after this morning's episode. You're finished, we may as well go home now, eh Larry?" Lambartus is stoked, he made up his mind way before he'd even got on the plane.

Larry doesn't say anything, the penny is dropping. The neck-jerks-back, the arm-twitches-front and it finishes-in-the-fingers.

"The whole reason we came here in the first place, Larry, was to see if you were running a fit and proper operation, and you know, I'm loathe to say it, but I don't think you are," Nazreen says.

Chapter 44

THE BATHROOM SCENE

Friday, 20th December - 11:14

Melody has found something in the toilet bowl and she is waiting for the cistern to refill. "It's the prick with the man bun. He's marking his territory. The animal."

"This is the guy who barged in on Ken Oath's show right?" Mark says.

"One of them."

"Oh, that is rank," Mark says, holding onto the R part of the word a little longer, so as to emphasise the rankness. "Whoever did this needs to see a doctor."

"It'll have been the guy that intruded on Ken's show?" Melody says.

"This is the guy who got into the Range Rover right? Soul patch?"

"Yeah... well, the soul patch guy was the *other* guy. The main troublemaker would've been in here by the time *you* arrived. Must've slipped away in Nazreen's commotion," Melody adds. "You'll need to piss that caked-on-shit off. Save on detergent. I mean, it's all you men are truly good for anyway. Pissing caked-on-shit off the sides of a toilet bowl. Other than that, you're useless."

"Harsh," Mark says with a laugh, "I guess I could give it a go. Do you remember what his name was?"

"What, the prick with the man-bun?"

"Yeah."

"Rick Bricks, something like that. I mean it wasn't that, but it was something *like* that. Looked a bit like Conor McGregor. You know, the boxer? I couldn't believe how rude they were being. Bastards."

"Rick Bricks. Nah, doesn't ring any bells."

Just then Big Bill Tong arrives for his show and seeing the commotion at the loo, approaches, pops his head around the door, considers the mess in the bowl, and says, "what have you been eating boy? Ooh, that looks like a negative photo of a plasterer's bucket that does. Did your mate's monkey do it?"

Chapter 45

THE SANTA PARADE

Saturday, 21st December

They'd never been closer. Melody on the colour stick, whitening Mark's eyebrows, making them look snowy. Blusher on his cheeks too, making them look rosy. She's lingering on his face with her eyes. Displaying the concentration of a tightrope walker. She's lingering longer than she needs, he can tell that she is listening to him breathing. There's eye contact. He smiles.

Right Shoulder – Boner!
A tingling sensation up the spine for a half hour or more.
Left Shoulder – She's seen it.
She's smiling when she packs him off to the toilet with two bags, one belt, and a YouTube video called How to get Dressed Like Santa. It takes about ten minutes to follow the instruction, but by the time Mark is ready, he emerges from the stall a new man. A new man with a new name. Santa Claus is now how he goes.

At ten to noon, Santa straightens his belt and slings an oversize red felt bag of one thousand Fruit-Bursts over his Left Shoulder. It is uncomfortable wearing a big white polyester wig and beard in the heat of a mid-summer's day, much-less when also having to wear a wool-implanted home-made fat suit too. The weight of the Fruit Bursts is deceptive. Heavier. He walks away from the radio station, and down the ramp by Ajadz Restaurant. Suddenly, he sees it. He stops. Behold, Santa's Sleigh. The vehicle in which he will die.

The sleigh is parked outside the main entrance to the Waiheke Library next to the Christmas tree. It is a single axle flatbed trailer, embellished in tinsel. On the flatbed, eight bales of hay are decorated to look like Christmas presents. They surround Santa's Throne which, rather than being an actual throne is just a rickety wooden chair spray-painted gold and fastened to the trailer's frame with a chain of plastic cable ties.

Left Shoulder – You will, be killed.

Right Shoulder – She'll be right.

Just nine floats in the parade this year, crawling down the Oneroa strip. Top roundabout to bottom, then doubling back up the hill. Three thousand locals and day-trippers line the route, standing on the pavement, gathering on the grass by the zebra crossing and the selfie penguins. It's easy, throw lollies at children, point, wave, shout.

"Merry Christmas, kids!"

It is the hottest day of summer so far. No wind. Only a warm curtain of air filled the air with the scents of Christmas. Sunblock, charcoal and fresh cut grass, mince pies. Music is playing. All down the main strip are loudspeakers, all connected to DJ Lalo, Nacho, and Pablo Techno, performing from the shelf by the gelato place after Andre's barber shop.

Some three hundred metres from the end of the parade, the sleigh is crossing the zebra by the Four Square, *when* a wisp of air draws the scent of frying meat to Mark's nose. He follows it with his eyes. It takes him to Larry, serious on a sausage sizzle by the Oneroa Chemist. Nazreen and Lambartus standing with him. Deep in conversation with Sylvia Park and Lynn Mall. The latter of the pair eating.

A turn away from the end of the parade route, just by the butcher and cop-shop, a man on the other side of the road wears a black wife-beater, black jeans and jandals. He is being manhandled out of a patrol car by two uniformed police officers, he stops struggling to shout, "Hey Santa Claus ya cunt, where's me fucken bike!" It's as rough as arseholes and it's all packaged up with an Australian accent. A cruise-ship drop-away. Munted on a wine tour. Twelve toddlers, tweens and pre-teens hear him.

"Merry Christmas!" replies Santa, furiously waving at the dog-end of the parade.

Two metres square, the grotto has straw spread across its floor and is positioned next to the library's Christmas tree. Three metres in front of the tree, Melody is working the camera, face pressed against her Nikon D800 that stands on a tripod. Monitoring the queue and helping Melody marshal the children for her photos are the GLITFAB pair, Albany Westfield and St. Luke Small. They are dressed as elves and the line they're monitoring consists of about fifty snotty-nosed, piss-stinking, puked-up minors.

Rank as fuck, no doubt, but, one hour into it, a four-year-old boy almost breaks Santa's resolve. That poor child, his saturated nappy dampening the festive lap, inside the diaper, a mashed shit paste with three cycles of piss kneaded through. As the Nappy Child poses for their picture, Santa gags in revulsion, and in that moment, Melody opens the shutter on her camera to take the picture. When developed, Santa's epiglottis is clearly visible trying to escape the confines of his throat.

With the crowds now petering out, a woman approaches the grotto. One of her hands is holding that of an eight-year-old girl with Down Syndrome. The other is pushing a red-framed positioning wheelchair. Going off size, the girl in the chair would've been about eleven. She appears to have no movement from the neck down and is almost horizontal in the chair. Her head is cocked to the right. She isn't able to tend to the dolly in her lap. All she can do is have it next to her, trapped in her own body as she is. It's obvious though she's happy here. Excited. They both are. You can feel the electricity of it.

"Hi Santa, I'm Jo, this is Vicky," says the children's caregiver. She is gently coaxing the girl with Downs towards him, "She wants to show you her Starship dolly," As Vicky offers the dolly, Jo continues in a babying voice, pushing her own face into the wheelchair, "and this is Dominique."

"Can we have a photo?" Vicky says, smiling, exuding the purity of soul that kids with Down's syndrome often seem to have.

"'Course we can. D'ya wanna to bring the chair round? We'll get your Starship dolly in too, eh?" Voice booming, keeping Vicky in the picture.

"Erm. Actually Santa," there is a real earnestness in Jo's voice. She wants this for Dominique more than she ever wanted anything from anyone for anything else, ever.

"You have to hold her head and she is a bit heavy, but it'd make her day if you could cuddle her."

"Of course we can!"

As Jo unstraps Dominique and hauls her up, out of the chair, Santa prepares to take her weight. Limbering up mentally.

Left Shoulder – Straighten the back / Push through the knees.

Right Shoulder – Heave!

Dominique is heavier than she looks, sixty kilo easily. A test for the lumbar. Once she's been wrangled onto his lap, Mark is effectively cradling her. Peering down into her brown eyes through the curls in his uncomfortable white polyester wig. Then, theatrically he says "Well, Merry Christmas to you Dominique. Now, two months ago I got a letter from Jo here, and it said that you'd been a very good girl. *All year!* That's right, eh?"

Dominique couldn't reply by way of words, but everything anyone ever needed to know about how she felt was right there in her eyes, which were alive with a million variations on the word 'happy'.

As Jo, Dominique and Vicky are being entertained in the grotto, no one notices Melody's reaction. It isn't obvious, but, underneath her elf costume and behind that Nikon camera, she cries. She thinks of Cadence, imagining her twin, unencumbered by any affliction, dancing in a meadow in heaven with Nana. This is the magic of Christmas. Right here in the way Mark is interacting with these children.

Around five minutes later, the last customers of the day rock up. Santa had noticed three kids from the grass steps by the Artworks Theatre. They'd been there all afternoon. Each seemingly removed from the festivities. Distant. It was only when the market was packing down that Mark saw them smile when a woman from the ice cream truck brought them each a ninety-nine. Then, with her, they approached the grotto.

"Merry Christmas, children!"

"Merry Christmas, Santa," they chorus, a little downcast. The three go to Waiheke Primary in Ostend and their names were Faith, Liam and Destiny. Nine, seven, and five respectively. The woman is their mother. Her name is Hazel.

"And what do you want for Christmas this year?"

These kids all want the same thing. They know they can't have it though, and so the three of them just stand there before Santa, unable to express themselves.

"Santa, these kids lost their dad in a car crash last month. It was on the Onetangi Straight. It was on the front of the paper," Hazel says, her voice cracking on the word 'Onetangi'.

"Oh no," Santa says, momentarily stunned, the wind knocked from within him. The Seven Step Process to being Santa Claus hadn't covered this. Then, humanity takes over and he reaches out to embrace the whole family in his arms, pulling them close with his white gloves.

"Do you know what I get asked for the most?" Santa says, leading the huddle. Fixing the gaze of each child as he speaks, choking up, before a steadying breath.

"No, Santa." Destiny replies, tears carving tracks through the vanilla ice cream that is smeared across her little cheeks.

"A brother or a sister, that's what. You wouldn't believe the amount of letters I get asking for a brother or a sister, so you know what? You've already got the best present there is. I can't bring your dad back, but I do know he's right here, right now, and he's telling his mum and his dad how proud he is of you three." Santa, keeping the family in the huddle, takes a deep breath. He is about to round things out when little Destiny interrupts him again.

"Santa, we don't live in our house anymore, how will you know where to find us?"

"Well, where are you living now?"

"We stayed in Pūtiki Bay last night," Hazel said.

"Which house?"

"Oh, no, erm, no. We're living in our car."

"The four of you live in your car?"

"Yes, Santa."

"Are you getting any help from anywhere?"

"No, Santa. It's just me and the kids. I've got the job on the ice cream truck. It's only part-time though."

"Would you want some help if it were there?"

"Yes, Santa." Looking at the floor, as her voice begins to crack again.

"See the Artworks Theatre there?"

"Yeah."

"Well, there's a building behind it. It's the radio station. Go up there in about fifteen minutes. I'll introduce you to some people who might be able to help."

Chapter 46

THE HELPING HAND

Monday, 23rd December - 11:03

It is debriefing time and Nazreen Rahman perches on the green two-seater in Larry's office while he sits upright in his swivel chair. Outside, horizontal rain is teeming onto the asphalt on Kororā Road. It makes a droning sound as it pulses upon the roof. As usual, the radio is playing, it's Massive Attack with *Unfinished Sympathy* at no more than fifteen percent.

"You know, Larry, I can't lie. You needed an exemplary report, and perhaps without the two incidents from last week, I'd have gone back with one. I've seen some incredible things this weekend, things that wholly justify what Access Radio is about, but at our meeting in Wellington you agreed to put systems in place to prevent breaches." This isn't the angle Nazreen wants to come in from, but it needs honesty.

"We did," Larry protests, triple ticcing.

"These things still got through, didn't they?"

"Nazreen, we're being sabotaged."

"Willie Hamilton wasn't being sabotaged when he accused Caleb McGill of a crime live on air was he? Larry, this is a training issue, your PD should have been across it before it even happened."

"But he's new."

"He's not that new. He's been on staff for a few weeks now Larry. Does he go through the BSA rules before he lets broadcasters on the air?"

"He should be."

"Well, I'd suggest he runs a refresher course. Seems like Constable Willie Hamilton might need reminding." Then Nazreen fixes Larry's gaze again, this time with a mixture of pity and encouragement, "Look Larry, I've got my NZOA hat on. Taking that off, I really want the station to succeed. *You know that.*"

"Yeah, I do."

"Look, I've read your report and I'm aware of the extraneous factors at play here, but honestly you need to be realistic, there's very little chance the board will agree to fund the frequency renewal now. Ever since the new government came in, they've been looking for excuses. Minister Saddleback's made no secret about that. You've only got to look at how the board's changed to see the intention," Nazreen pauses, "Lambartus Butler's not even here. He left the island yesterday. That should tell you all you need to know. Truth is Larry, you've two options, either you raise a lot of money in a short space of time and you pay for the frequency yourself, or you prove you've been the victim of a conspiracy. If you can't do either of those things, I'm afraid the station's finished."

"Now sports," Larry says sardonically. Then he casts his gaze back to the rain outside. It gives him a moment to internalise. Things are stark and he knows that if the station folds, all of his professional inadequacies will be laid bare. He'll be pegged as a gimp, known locally as The Village Idiot, the one to have mince where his brain should be. It is probable now too. Hard to stop. "That's it then really, isn't it?" Tics.

"Well, I can't confirm it yet, and if I were you, I wouldn't be talking about this with anyone else until you hear from me, but, honestly, I'd be working under the assumption that it'll go to auction on February fourteenth."

"We're not going to be able to compete?"

"You're not meant to."

"It's just too much money?"

"Well, I did hear something the other day regarding that, and I probably shouldn't tell you this but apparently there's a small chance it might go for a lower amount this time. A lot lower."

"Really, how so?"

"I've heard Radiohub and UNZ might not be bidding."

"What?" Larry looked befuddled, "nah?"

"Yeah, they're both in a spending freeze. It's the recession."

"Really?"

"It's what I've heard."

"You're saying there's a chance then?"

"A small one, but you need to start fundraising, Larry. Today." Nazreen then leans in as if about to whisper saying, "you know, between you and me, I might actually be able to help with that. I've a producer friend who works on *Good Sorts*. You know, Sunday nights TVNZ? Maybe I could pull a few strings, see if we can get you on there. That'd bring your profile up."

"You reckon?"

"It's possible, I mean this station is perfect for a show like Good Sorts. They shine a light on people who do good in the community."

"It's a nice idea, Naz, but I just can't imagine we'll raise the money we need for a full-power FM frequency on the Auckland spectrum from going on Good Sorts once."

"We can but try Larry. God works in mysterious ways and I'm a woman of faith, so you know."

"And what do you reckon we should do about Mr McGill's Letter Before Action?"

"I'd leave that until the New Year, Larry. The courts shut down over Christmas anyway. Take a break, gather yourself, it'll be a hard fight, but you've been through harder times than this, you can get up again."

Chapter 47

THE LIFE AS LIVED BY

Monday, 23rd December - 15:45

Whenever the station is between shows, all programming reverts to what is known as the *autoDJ*. This is an automatically generated playlist of songs, split into high, medium and low rotations. Using *autoDJ* a station can find its sound, and the sound most would associate with Waiheke Island Radio since *autoDJ* came in would've been Alt-*Soft*. The 'Alt' bit was Larry. The main driver of the station's sound. He said it was 'intelligent' country music. Music by all his favourite artists.

The 'soft' bit is because listeners can nominate songs for the playlist via the website and they nominate the likes of Mariah Carey, Ed Sheeran, Demi Lovato, Coldplay. Mark had begun deleting them the week he'd started, cancelling them from the station by quietly ushering them into the recycle bin. Larry would never do such a thing. He was too hooked into the ideal of 'common decency' and democracy. Being a music-Nazi, Mark is comfortable with it. He is doing it for the betterment of the listeners, and consequently, whole swathes of music are slowly being purged from a database of fifty thousand songs. AOR, gone. MOR, gone. Hair metal, gone. Jazz funk, gone. Every version of *Unchained Melody* and every version of *Hallelujah,* despatched. Michael Bolton, gone. Simply Red, gone. Boyzone, gone. Roxette, gone. Robbie Williams, gone, well that is except for *Angels* which Mark had been forced to put back after receiving a death threat from a 'Karen' called Karen in Palm Beach. She'd sent him a finger in the mail, and he suspected she wasn't called Karen at all. Anyway, *Angels* is un-droppable.

Karens notice when it doesn't play for a few weeks. *Someone Like You* by Adele is another such tune, and as Larry loiters in the kitchenette it takes his attention.

"Ah, Adele," he says wistfully.

"Adele? *You?*" Mark replies.

"Yes, I'll always be grateful to Adele."

"Grateful?"

"Well, two and a half weeks I was in that coma," Larry says as he leans against the edge of Melody's desk. The rain is heavy on the roof now, has been all day. Cyclone Frank is here.

"Coma?"

"Yup," Larry inhales through his mouth and loudly exhales through his nose, "two and a half weeks and it was Adele that saved me."

"How so?" Mark queries, confused.

"They kept playing it," Larry says, pacing, trying to find a moment to make a break for it. Looking for a small let up in the downpour. He jangles his keys in his right hand. "Yeah, it was that *21* album. I had to wake up to get someone to turn it off. It was doing my head in."

Mark laughs but Larry is serious. "You know, I don't think they're gonna show. Bruce said they'd be here at two. It's a quarter to four now. I can't believe they're making us go through with this."

"I thought you were mates with Bruce."

"It's not him. It's the Tories on the local board."

"Fuckers."

"Hear hear."

"You know, Larry, maybe you should get off now then. I mean this weather's not getting any better. You don't want to get stranded on this side of the island."

"Hey, er, before I go, what are you doing for Christmas?"

"I'm not doing anything. I've got no plans."

"Well, you know you could come to our place if you want. There's plenty of room and Melody'll be there too."

"Serious?"

"Yeah, come down on Christmas Eve, get a lift with Melody, crash on the couch, then you can have a drink eh."

"Yeah okay, I think I might."

Ten minutes later, and underneath the combined sounds of roof–rain and Echo and The Bunny Men's *Killing Moon*, Mark hears a car door slam. Then another. Two men are climbing out of a silver Mercedes rental car out front. One has an orange turban on, black silk angrakha and cream-coloured trousers. The other is dressed like a pirate.

Left Shoulder – It's them.

Mark watches on as the pair shield themselves from the downpour under an umbrella with UNZMedia branding. They're approaching the front door. Something looks familiar about the pirate, but his face is obscured by the brolly. Within a minute, Mark, activated by the reception bell, is through the partition where he instantly recognises Jay Dicks, his old boss from UNZMedia. The one who'd called him a 'fucking idiot' in front of an audience of half a million Sport Radio listeners. Mark's throat dries up.

"Markie, Markie, G'day, mate?" Jay's voice dripping with patronising insincerity, "I wondered where you'd wash up." It's the first time they've spoken to one another since the night of *The Dead Air Incident*. Both were sacked in its wake. Both have a personalised emergency-eject phone call from Gordon West. Mark's call had been a good deal shorter than Jay's. At no point during his sacking, nor since, has Jay Dicks taken responsibility for his part in the episode. Even after Gordon had bullet-pointed Jay's laundry list of indiscretions.

Homophobia (on air)

Ageism (on air)

Insubordination (on air)

Workplace bullying (on air)

The word 'cunt' twice (on air)

The word 'fuck' three times (on air)

Audible drug use (on air)

Lies (on air)

The fact that he was AWOL during the biggest event the station had ever been a part of.

"You know each other?" The Indian man says, confused.

"He worked under me at UNZMedia, didn't you Markie?"

Ignoring the question Mark responds, "well, what do you want to know then, Dicks?"

"Er, it's Mr Dicks to you."

"Pfft."

"Markie, this is Mr Singh. I'm showing him the building." Jay pats Mark on his shoulder blade.

"Don't touch me," Mark spits, shrugging off the touch.

"Ooh, autistic much."

"Can we have a look in your studio?" Mr Singh says, sensing the needle between the two.

"Afraid not."

"But we're here to see the property," Jay says.

"It's in use."

"No, it's not. It's empty," Jay nods towards Mr Singh. "Let him in."

"Nah. That desk is primed for the four o'clock show. Anyway, if it's the property you're interested in, you can see what you need from the door."

"He wants to see the main studio."

"Look, look, there's no problem gentlemen. It's all good," Mr Singh says.

Mark reluctantly guides the pair around, starting at the kitchenette.

Mr Singh is enthused. "How many listeners do you have?"

"We don't count our audience, but it will be in the tens of thousands."

Jay sniggers, sarcastically saying "*Sure* it is."

"Do you get a lot of advertisers?" Mr Singh ignores the Dicks comment.

"Well yeah, we do have some, but there's actually a ceiling on the money we can bring in through advertising because we're an Access station. Our advertisers have to make more of a commitment to the station, you know, sponsor a show. Then we can give them adverts as part of the sponsorship deal."

"Well, it's a function of democracy for ordinary people to have access to traditional media, that's why Access Radio stations like ours are paid for by the Government. The idea is to engage as many unique voices as we can. Things like religious programming. We have several shows for a variety of faiths. We cover foreign languages too. We actually have shows in fifteen languages at our station. We have Rainbow programming, youth programming, and programming for senior citizens. It's my job to to find those diverse voices then train and support them to host shows."

As Mark goes into more detail Mr Singh's question their rapport seems to grow. It looks like Mr Singh is more interested in Mark than in Jay Dicks. Dicks, the suitor, feels the isolation. It jolts his insecurities being locked out of the conversation like this and he feels spooked. The IBS (for it is real) causes his stomach to drop-a-floor. Now, it's resting, precariously at the mercy of his ring piece. He'll need to action it right away.

"Where's the loo?"

"Over there," Mark is pointing at it, "but that one's out of order."

Pure panic descends though Jay's face. "Do you know where there's one that's *not* out of order?"

"There's one at the library."

"Where's that?"

"Left out the station, down the ramp in the courtyard."

"Are you okay to hang on here, Mr Singh?" Jay speaks slowly and loudly to his quarry. He'd probably talk to a deaf person the same way, or a pensioner, or a toddler, "I'm feeling a little queasy, might've been the boat. Seasick. I'm just going to the bathroom quickly." Then he scurries down to the library toilets.

"You don't mind if I wait for him here, do you?" Mr Singh says. "I've got many questions. You know I had no idea something like this even existed. Tell me do you have any shows in Punjabi?"

"One of our most popular shows actually. It's called *Punjabi Time*. We air it every Thursday night at eight. A guy called Kuldeep Chahal hosts it. The podcast of it gets more than three thousand hits a week. They're looking for a sponsor at the moment."

"This is a New Zealand audience?" Mr Singh says.

"Oh no, all over the world. In fact, we probably get more hits in India than anywhere else."

"Well, you learn something new each day. You know, Mark, I love radio. I used to listen to it growing up in Hamilton, but there is no dedicated radio station in my mother tongue. I'm going to change that."

"Oh, you're starting a dedicated Punjabi language station?"

"Hopefully."

"Have you got a frequency?"

"Well, not yet, but he's going to set me up with one," Mr Singh says, nodding his head in the general direction of the library.

"Who, Jay Dicks?"

"Yes."

"A full power frequency?"

"Sure."

"In Auckland?"

"Sure."

"But there's none on the market." As Mark utters those words the penny drops.

"Well, I'm afraid that's all I know. Mr Dicks is working as a consultant for me to try to find a frequency."

"So, you're not here to look at the building then?"

"No."

"Oh right, I was under the assumption that's why you were here. Maybe you wanted to lease it from the council."

"No, I was told that I'd be shown a working radio station. I'm not interested in this building."

Jay returns ten minutes later looking like he's had a light workout. Soaked with rain and flushed around the face. As he comes through the partition, Mr Singh and Mark are enjoying a cup of tea.

"Sorry to interrupt, Mr Singh, but I need to get back to Auckland. I'm afraid the weather is closing in and I don't want my boat to be cancelled. Shall I take you back to Burrell Road?"

"Yes, Mr Dicks, that would be lovely."

Chapter 48

THE STORM

Monday 23rd December - 20:30

Jay Dicks has gone the whole hog for Mr Singh. Rolling out the red carpet. Covering all the expenses. Transport, food, lodgings. A small blue Airbnb on Burrell Road is what he'd hired. Baby blue with flashings in white. Still, easily the most prominent property in Surfdale. Still, perched high on the ridge of a steep section next to a large pine tree. Still, defying gravity, sixty years after having been put there. Mr Singh is just getting cosy in it.

Outside, Cyclone Frank is intensifying. He's downed his sleeping pills at half eight while listening to talkback titan, Larcus Mush. Half an hour of Mush and he'll be away by half nine. He struggles to get a fix on Larcus's topic because of the sound of the house creaking around him. It's one of the louder houses. Flexing in the wind. Banging. The light in the bedroom flickers sporadically too. It unsettles him, but 'maybe' he thinks, this house 'always does that', how would he know? Maybe it's haunted. And then his spine starts to tingle, and he loses touch with the day in a slumbered haze.

The wind is what wakes him. Eleven p.m. and Frank is howling through the gutter. Yes, a bit of banging. Close too. Repeated banging on the roof. Glass breaks. The ceiling gives way. Now it's rain. Rain inside and sparks and shrubs. Leaves in bed, but the house is moving and now there's leaves on his pillow. Confusion. Darkness. A stick to the face. Too dark to see. Picking up speed now, it's moving. Not just the bed. The whole house. Moving off the hill. Until it drops. Shear. Down through the stilts that held the home to the cliff. Down through the section. It stops in time, violently. He's cold, wet and he's covered in debris. Hurt. Sleepy. 'I'll just have a little rest,' he thinks to himself. And as he lies there in the septic field, underneath some cladding and skewered against a tree at the bottom of the garden, Mr Singh's life starts to flash before his eyes.

Being a kid, Mum, Dad, brothers and sisters. Cricket in the slums. School. Moving to New Zealand in the 70s. The comments from the school bullies, shouting 'fucking raghead' as they beat him. Selling and buying. The moment he met his wife. The birth of his kids. Walking his daughters up the aisle. The successes in business, the failures too. Walking on the beach with his family. Trips back to India.

Chapter 49

THE STAND IN

Tuesday 24th December - 05:18

It's Christmas Eve morning and after a sleep interrupted by the sound of Cyclone Frank bearing down on his roof, Mark is woken abruptly by a phone call from teenage broadcaster, DJ Remington Dill.

"Boss, boss!" Remi sounds stressed, and the background is noisy.

"What's up, Remi?" Mark says wearily. "You know you've woke me up, eh?"

"Sorry, boss, sorry, look I can't do the breakfast show. There's a tree across Donald Bruce Road. I can't get past it. The road's been closed."

Twenty minutes later and Mark is on his scooter heading to the station to host the breakfast show himself. At the bottom of the drive, and in the dark in the middle of a massive weather event he runs into Bento.

"What the fuck are you doing out here?" he says.

"Exercising."

"What about this cyclone?"

"What about it? Man's got to keep fit. Question is, 'what're you doing up?', why're you up?"

"Oh I've gotta do the breakfast show, the usual guy can't get in to do it. I better go though. I'm late already."

Mark doesn't take the detour up Glen Brook Road to avoid Liz and Gavin Gregson's place. In fact, he never does that anymore. Instead, he takes the left to go straight up the hill on O'Brien. Within 20 minutes of doing that, he is keying the door at the radio station. He disarms the alarm and makes himself a coffee. He checks X and Facebook to see what information he can gather on Cyclone Frank as it rages away outside.

Despite not having hosted a show since doing *The Wire* on 95bfm more than a year earlier, there's no nerves, just adrenaline, muscle memory and producing a radio show on his feet. He lets the BBC International News play out and then he hits play on some generic news music which lurks at a bed of fifteen percent volume.

"Good morning, it's seven o'clock. You're on *Waiheke Island Radio*, 89FM. My name's Mark Goodenough. It's Christmas Eve, and what a night it's been. Cyclone Frank's been a big one what. There've been no ferries, either on or off the island for more than fifteen hours. There's power outages all over the island and there have been reports of flooding on many properties.

"A house looks to have been destroyed on Burrell Road. Emergency services are still in attendance there. It looked horrific when I went past it earlier. Hopefully, no one was in it. Anyway, Waiheke, I'm going to make a few phone calls, find out what I can, and while I do that, I'm going to play the extended version of *Fools Gold* by The Stone Roses."

In the ensuing nine minutes and fifty-three seconds, Mark speaks to people at the local board, the fire station, the police station, the coastguard, and the people at the road maintenance company, Downer. Five listeners had each phoned in, taking their turn to give first-hand accounts of Cyclone Frank from all around the island. It was all recorded for use during the broadcast.

"Ok, this is Waiheke Island Radio, 89FM, and you're listening to *Island Breakfast* brought to you by *I Believe I Can Fry*, the island's number one fish and chip shop. Okay, so the far end is cut off. We're getting reports of trees across Orapiu Road, near Passage Rock, and also Waiheke Road near Talking Tree Hill school for kids. Our Station Manager Larry Minto lives down in Otakawhe Bay. We'll get him on the phone as soon as we can to have him tell us how things look on the ground down there. He always gets cut off.

"I can tell you from personal experience the roads are a mess. There's a massive puddle near Waster's Corner down by the Dirt Track, where the road bottoms out, there's another monster puddle at Little O Junction too. There are several small landslips all down Ocean View Road between Burrell and Goodwin. A tree's come down on Donald Bruce, that's blocking the school, good job it's holidays. I don't have any report from Mātiatia yet.

"My advice. Stay in, don't drive. Leave the roads for the emergency services. We'll have another song, and I'll see if I can get us some guests, this is The Chills with *Submarine Bells*."

By a quarter to seven, the switchboard is alive, and texts are flying in from all over the island with people reporting what's going on in their area. With this kind of engagement, the show practically runs itself. This is local radio, doing what it is supposed to do. It isn't lost on Mark that the last time he'd seen a full switchboard, was during *The Dead Air Incident*. That night he was playing to a much larger audience, but to have this many callers tuned in to a local radio broadcast suggests that a lot more people were tuning in than they'd previously thought.

"Ok, I have a statement here from Kane at the fire station. A man in a critical condition was flown to Auckland hospital after the Burrell Road Airbnb he'd hired was smashed down a steep embankment by a tree in the early hours. The man, known to be from Hamilton, was freed from the wreckage by the actions of local fire-fighter Bella Lasagne, who risked her own life to get to him. The tree which had already been flagged by the council as dangerous succumbed to the one hundred and twenty kilometre per hour winds that lashed the island through the night. Let's hope he pulls through." Mark pauses. "So, two hundred residents on Kennedy Point Road, now cut off by a tree. We'll get Remi D on the line in a few minutes to give us the details on what's happening there shortly.

"Enclosure Bay and Sandy Bay are both accessible only by foot, again that's probably another thousand of the island's residents. Rocky Bay is only accessible by bike. There are three considerable slips on O'Brien Road. One is around a blind bend, so drive very carefully if you're in that area. I'm also getting reports of extensive flooding in Blackpool, and we'll get another of the Waiheke Island Radio team, Melody, to give us a report from there as soon as we can. There are power outages the Te Toki Road, Junction Road, and Bay Road areas, as well as parts of Surfdale and all of Palm Beach is out.

"Wow, there's going to be a lot of frightened people out there, so if you can check on your neighbour once this dies down, you should. Now, we've got a report here from the MetService that says the storm will have passed by nine o'clock."

At five to ten, Mark plays the last song of that morning's breakfast show, *Here Comes the Sun* by The Beatles. "Well folks, thanks for listening, it's been a wild ride, probably a bit of damage, but you know, at least you won't have to worry about filling your tank for Christmas anymore. I've been Mark Goodenough and you've been listening to Waiheke Island Radio 89FM."

Melody is waiting at the door for Mark to turn his microphone off. "That was a bloody brilliant show Mark, good on you, I've never heard you present before, you're really good at it. You should do it more often."

"Thanks, Melody, you get any damage at yours?"

"I had some water coming into the garage, but I managed to divert it."

"See that house in Surfdale?"

"No, what house?"

"A house on Burrell Road slid off the side of the hill. A tree fell on it. Apparently, Bella pulled someone from the wreckage. An Indian man, he's supposed to be at death's door."

"Oh my God!" says Melody as she covers her mouth with her hands.

"Yeah, and you know those visitors who were meant to be coming in yesterday?"

"Ricky Bricks?"

"Yeah, but his name isn't Ricky Bricks. It's Jay Dicks. I know him. I used to work with him at UNZ. The man's a prick. First class tool. Well, he eventually turned up with this Indian fella. It was just after Larry left. I'm pretty sure the guy they took out of the crashed house is the same guy that came with Jay Dicks. He was Indian, said he lived in Hamilton. And Dicks asked him if he wanted a lift to Burrell Road."

"Really?"

"Yeah. He was a nice guy too. I hope he's okay. I felt sorry for him, it'd have been awkward for him."

"So, what's a nice guy doing with that Bricks prick then?"

"Dicks."

"Yeah, that too."

"Well, get this. Dicks is trying to pimp our frequency off to the Indian fella."

"Serious?"

"Yep."

Chapter 50

THE NIGHT BEFORE CHRISTMAS

Tuesday 24th December

At nine o'clock on Christmas Eve the Mintos put their children to bed, while Melody lays out the Scrabble board on the coffee table. The teams are set, Larry and Holly, Mark and Melody, Derek Barnaby and Barry Twelvedogs. As Larry dips his hand in the green felt bag, to draw out his seven tiled letters, Holly is still on her feet, pouring wine in the kitchen for her and Melody. With the seven tiles in his hand, Larry places them on the rack. One vowel, six consonants.

YRNCGRI

Straight away, he knows what he has. The six-letter word, CRYING with a spare R left on the rack. What a way to start the game. He is raring to show teammate Holly, who is about to sit down, just as she does, her phone lets out a bing, prompting her to pull it from her pocket to read the incoming text.

"Oh my God," she utters, sounding shocked.

"Everything alright?" Says Melody.

"Mum's been taken to hospital."

"Bluebell?"

"Yeah."

"Oh my God. What's happened?"

"I don't know, your dad just sent this text now. He wants us to call him."

"Now?"

"Yeah, shall we go out to the granny flat to make the call?" Even though Melody hates Bluebell, she loves Holly, and she loves her dad too. This is most definitely her business. The game of Scrabble would have to wait, but as the pair walk to the ranch slider Larry says. "Should we carry on?"

"MMMM maybe we should wait a few minutes," says Twelvedogs, sounding like a Cylon off the 80's sci-fi television series, Battlestar Galactica.

"I think we should carry on. They might be a while," counters Larry.

"I'll play. They can jump in when they get back," says Mark.

"I'm with them, Dogsy. Let's keep going," Barnaby says.

"MMMM okay then. MMMM who's going first AAA?"

"Draw a letter out of the bag and the one with the highest value letter goes first, then it's clockwise from there," Larry says.

"MMMM righto AAA."

Larry is gutted that he can't start the game with CRYING after Mark wins the draw to go first. Mark's first word down is CART which he racks out across the star in the middle of the board. Then Larry sees it. He can use the A in CART and his spare R to make the word CARRYING. Larry, quivering like a bull in a stall at a Texas rodeo, is raring to go. It's a catch-22 though, a crowd-pleasing hand for a passive audience. He needs more eyeballs on this play.

"I won't play just yet. Let's wait for Holly," Larry says, pretending humility.

"All good."

Ten more minutes of beer, wine, cheese, and biscuits pass before Holly and Melody return from the granny. "I'm sorry everyone. Should we carry on?"

"Yes, let's," Larry says eagerly, and just as his wife is about to take her seat, he leans excitedly in and whispers into her ear, "here, look at this."

Before Holly can look at the tile rack, she is intercepted by a comforting squeeze on the shoulder from Derek Barnaby. Just a simple act of humanity but it brings on the waterworks and the pair embrace platonically.

"Bless you, my child," says Derek.

"Thank you, father."

Time is passing while they embrace, and Larry can feel the sting going out of the game. Here he is sitting on the greatest hand of Scrabble he's ever had. This is not a time for grief. Besides, no one's dead yet.

"Okay, I'm just going to play on here."

By the time Larry puts the letter I down, people start seeing it.

"Yeah, now you're interested huh?" Larry says, going full Asperger's, his voice getting louder as he starts crowing, "how's about a bit of this then eh? CARRYING. A mere fifteen points you might say," he gloats while his wife dries her eyes, "but with a fifty-point bonus for using all our letters that nets us a whopping sixty-five points."

🐶

By the time Larry climbs in bed a few hours later, he's deflated, gutted about the game petering out in the way it had. All he wanted was a win, something to crow about. Something. Anything. Holly is still on her feet, pottering around the bedroom, preparing herself for bed.

"Didn't she play sports when she was younger?"

"Who?"

"Bluebell."

"Yeah, she was a Silver Fern in her day."

"So, generally a competitive person, you'd say?"

"What are you getting at, Larry?"

"Well, I'm just saying, she'd have probably wanted that Scrabble game to continue, wouldn't she?"

"Are you still on about that?"

"Well, it was a good hand."

"She's had a stroke, Larry. She might die."

"But you don't seem to understand, Holly," Larry implores, his palms outstretched. "That was the opening gambit of a lifetime."

"You're autistic. You must be."

"Well, it didn't get the credit it deserved, and anyway, it's what it represents, isn't it?"

"What do you mean by that?"

"Well, Christmas is about to turn to shit because your difficult mother has died." It's a Freudian slip, alright.

"Larry, she's not even dead yet. And that's my mother you're talking about. She was a lovely woman, and now she's at death's door, and all you can worry about is a word in a game of bloody Scrabble. This is ridiculous. I can't believe we're even having this discussion. This is crazy and you're drunk and you're autistic too."

"Look I don't want to be a grammar nazi, but you've just put her in the present and past tense in that last sentence, and you did it while you were correcting me on the tense, I'd used to describe her in the first place."

"Oh, fuck off, Larry, you insensitive prick," Holly says, shooting daggers at him.

Drunk, the pair sleep back-to-back that Christmas Eve, stacking zeds, while Chunk snores rhythmically at the foot of their bed like the Wookie with the apnoea.

Chapter 51

THE CHRISTMAS MIRACLE

Wednesday 25th December - 10:02

It's Christmas morning and at around 10 a.m. Mr Sidhu Singh comes to, and he does so with a quick realisation that he can't move much of his body. There's a tube up his nose and only one of his eyes seems to be functional. Through it he can see that both arms are encased in plaster and are stretched in front of him. Beyond his rigid arms, he notices the red, green, and silver tinsel that traces the frame of the door to the room. The sounds of indistinct voices and random footsteps woke him. That and the mechanical beeping of medical machinery. All these realisations, coupled with the pine bouquet of chemical disinfectant tell him where he is. His next interaction will tell him why.

"Merry Christmas, Mr Singh. It's good to see you're back with us. My name's Gloria. I'm one of the nurses here in the intensive care department at Auckland General Hospital." Gloria speaks at pace in a Filipino accent as she changes the morphine drip, close to the left side of Mr Singh's head. "Mr Singh, you've been in a coma for thirty-two hours. You are a *very* lucky person. If it wasn't for that helicopter and that fire-fighter on Waiheke, you'd be dead now."

To Mr Singh, this all figures, because he feels like shit. Besides not being able to move, he can't speak, and he has a headache and a ringing in his ears. All he can do is listen.

"Mr Singh, your house collapsed in a storm, with you in it. You've got lots of injuries." The intake of Gloria's breath tells Mr Singh the list is going to be extensive. "Collapsed lung, broken ankle, two broken arms, broken wrist, and four broken ribs. Blunt force head trauma, lacerations about the face and upper torso. Three puncture wounds in your side. You've broken your femur, lost a finger and a bit of your ear is missing.

"Now, most lacerations were from broken glass, and you were impaled on the tree that fell through your house. That's what caused the puncture wounds. The head injury was most likely sustained when you hit the ground. We don't know why you lost your ear or where your finger went. It's pretty big news, Mr Singh. You made the front page of *The Herald*."

Gloria is right. It is big news, and a picture of the destroyed house on Burrell Road dominates that morning's edition. Above it, the slug line *BLOWN AWAY*. It is the kind of image that sells newspapers and garners clicks. The team in *The Herald* newsroom were overjoyed when they saw it. Christmas Day is always slow. Advertisers love that stuff. They don't even have to send flowers.

"Now we've informed your family and they're on their way over. We've had another call asking about you. It was from a guy called Mark. He said he was from the radio station on Waiheke. He seems quite concerned for your welfare."

Chapter 52

THE SPECIALS

Sunday 5th January - 18:30

Two Sundays later, at six-thirty in the evening, Mark, Larry, Melody, and practically everyone else connected with the station are glued to their television sets. Waiting on that week's edition of *Good Sorts*, the ten-minute piece tacked to the end of the six o'clock news on Sundays. A pat on the back to Kiwis who consistently go above and beyond for their communities.

It starts with a drone shot, fifty feet in the air, moving down the beach at Little O, and crossing the headland. A ukulele starts strumming along to a xylophone. It's the kind of music one hears in adverts for banks, insurance and pension schemes. Unboxing music.

"Waiheke Island," female narrator, twenty years a smoker, "the third most inhabited island in New Zealand," pause, "a home in paradise to a diverse community of around nine thousand people." A piano kicks in on the offbeat, giving a suggestion of naïve fun, and primary school reggae. The drone shot continues. It moves along the beach at Big Oneroa and veers up the hill towards the mid-to-high-end properties next to the library. And then, the radio station comes into focus as the drone slows down to a stop.

"And on today's Good Sorts," you wanted to cough for her, "we're going to introduce you to some of the people who hold that community together with some old-fashioned *Good Sorts* glue. Today we are looking at the community radio station, Waiheke Island Radio."

With the station house in full view, the drone stops and zooms in onto the back deck of the building. Standing upon it and waving, there's a group of about fifteen staff and broadcasters. The shot lingers on the group for five seconds before cutting away to Larry. He is sitting upright at his desk.

"It's not just about what we do on the radio. We're a community hub. We help people with all sorts of things."

A succession of vox-pops follows. These are personal, to-camera testimony. In this case, by people standing on the beach at Oneroa with the sea in the background. All of them unanimously lauding the work that the station does.

Pablo, Lalo and Nacho Techno are up first, "We're from Argentina and we love Waiheke Island. There's a large South American community on the island and this station helps us stay informed about what's out there for us, in our language. It helps us learn English and it lets us engage with the wider community."

The next face is that of Tui James from the marae. "There's no iwi stations on this island, and you can't really get the Auckland ones too clearly, but at Waiheke Island Radio, we can let our people know about the services that are available to them and we can get the message out about the events we have down at the marae. This station means we can be heard."

Melody is standing by the tree in the courtyard outside the Artworks theatre, "I've worked at Waiheke Island Radio for five years now. This is a great place for kids to come and learn to speak publicly, to organise and to create. There are heaps of skills they can develop through doing that. Plus, it's free to them. We've turned around the lives of many kids who were flirting with trouble."

By the beach again, "Hi, I'm Fire-fighter Lasagne, with Waiheke Volunteer Fire Brigade. Waiheke Island Radio allows us to educate people on fire safety and awareness, and to update our listeners on any news we might have for them."

"My name's Willie Hamilton and I'm from Waiheke Police. This radio station does so much good for this community. We can help people feel more secure with our regular updates. We'd hate to lose it."

When the vox-pops finish, the shot cuts to a short of the Palm Beach barbecue area by the playground, then a shot of ANZAC Bay from the entrance to the retirement village carpark, and finally a long shot looking back to Auckland City from Vintage Lane. Over these images, the gravel-voiced narrator continues, "but it's all under threat because the station needs to raise enough money to retain their frequency which comes up for auction next month."

More vox-pops follow, this time from Waiheke residents. Again, the testimony is universally positive. A longer interview with Larry follows. Framed by his trophies and his Brother Brothers and the Brothers Brothers poster, he explains how the station is under threat, and he makes the call to action, asking viewers to donate towards their fundraising drive. He says that they might even end up needing the money for legal fees given how bad things are getting. He is completely honest.

A sombre piano plays a heart-rending tune. A woman and her three young children hand in hand, walk down the Esplanade between Surfdale and Blackpool. They have their backs to the camera as the waves crash against the rocks in slow motion next to them. The smallest of the children dangles a dolly from her right hand. A different woman's voice trails in over the wide shot. "I lost my husband back in October," the music then fades as the shot cuts to a woman facing the camera. It's the woman from Santa's grotto, Hazel. Her name appears at the bottom of the screen as she tells the story of how she couldn't afford the rent after Troy drove his car into that pōhutakawa on the Onetangi Straight on purpose. He left a note on the passenger seat. Now, she's had to move the family into the back of her car.

A guitar kicks in, acoustic. Major key and sleigh bells. The narrator's voice returns. "Then, a chance meeting with Santa Claus turned things around."

Hazel comes back to the camera. "It was like a Christmas present. Ever since we went up to that station, and were introduced to their network of angels, I've been able to start to piece our lives back together. Now we've got emergency housing on the island, and I've got a new job too. It's still tough for us all, but these people have been awesome. They just wanted to help. They didn't want anything in return. I think they should all be knighted. I can't believe that the station might not even be here in a few months. I hope they can turn it around."

At the end of the piece, the address to the station's *Give a Little* page is displayed in large letters on the screen, with the narrator's voice imploring, "Go on, give them a helping hand. They'd do it for you."

Chapter 53

THE FOLLOWING FRIDAY MORNING

Friday 12th January - 07:53

Darcey Knight, Lynn Mall, Sylvia Park and Albany Westfield of the GLITFAB Crew are standing-in at short notice for Anderson Yogamum on the Island Breakfast. Mark asked them the day before. They've been good lately, stayed on the right side of the rules. Even so, Mark rocks up early for work, concerned about the prospect of casual lewdness during the school drop-off. It's been troubling him since four. He needn't have worried, they've been very professional, and all the markers were met. Weather at seven, then a throw to the surf report. Celebrity birthdays at seven fifteen, listeners' birthdays immediately after that. At seven forty Cathryn Katzenfrau from WISCA comes in to tell listeners about three lost cats and a misplaced pit-bull.

Just before eight is Darcey's favourite feature, *Celebrity Sightings*. They've scripted it themselves and read it out over a bed of the Theme tune to Cilla Black's *Blind Date*, which plays at no more than thirty percent volume.

"Danny of Surfdale saw a couple of pensioners helping James Bond actor Daniel Craig to his feet after he'd slipped on the grass by the selfie penguins in Oneroa," Darcey says.

Lynn Mall, singing, "He's got a license to spill."

Sylvia Park, "Bet he was shaken, not stirred."

Darcey Knight, "Taxi driving local Martin Chuzzlewit had non-binary Grammy winning behemoth Sam Smith in the back of his car last week.

Albany Westfield, "Had them where?"

Lynn Mall (singing), "Somewhere unholy."

Darcey Knight, "Christopher Luxon's been out on his Sealegs. He and his fabulous family, breaking the rāhui at Onetangi Beach. Dropping anchor and no doubt exacerbating the spreading of the noxious seaweed Caulerpa."

Lynn Mall, "Spreading what?"

Sylvia Park, "I'll bet he says he didn't know about it."

Darcey Knight, "And you'd be right."

Sylvia Park, "What can I say, Darcey? I'm a psychic."

Darcey Knight, "Former radio host and eyeliner spokesman Michael Laws has been over. Dominic Catlove of Kennedy Point says he saw him struggling to control his giant Spoodle as it chased a nesting dotterel at Whakanewha last week Wednesday."

Lynn Mall, "Giant what?"

Darcey Knight, "Spoodle."

Sylvia Park, "Spoodle?"

Darcey Knight, "Spoodle. Moving on. Jason Gunn's been over. Shellfishly parking on the pavement in Palm Beach and forcing families to walk in the road. Brow of a hill too. And finally, the Dalai Lama was seen down the Little O chippy eating a deep-fried Moro bar. Apparently going back half an hour later for a couple of fishcakes, a fish and a pot of vinegar."

🐶

As *Celebrity Sightings* concludes it segues perfectly into a commercial for a firm of local undertakers and then an advert for a local cobbler called Sue. There's a five second pip and then the BBC International News on the Hour does its five-minute stint of dog whistle balance and war propaganda. After that Sylvia Park reads the weather, then, at ten past nine there's an interview with two local activists. They're in to persuade people to sign their petition against the opening of a Carl's Junior in the car park outside Placemakers. One of the activists is called Hans. The other is called Nees.

"So, what's this about the soccer player Rolando? Is it true he signed your perdition?" Darcey says.

"Ronaldo," corrects Hans.

"Yeah, that's what I said."

"No, you said Rolando."

"Cristiano. Right?"

"Yeah."

"Are you sure it wasn't just a Rolando look-a-like?"

"Ronaldo."

"Yeah, that's what I said."

"No, you said Rolando again."

"I did?" Darcey flexing a little here. This liberal-windsock pensioner might need to be shown who the alpha is.

"Correct."

"And what of your perdition, how many people you got signed it now?" Darcey says slightly ruffled.

"Petition," corrects Hans again.

"Yeah, that's what I said."

"No, you said 'perdition'."

As Darcey sinks further into batter mode, Nees picks up on it and interjects, "nearly ten thousand."

"Really? That's good. Any other celebs sign it?"

"Yeah, loads, Sir Graham Henry, Marc Ellis, Lizzo, Bez, John Campbell, Lorde, Johnny and Big Hungry from 95bfm, Big Bill Tong, Jonathan Bree, all of Phoebe Rings, Dubhead, Paul Rutherford, Gary Farrow, all of INXS, Taylor the Swift, Ryder the Eagle, both Kevin Sheedys, Troy Ferguson, The Weeknd, Mikey Havoc, Princess Chelsea, Noora Te Hira, Brandon Smith, Josh Emmet, Matilda Rice, Arthur Green, Bruce Davis-Goff, Linda Savage, Leighton Baines, all of Simple Minds, both of Tears for Fears, both of Go West, one of Five, two of Queen and one of Robbie Williams."

"Robbie Williams? He's a tool. Was there anyone what didn't sign it?" Lynn Mall asks.

"Well, yes there was actually. The Mad Butcher, said he had a conflict of interest,"

"Oh well, I supposed he would've, being a man of meat," Sylvia says.

"Actually, we were hoping to get your signature today," says Nees addressing Darcey who is still flexing.

"Me?" Always modest.

"Well as being Waiheke Island's eighth most famous person."

"Well, I suppose I could," Darcey replies, flattered.

"Don't worry, we'll all sign it, darling," says Albany Westfield and to the sound of rustling paper and arms moving microphones they do, until it gets to Lynn Mall.

"I'm not signing that."

"No?"

"No, I like Carl's Junior. I want one on hand. I mean just imagine it. You wouldn't even have to go in. Just stay in your car and place your order. What's wrong with that? It's a bit of me is that. I mean, I just don't get it."

"You know, now that you come to mansion it, I quite like the idea of being able to get my Phillip of fish and my decapitated coffee without getting out of the car. Yeah, actually I think you're onto something there Lynn. In fact, pass me that perdition, I've changed my mind. I'm going to rub it out."

"You can't do that. You've already signed it."

"Oh yes I can."

Sensing blood, Lynn Mall continues the assault, "I don't know why you people have such a beef with meat?"

"Well, for one, it's very close to Waiheke Primary and also, according to our research, people just don't want drive-thrus here. We've got the healthiest kids in Auckland on this island and it's because we've resisted American helpings for years."

"American helpings?" Lynn says, swallowing an excess of saliva.

"Yeah, American Helpings. They're putting five patties on a burger. It's disgusting"

"Five patties on a burger," Lynn adds picturing it in the mind.

"Yeah, and they want to bring it here, to our island to fatten up our tamariki."

"Have you got kids?" interjects Sylvia.

"No."

"American helpings, eh? I'm not sure I see the problem," Lynn Mall says out loud again.

"Well of course some people want these American helpings, don't they?" says Hans, laughing smugly to himself and looking directly at Lynn Mall.

"What do you mean by that?"

"Oh, you know, nothing."

"Saying I'm fat?"

"Well, I'm not saying, you're thin."

"Not thin?"

"Well, you're not."

"But."

"Wait a minute, Lynn," Darcey interrupts, "are you going to be eating all five of those Mars Bars you've got there?"

"Well, I might," and with that, the whole room belches out a wave of laugher that ripples through the room a wee while longer than it might've, had the tension not been there in the first place.

"Wait a minute though," says Sylvia, "I'm also starting to agree with Lynn and anyway, don't we already have fast food outlets on the island? What about Tsing Tao, Mint As, Two Fat Buns? How come you're not out protesting them?"

"Erm, well, they're locals. That's different."

"Oh, I see. Local shops for local people, eh?"

Before Hans or Nees can reply, Darcey, composure regained, says, "well, running short on time, how many signatures do you need, and where can listeners sign your perdition?"

"Well, we're up to nine thousand eight hundred now, we need ten thousand for the Government to look at it, so only two hundred short."

"Yes, but where can people sign it?"

"Well, we'll be at Mātiatia tomorrow afternoon, and Ostend Market in the morning. I'll be going to the Dirt Track on Sunday and if you don't see us there it'll be at the library."

"Well, we at Waiheke Island Radio also need you. What we need though is your money so we can buy our frequency back. Now, I can see that Melody has just arrived for work, maybe we can have a quick word with her on the air so we can tell listeners where we are with our fundraising drive."

Two minutes later, Melody is on the air. "So, our Give a Little page needs to keep ticking over," she says, obliviously holding a piece of paper showing a graph to an audience that can't see it. The X axis on the graph started on Saturday morning and went through until seven thirty that Friday morning. The Y axis shows money raised. "As you can see, it was a flatline 'til Sunday night, and it spiked when we were shown on *Good Sorts*. It goes up again the next day, that'll be when it was shared on the internet."

"So how much are we at now?"

"Well, we've had a stellar week, and the tally stands at eighty grand now.

There've been several big donations. The Argentine consulate donated ten grand. One Peter Leitch of the Surfdale Bowling Club very generously put in five grand, a Ms Rahman donated two thousand bucks. Darcey I can see you've given a one hundred bucks, good for you. Big Bill Tong gave one fifty, Paul Rutherford, two hundred. Derek Barnaby two hundred, Devast8er, three hundred, Ken Oath, two hundred. It's unreal. Still a way to go though."

When Melody says, "a way to go" she grossly undersells it. What the station actually needs is a miracle.

🐶

It's time for another emergency meeting, and as soon as the Friday edition of Island Breakfast is finished, Larry calls it, as usual, at the kitchen table.

Before he can convene it to order, Melody comes straight in with her own question. "So have NZOA confirmed that they're not putting anything in at all now?" She knows she's reaching.

Larry already has the answer, but he also knows he is going to have to exercise every ounce of diplomacy that he has. "Nothing's been confirmed yet, but I've got to say, there's a good chance they won't."

"So, we need to raise what? About eight million dollars, right Larry?" Melody is indignant, annoyed, "It's not going to happen, Larry. Be realistic."

"Cards on the table," triple-tic, "right? Look, I know things look bleak, but you know, I've known bleaker." It is rhetoric on Larry's part, pathos and ethos and it is coming in hot. "I know what real hopelessness is, and this, it isn't." He pauses to breathe in through his nose, seemingly angry. It's clear he isn't finished. "For the last two weeks of my coma, I was awake. I could hear and see everything that was going on around me, but I couldn't engage any of it. It was the most frightened I'd ever been. I couldn't feel my body at all. I was just eyes in a head."

Larry pauses, and he seems to be reading the words on his Battered Bastard mug. "When I heard the doctor tell my mother, I'd likely be a vegetable for the rest of my life, I had to listen to her wailing," tic, a sudden emotional choke in Larry's words and he pauses to swallow, "*I couldn't wail,*" another pause, and a tic. "I wanted to, but I couldn't even cry and I lay there, fully alive in my head for two whole weeks not knowing whether I'd ever move my body again the whole time."

"That was hopeless. This is bleak, but I don't know. I just have a feeling we'll be okay. I know it sounds mad, but I think we can fix it. We've got to keep up the guerrilla tactics on the prick, keep checking his voicemail, try and get that phone of his. Are you still hacking their voicemails Mark?"

"Not for a few days, boss, last time I did, it was all tickets and gardeners, you know the drugs? He must be dealing though. Maybe we can use that against the prick?"

"Chance'd be a fine thing. I do think we should keep on digging at his phone though." Larry takes two deep breaths. "Look, there's something else I need to tell you. It's more bad news, I'm afraid."

Mark sniggers, saying, "More?"

Larry sniggers too, tics twice and says, "You know I can't believe I'm having to tell you this, but remember that Caleb McGill joker?"

"The neo-Nazi?

"Yeah,"

"Well, Mr McGill is suing us."

"Caleb McGill?" Mark says, belching on a ball of indignant laughter, "The nazi? Suing us?" Mark is completely confused "How does that work? That show wasn't ever broadcast, was it?"

"Nah, it wasn't that. It was from the day before that, remember those racist flyers?"

"Yeah."

"Well, you know Constable Willie Hamilton?"

"Yeah."

"He's accused Mr McGill of disseminating those racist flyers. He's also given away Mr McGill's whereabouts live on air. Happened during Remi's breakfast show. You must've missed it. I know I did."

"Oh brilliant," Melody sarcastically replies. She'll be looking for a new job tomorrow. "Why didn't you mention this sooner?"

"I didn't want to ruin Christmas."

"Ruin Christmas?" she was astounded, flabbergasted, "Y-you've known about this since Christmas?"

"Oh, I've known about it since before Christmas."

"But that's three weeks ago."

"One week before Christmas," tic.

"You've known for a month?"

"You should've said something, we could've started looking for other work," says Melody.

"I'm really sorry Melody. We all needed a break. I didn't want to destroy yours before it had even begun. Look, all I can say is I'm sorry."

"I don't know what I'm going to do now, Larry,"

"Well, I'm not going to give up."

Larry's phone sings out and he takes the call, ushering himself away into his office. It is as if he left a bad fart behind him and Mark turns to Melody, saying, "What the actual fuck?"

Melody gasps, "I think we're done for."

"Well, I'm glad Larry has a good feeling about it. I know I don't"

"Jesus,"

"I wouldn't mind but I've only been here a few weeks. I was beginning to like this job."

"Maybe we should all get drunk," says Melody.

"What, you and me?"

"Well, we are in the same boat."

"I suppose."

Chapter 54

THE DIRT TRACK

Sunday 12th January - 11:00

Mark, Bento and Bubbles are sitting in the viewing area at the Waiheke Dirt Track as the day's racing commences. Bubbles is on a lead. Bento is trying to keep the monkey's profile low. Animals aren't allowed in the viewing paddock. The humans are sweating profusely after their fifteen-minute uphill tramp through the Kauakarau Forest. This, right at the business end of another New Zealand summer. Bento'd done the bulk of the work, hauling the cooler-bag backpack on his shoulders, up through the bush and over the saddle. The cooler-bag is four beers over its six-beer capacity, and the extra four bottle tops are pushing the fabric like snapped bones under stretched skin.

From their vantage above the back straight, the pair have a splendid view, it takes in the whole of the egg-shaped circuit, the pits and the finish line which is framed majestically by a steep bush that rises sharply to the summit of Rangihoua Hill, some two hundred metres above. It's early in the racing programme and many of the spectators have yet to arrive. That said, Hans and Nees, the Carl's Junior cockblockers are there, working from a trestle table next to the food truck and hustling for signatures with little success. As usual Big Bill Tong is there too. He's sitting on the other side of the course, calling the races from a black and white chequered structure that stands on the finish line.

The most popular place to watch the racing is at the top corner before the home straight where a chain-link fence separates the on-track action from about fifteen spectators. They call it 'Waster's Corner' and it is here that you'll find the hard-core car crew, the beer-swilling, weed-smoking, funeral-burnout bad boys of Waiheke Island.

"You know a car went over that fence once? Landed on a cunt's bonnet." Says Bento, about Waster's Corner.

"Yeah?"

"Yeah, they had to get a crane in to pull it off."

"Pull it off."

"Yeah, pull it off."

Whenever Big Bill has something to say about Waster's Corner over the P.A. a large drunken cheer can be heard from those on it. This only happens between races. Also, between races, music blares from the daisy-chained speakers on top of the chain-link fence that surrounds the track. The music they play is music of an aesthetic you'd expect. Grown men with beards screaming for the pleasure of grown men with beards.

"Here she is," says Mark as he looks across the track, recognising Melody's silver Mazda materialising from the greenery on the other side of the valley. The car offering flashes of its paintwork as it moves laterally along the road and through the bush some two hundred metres away. He continues to trace the car as it moves down the dip and around the bend that hugs Waster's Corner. He can hear it too, the loose fan belt screeching it along the road before she parks it on the berm. Mark is trying to be cool, pretending not to notice as Melody climbs out of her car. She's seen him though. Green and white hooped shirt, khaki shorts, white cap.

No one else was supposed to have been in the picture in Melody's mind. It was supposed to be her and Mark. Just them. When she sees Bento getting high in the family enclosure, she's gutted. He looks like a dickhead too. Lain on his side, spatchcock, like Michael Jackson on the inlay sleeve of *Thriller*, the monkey replacing the lion cub. Mark is sitting next to him, leaning back on his elbows, legs crossed, and drinking beer on a large green patio rug made from woven plastic.

"Kia ora!" She says stifling her disappointment, "you'll never guess who I just saw at the refuse station."

"Go on."

"Guess."

"Elon Musk," says Bento.

"No."

"Hilary Barry?' Mark offers.

"No."

"Nelson Mandela," says Bento.

"No, he's dead."

"He's not."

"He is. He's been dead ages."

"Oath?"

"Yeah."

"I don't remember that happening."

"It was Miley Cyrus," Melody spits. The tone of her words, best complimenting her resting bitch face.

"*Miley Cyrus?* Naaah," Mark says.

"What's she doing at our tip?"

"Getting rid of an old telly."

"What kind of telly?" Says Bento.

"Sony Bravia. Wasn't even a flat screen."

"They're heavy them."

"Yeah, they had to help her. They all got selfies."

"It's the least she could do," Bento says.

"Melody, have you met my friend Bento?"

"Yeah, we've met," she says, underwhelmed.

"Hi Melody," Bento says, theatrically, "fancy a beer?"

"No thanks, I brought wine."

"What'll you do with that? Swig it from the bottle?"

"No, I brought two glasses in my bag," she snaps.

Mark is standing now, offering space on the rug. As Melody sits down, she scans the four empty bottles of beer next to the chilly bag.

"How long ya been here?" she asks.

"Since eleven," Mark replies.

Bento has a pull on his joint, and the fumes of it carry on the breeze, giving the monkey a pop, while drawing a veil of cannabis smoke across Melody's nose. It forces her to wince.

"Saw ya on telly. You look thinner in real life," Bento says, thinking this is endearing himself in some way, but instead it is just another example of his high impact insensitivity.

"Saying I'm fat?"

"No," Bento replies defensively.

"What is it with you men and your inappropriate comments anyway? You're all the same."

Stoned, and a little bit drunk, Mark is alarmed. He needs to do something. Take control. He tuts saying, "Ignore him Melody, he's always like this," then he ruffles Bento's hair, "probably undiagnosed Asperger's, eh?"

The Jalopy category is finishing their ten-lap race by the time talk turns to the station's woes,

"Is it really going down then?"

"What?" Mark replies.

"Your station."

"Oh, you know, just a few weeks to raise millions of dollars," Melody interjects sarcastically.

"And to cap it all we've got a summons to court over defamation and breach of privacy, where the accuser is a nazi and our co-defendant's a policeman."

"What?"

"Couldn't make this shit up, eh?"

"We cloned his phone though. Didn't we? What happened to that?"

"Whose?"

"The nazi's"

After a small pause Mark says, "Well I don't think we checked. We were going after Sarin, not him."

"I cloned both of those phones., and I gave them both back to you. I'm sure I did."

"Probably in my desk drawer at work." Mark says.

"Can you get it?"

"Yeah."

"Today?"

"Sure, I'll head up there after this."

"Do you think you'll be able to pull him off?" Melody says.

"Who? The Nazi?"

"Yeah."

"You can pull him off. I'm not going anywhere near his bellend,"

"Jesus! There it is again. Is there no end to your inappropriateness, Bento?

Oh my God. I can't believe you'd say that."

"Come on, it's not aimed at you. It's aimed at me."

"How's it aimed at *you*? How? You're the one that keeps mentioning dicks. It's inappropriate."

"Look I'm sorry. It's just my terrible sense of humour."

"Pfft, sense of humour? I think you're a weirdo, and that monkey thing isn't right at all, either. It's cruel."

"But he loves me. It's not his fault he was kidnapped and forced to work in a cigarette testing facility. How would you like that? He's happy now. I cater to his every whim. If he went back into the wild, he'd die. It's too late for him." And then Bento pauses to stroke Bubbles on the back of the neck, but the monkey enjoys it too much, and he starts to develop a boner. "Go on, have you not tried feeding him? Give him a banana. Go on."

"Fuck no!" She's seen it.

"Make friends with him, go on.

"You're smoking cannabis next to him."

"He loves it."

The monkey chitters.

Since they arrived, the water truck has been past umpteen times, dampening down the clay for the races of the day. As quickly as the water is being put down though it evaporates in the sun and in no time the movement of the race cars agitates the land, raising a plume of dust from the earth which rises, and gathers, spinning and moving on the gentle breeze. Slowly the cloud approaches the family enclosure, turning like a slow-moving tornado. As it moves past the fence, some of the kids watching the racing turn their attention to it and playfully jump into the swirling bank of dust.

One spec of it had always been destined for Mark Goodenough's eyeball, it is a destiny fulfilled. Now the spec of clay dust is disturbing his contact lens, detaching it before it can be caught. It falls into the long grass. Instinctively Mark reaches forward to recover it. He squats, leaning down towards the floor and scanning the terrain for the lens with his hands. With his impaired vision, he sees something and prods at it with his index finger. Just as he does that, a heavy-set dude in a Warriors' top is walking past the three of them.

Perhaps it is the colour of Mark's attire, the white cap, the green and white shirt. Maybe it is the angle from which he views this, but Warriors Top is of a mind to stop. Then, pointing with both index fingers in Mark's direction, he shouts playfully.

"Uce! Still looking for ya drugs, eh?"

"Sorry?" says Mark.

"Looking for your drugs? I'll help you find them bro. Seen you off TikTok, uce. *Waster in Emu Suit Looks for Drugs in Own Vomit.* I'd recognise you anywhere, my brother."

"What's this?" Melody says, as she turns to Mark looking for an answer.

Before Mark can reply, Wariors Top continues, "Yeah, its crack up, sis. He's in an emu suit, fingering vomit. Hard case eh." It's a hearty laugh and it sets Bento off.

"Nah, wasn't me, mate."

"Yeah, it was. Don't lie," Bento contradicts, laughing.

"What *are* you?" Melody says indignantly.

"It *wasn't me,*" Mark giving Bento the look that says 'shut the fuck up'.

"Reckon I can get a selfie, maybe get the monkey in it too?" Warriors' Top asks. Bento cracks up.

"But it wasn't me."

Warriors' Top points at Bento, going, "He says it is."

"Well, it isn't. I'd know if it were me." Mark is flapping, "now, where's that fucking lens?"

"Fucken was, bro," Bento, in shit-stirring mode, is completely enthused.

"Can you *please* help me find this lens?"

"*Was* it you?" Melody says, familiar with the video because she'd emailed it to Wendy a couple of months earlier.

"No."

"Bullshit, bro, I've got proof." Bento is still laughing.

"You do? Let's see it then," Melody says, ignoring Mark's plea for help.

"Oh man, what a night. What a night that was, yeah, we all went to the Sun Festival, we got dressed up for it. Here look, I've got the pictures on my phone. Look, we were all on MDMA. Unforgettable."

Bento then passes his phone to Melody, as Warriors' Top says, "Yeah,

226

you'll have to give me that selfie now, bro."

And as Mark poses for the selfie with Warriors' Top and the monkey, he feels just a little more comfortable doing it than he ought to have, especially since Melody is pulling out her phone to do a search on TikTok for *Waster in Emu Suit Looks for Drugs in Own Vomit.*

"It is you!!" She says when it finishes. "I knew I knew you from somewhere the day I met you. Jesus, Mark, you're even wearing the same clothes." She's disgusted. Coming off as austere. In the twenty minutes that follow, very little is said until Melody abruptly stands up.

"I'm going now."

"It's not finished," protests Mark.

"Well, I've got stuff to do."

Once Melody is back in her car, Mark turns to Bento, and angrily says, "the fuck was that?"

"Just a truth-teller, bro."

"Man, she's my colleague. I work with her. She doesn't need to know what I get up to outside of work. Then you start sexually harassing her."

"I didn't sexually harass her."

"You did, talking about pulling off Nazis, you said, 'you can pull him off, I'm not going anywhere near his bellend.'"

"I'll bet *you've* done it."

"What?"

"Accidentally said something about your dick to a woman you fancy."

"Nah. Never."

"Yah, whatever man. Anyway, you fancy her. This isn't about her being your workmate, it's about you wanting to get with her."

"Look Bento, stop doing this mad shit please. Don't you have any idea about reading the room, ya fucken idiot."

"I wasn't the one who brought it up. It was that dude in the Warriors top, man,," Bento says as he motions with his head in his direction. "And ultimately it was you that fingered your own vomit man, no one asked you to do that eh."

"Yeah, but you didn't have to draw attention to it, did you?"

"Okay, man, look, I'm sorry. I thought you'd see the funny side. I thought it might break the ice with her. I'll tell you what," Bento says, looking for an olive branch, "if you can get that phone to me today, I'll have a look at it later?"

"Whatever, man, I'll get it," Mark says downcast, "but I'll be getting an early night tonight. I'm sick of this shit."

The monkey makes a crying gesture, by pretending to wipe both eyes simultaneously.

Bento has a filter on one of his burner phones. It's called a MagicMic Real-time Voice Changer. It takes the pitch of his voice down a couple of octaves and adds a small amount of vocoder to it too. Ten percent Cylon warrior from Battlestar Galactica. He tests it out by phoning Mark who's asleep because it's one in the morning.

"This is Darth Vader," he says, after Mark answers it. "Come to the dark side!" Then he terminates the call.

After putting the phone down, confident the filter would do what it should, Bento enables the VPN and phones the number of Caleb McGill, leader of the New Zealand National Front. As he does this, he pushes record on four different devices positioned at four different angles, one for a TikTok livestream, one for a YouTube livestream, one for an X livestream, and one for a Twitch livestream. He wears a pigeon-head mask to disguise himself. The dial tone rings out five times 'til it connects with a voice that projects menace.

"Yeah?" the voice barks, tired, "What time do you call this?"

"It's one o'clock in the morning my friend and I'm looking for Mr Caleb McGill," in addition to the filter's voice-disguising properties, Bento also speaks in a New York accent and plays circus music at fifteen percent volume in the background.

"Who is this? How'd ya get my number?"

"Hey, buddy, ya need ta wise up man! You, my friend are the owner of a secret X account called *South Island Snakey*, right?"

A few seconds of silence then Caleb utters, "I don't know what you're talking about."

"Yah, you do."

Caleb says nothing.

"See, Mr McGill, on every photo anyone takes, there exists something called metadata. It's on all of the photos on your phone. It's on all of the photos you've published to South Island Snakey. Metadata is data about data. By reading this metadata, it's possible to ascertain where it comes from. Let me give you an example. Your phone, also known as 'Caleb McGill's iPhone', shows the date and the time and the location of every picture you published to South Island Snakey."

"What?"

"Yes. And looking at the patterns, I'd say you lived on Littleton Street in Spreydon, right? Well, you did when you took these. Right, buddy?"

Silence.

"Man, I'm swimming in pictures of your dick here Mr McGill. What am I supposed to do? Up to my eyeballs in your ball bag, I am. Your cock in various states of arousal, Mr McGill. You've got a tattoo there, right? A pair of snake eyes and a red forked tongue off the side of your foreskin. That's an interesting choice. I wonder what your family would think, indecently exposing yourself on the internet, where kids can go. I wonder what the Police would make of it. I mean, there's close ups, extreme close ups, mirror shots, there's even a psychedelic kaleidoscopic image of your dick. That one's on TikTok too. I just put it there. I mean, it's not even that big a dick. Why would you want to advertise it? Four? Maybe four and a half inches, right? Slightly bigger than a Hellers breakfast sausage. Right, buddy?"

"What do you want?"

"Well, I've got other pictures too. You've got machine guns, real ones. Not a good look. Not now? Certainly not in Christchurch, eh? You could go to jail for this stuff."

"What do you want eh?"

"Well, you know I'm live streaming this?"

"Turn the live streams off and tell me what you want?" panic in the voice.

While Bento works his magic with McGill, Mark lies in bed. He's annoyed now. He was asleep before Vader phoned him. Now he's awake and struggling to get back to sleep.

Right Shoulder – What were you thinking? You stupid gimp. What woman wants a drongo like you. A fucking idiot. She's out of your league anyway, dickhead.

Left Shoulder – Work. Melody. Viral shame. Ken Oath. Jay Dicks. Sheba. The Dead Air Incident. Liz. The Walk-In.

After two hours of juggling messages from either shoulder Mark has an idea.

Part Four

Chapter 55

THE CRAZY IDEA

Monday, 13th January – 08:00

At eight o'clock the following morning, the chirping sound of Melody's approaching fan belt intrudes on the upper Oneroa area. Mark hears it first. Larry is a little slower to register, due to the waxberg against his left eardrum. In actual fact, everyone with a mid-functioning aural faculty within two hundred metres hears it until she parks the car out front of the station. They've also heard her slamming the car door behind her. She did it loud enough.

As Melody pushes past the partition, she sees Larry sitting at her desk, his chair turned sideways to face Mark.

"Morning, Melody," Mark says, craning his neck towards her.

"Why did I have to come in early? What's so important?" Her curt-lip is back. It's a self-defence mechanism. She started 'checking out' as soon as Larry mentioned Caleb McGill's court action the previous Friday. What she learned at the dirt track only served to hasten it. In fact, she already tarted up her CV and applied for three jobs off Seek since then. Maybe she'll leave the island.

"He's got an idea," Larry says, pointing at Mark with a pen.

"And? Does it involve his monkey?" Melody glares at Mark, arms folded.

"What?" Larry, quizzical while Melody fumes

Mark interrupts, "I think we should make a video, see if we can get it to go viral. Maybe we could raise the money. It'll get back at Dicks at the very least."

"Oh yeah. Just like that?"

"Well, what ideas have *you* got?" Mark snaps back. It's the first time he's sent a crossed word back in Melody's direction, and he instantly regrets it. Melody doesn't say anything, and Mark continues, "remember when he stood on Sheba's tail?"

"How could I forget?"

"We should make a fake CCTV video. Use it against him." Mark says.

"What? How's that when we don't even have cameras?"

"Got the audio though, haven't we?'

"So?"

"We use the audio from the radio broadcast, and we recreate the CCTV video."

"Riiiight." Melody says in a sceptical tone, "what for?"

"It'll trigger people."

"Trigger them to do what?"

"Donate money."

"Pfft."

"He stood on a guide dog's tail Melody!" Mark pauses, "people love dogs."

"And blind people, people love blind people," Larry adds with a tic.

Positive discrimination there, Melody thinks to herself.

"We want to piss people off, trigger an emotional response. Make them feel like they're fighting a fight worth fighting."

"Well, I'm not sure," Melody says.

"We'd have to choreograph it, make sure it matches the audio. We'll need to get Ken up with Sheba. Who's gonna be the Dicks fella?" Larry adds.

"He probably has a similar build to Pablo Techno." Mark says.

"What about the bald fella, who's going to be him?" Melody asks.

Larry has a quick think before offering, "Juan Martinez, he's bald. Might be a bit taller though."

"Can you remember what they were wearing?" Mark asks.

"Well, Jay had a grey suit, paisley shirt, and brown shoes."

"Neck tatt, he had a neck tatt." Melody remembers.

"What about the other guy?"

"Blazer and jeans, brown shoes," Melody says, "a little weasel desperately trying to come off as a tough guy."

"Shall we do it then?"

"I'm a little worried about the illegality of this whole thing. I mean, I've had my dance with the Devil, and I don't want to dance with him again, but then again, it is for the greater good, so yeah look, I'm in too, but this might be a waste of time. It's hard to make things go viral," Larry says.

"Well, about that, do you remember that video you saw on Sunday?" says Mark.

"The one with you in it?" says Melody

"Yeah."

"I've thought of little else since. Gross."

"What's this?" says Larry.

"Oh, never mind." Melody says, keen to move the conversation on.

"Look, Larry, full disclosure, there's a video of me that went viral. It wasn't my finest hour."

"Ha! *Waster in Emu Suit Looks for Drugs in Own Vomit?*" Larry says, "I knew there was something familiar about you from the moment you came in for that interview," laughing as he says it.

Mark feels a mixture of emotions riding around his insides. Shame is there, so too is gratitude for Larry's laissez-faire attitude to it all. "So, what I'm saying is I've watched that video go viral. I think I understand how to make that happen."

"It's a long shot eh." Melody says.

"It's a shot, but you know what else?"

"What?"

"Well, Bento's got a couple of hundred bots, so we might be able to push it on using them too."

"Ok, I'm in."

Chapter 56

THE FAKE VIRAL VIDEO

Tuesday 14th January

It looks authentic now that it's been rendered. Grainy, monochrome, and split between three perspectives. One perspective is in reception looking back across the room towards the front door. Another encompasses the office and a third looks back across the main studio from above the decks. For its fifty-three-second duration, the hashtag #SAVEWAIHEKERADIO pulses in bold red weighting in the top corner of the screen. A ticker accompanies this, continuously pulling the words 'GiveALittle/WaihekeIslandRadio' from right to left across the bottom of the screen.

The action starts on the front door with 'Dicks' and 'Wentworth' entering through it. They approach the desk at reception and the action suddenly pauses.

"This man..." says the honeyed voiceover.

A large red arrow bordered in black thrusts down at 'Jay' who is coolly leaning against the reception desk, "is about to stand on *this* guide dog's tail..." A still image of a puppy Labrador, zooming into to a close-up, "on purpose, and you won't believe what happens after that." The video continues on again. It shows Larry guiding 'Jay' and 'Garrett' through the offices of Waiheke Island Radio in double speed. As that happens, and without actually naming any names, the voiceover really gets to the nuts and bolts of how much of a bastard Jay Dicks is. The entitlement, the drugs, the racism. The dirty tricks campaign at the station. Jay is painted as *The Man*. The station set up as *The People*. It is an odyssey of just thirty seconds, and as it forms its narrative a stopwatch counts down in the bottom-right corner of the screen until Larry spills the Blackpool Rock and Dicks and Wentworth slip into the On-Air studio with a tail stamp and yelp.

"FUCK! A dog! Shit! Get it away from me. Get it away from me," 'Jay' shouts twice jabbing his right foot out towards the dog's rear as Blind Ken Oath motions forward with an arm.

"Who's there?"

"Keep your dog on a fucking lead man," 'Jay' is moving towards the blind pensioner for a fight.

"Yeah, stupid fucken mut," 'Garrett' adds.

"Leave ma dug alone or I'll have it set aboot ye ya wee cunt. An then I'll be comin' in fae aftas fanny. Get tae fuck while a host ma radio show, cunt," the dog is growling. Snarling. Packed and ready to go.

"What the fuck're ya doing?"

"What does it look like?"

"I don't know, I cannae see."

"What are you? Blind or something?"

"Och aye ah fuckin' am ye wee cunt, dae ye want tae make somethin' ay it?" The Brigton fighting brogue, addressing the part of the room that neither 'Dicks' nor 'Wentworth' are standing in.

Again, the video is paused and by now, the portrayal of Jay Dicks is becoming a little bit overstated, Juan's portrayal of Garrett, however, is much more measured.

The voiceover continues. "The blind guy is having none of it, watch what he does now."

'Jay Dicks' says something to 'Garrett Wentworth' but this is inaudible.

"Who's there, what's going on here?" With proper Glaswegian menace.

"*What*? Are you fucking blind or something?" Spits 'Jay'.

"Och aye ah fuckin' am ye wee cunt, dae ye want tae make somethin' ay it?" says Ken, addressing an empty part of the room.

Reality has never been a feature of this episode, so it is hardly surprising that Mark has opted to augment Sheba's barely audible growl with the seething snarl of an angry pit-bull. An extreme close-up.

"Get that fucken' dog away from me."

"And with his guide dog by his side," continues the voice-over, "these two ableists are going to have a fight on their hands. A big one. And you can help by donating today to help us beat this guide dog-hating ableist douche. *GiveALittle /WaihekeIslandRadio.*"

It is a brilliant effort, and after being approved by Melody and Larry, all of the station's non-English language broadcasters come in to record versions in a variety of different languages. Arabic, Spanish, Punjabi, French, Korean, Russian, Samoan, and Mandarin. After that, each version is uploaded to the socials under varying translations of the title *Blind Radio Host Triggered after Guide Dog hurt by Hipster*.

Chapter 57

THE RASH

Wednesday 15th January – 10:06

"It's not enough." Melody says forlornly.

"Be patient," Mark replies, "all it takes is one person with lots of reach to see it. I mean look at Darcey Knight. They've got loads of followers. Two Kardashians, Kanye West, Hillary Barry, Larcus Mush, Gary Lineker and Walt Hooper. If people like that get on it, you never know what might happen."

"Gary Lineker?" says Melody, "who's that?"

"Oh, he used to play for Everton, but he's also got two Kardashians too."

"*Two Kardashians?*" Melody says louder.

"Yeah."

"Two what?" Shouts Larry from inside his office.

"Two Kardashians."

Larry has no idea what a Kardashian is. To him, the term 'two Kardashians' might as well have been the contents of a 'His and Hers" garage in a kit-set mansion. Larry is also ignorant of just how much influence Darcey Knight has in the global LGBT community, but it is they who unlock it. Reposting the video to their half million TikTok followers at one o'clock on Wednesday afternoon. Once they do, the views start racking up from there.

By six, the video has been viewed twelve-thousand times and shared by more than two-hundred people. Larry and Mark are excited, but Melody just assumes it will all peter out. It doesn't though, it keeps rising and by Thursday morning it has over fifty thousand views.

Going off the feedback, people are outraged. They're donating too, not a lot, but the *Give a Little* page is seeing an uptick in donations to the pace of a trickle. At twelve minutes past noon, the balance is tipped after Kiwi Facebook meme page, *Mean Bro,* shares the video. The spike in views is remarkable and by five o'clock, the video has been seen by an additional one-hundred-thousand people.

Melody is starting to come around, "Oh my God it's working, it'll be right up there with *Beached as Bro* and *Twenty Fucken Whacks.*"

🐶

Not long after, in a car park in Remuera, Jay Dicks sees the video on Facebook. He doesn't recognise himself at first watch, most likely because it isn't him, and he clicks the laugh-react on the post. It's only when the video is shared to him via Messenger from Garrett Wentworth asking, "dis us bro?" he instantly replies.

"No, don't be silly."

Then he starts to remember the whole episode, and he starts wondering. Perhaps it is them. As usual, his stomach drops. The IBS is kicking in. He is on the toilet by the time he arrives at the comments, and they are damning.

"*I know him, the man's a douche*" jaybenlaurel1981.

"*Anyone who attacks a blind man and his dog is gutless and cruel.*" lizzydixon.

"*Fucken' pirate cunt better not come to Mangere.*" Jucy222.

"*Guy was a doctor before losing eyesight, respect.*" TalSheppy55. In fact, Ken Oath had been a welder before he lost his eyesight

"*Classic dog there, fine animal.*" Manpus101.

"*Who's cleaning the shit up if the owner can't see it?*" EstelleCostanza.

"*Look at the state of that fucken man bun.*" Bastyflupps33.

"*I've just donated fifty bucks, you should too.*" DaveWekka12, this was one of Bento's bots.

"*What a fucken shit bracket, I'd love to knock the cunt out.*" StevenLorrimer88. There is a reply to this comment from a GibNutz345, it read *"I'd love to see you knock him out."* That comment had over 6000 likes.

"*Maggot.*" GunterDub22.

"*Shit Cunt*" OzzyFuq44.

"*Looks like Captain Pugwash lol.*" JeffBlack75.

"*Never show fear to an animal.*" PEastoe.

"*I'd eat that dog, I wonder what it'd taste like.*" Jen Ritchie.

"*Puss puss.*" Flavelicious23.

"*Cockflap.*" Robbiebdret.

"*Dick-Tit*" BertieMee56.

"*I've sent him a finger in the mail.* You should too!" Mahutma002

In the wee hours of Friday morning, a massive donation of two hundred and fifty thousand dollars comes in. Melody thinks it's a mistake when she first sees it and she isn't keen on getting anyone's hopes up, so she waits an hour before checking again. The figure now reads $335,450 and it is going up, all the time.

"Larry, *Larry*! I need you to look at something."

"Yeah?"

"We've had a large donation come through." Melody, seated at her desk, shuffling from cheek to cheek in excitement. Just then, Larry pops his head around the corner of the door. It is the first time he's done a whack-a-mole in a wee while. He climbs up from his chair and hobbles over to Melody's desk. When he sees it, his eyes almost fall out of his head.

"Who sent that?" He says in astonishment.

"Doesn't say."

"Can you find out?"

"No."

"Someone gives you a quarter of a million dollars and you don't even get to thank them. I can't get my head around it. Who has a spare quarter of a million?"

"Anonymous is who. Doesn't even say which country it's come from." It was the English singer Morrissey. He's riding a tax write-off, but he'll deny it if he's ever asked. Some people think he's a cunt, but the animals like him. In less than 100 hours since it was released to the world, *Blind Radio Host Triggered after Guide Dog hurt by Hipster* has pledges of $375,000 and has racked up a staggering fifteen million views and #SAVEWAIHEKERADIO trends worldwide

Chapter 58

THE GOOD NEWS AND THE BAD NEWS

Monday, 20th January – 09:00

By nine o'clock on Monday morning #SAVEWAIHEKERADIO is still trending at number one worldwide and has been since Saturday night. Gordon Ramsay has shared it. So have Lorde, both Ronaldos, Barack Obama, Elon Musk and Russell Crowe. Even though the station has gone viral the mail still needs bringing in, and just as if everything was normal, Melody is standing at the mailbox, flipping through the letters at the end of the path. One package, one bill, and one letter with the logo of the law firm Mussell Decker Biggs in the top left corner.

All the desk phones are ringing as she walks through the partition. That's all they do now. Ring. She ducks over to her desk where she puts the bulk of the mail. "Larry!" she says as she walks over to his office ignoring the ringing of the phones.

"Morning."

"Larry, it's another letter from those lawyers," she says as the call coming through to Larry's phone rings off.

"Oh no. Really?"

"Yeah."

As Larry goes for the letter, he breathes in sharply through his nose saying, "What now?" Then he opens it and scans it, top to bottom. Now, a look of relief is pouring across his face.

"Caleb McGill's dropped his claim."

"Really?"

"Yeah, *and* his BSA complaint."

"*Really*? Here, let me have a look at that."

"Here."

Melody grabs the letter from Larry and reads it for herself. "This means we're back down to four complaints then, right?" There's a sparkle of jubilation in her eyes, "We're off the hook."

"I guess."

Larry allows himself the cracking of a smile. Just then his desk-phone begins to ring again. Melody takes this as a cue, and she sees herself gleefully out as Larry plucks the phone from its cradle.

"Larry Minto," he says.

"Lambartus Butler here Larry," To the untrained ear, Lambartus's voice has that weathered sound about it. Like his larynx had been hammered by the elements for years. Farmer-like, direct, masculine. It is a put-on. The man had been elocuted at New Zealand's most exclusive school *Prince's* in Remuera. To him sheep herding amounts to no more than ordering a lamb rack at a five-star school camp in Queenstown. "I'm calling about the outcome of our meeting last Friday aren't I Larry?"

"Oh."

"Listen, erm, afraid the board has decided to withhold funding for your frequency renewal. We're moving forward with the *TradeMe* thing. It'll run for one week commencing 7th February. We're also withholding any operational funding that we'd earmarked for your station subsequent to the 14th of March. As a result, the station will lose its Access status one month after the auction."

"Look Lambartus, erm, I've had some news come to light earlier this morning, regarding one of the complaints."

"Yes?"

"I've got a letter here from Caleb McGill's lawyers. He's not proceeding with his action, and has withdrawn the BSA complaint too, so that puts us back under the threshold."

"Yes, I'm aware of Mr McGill's position, and if you'd only had five complaints it would've been different, but you actually had six complaints until McGill withdrew his complaint last Friday."

"Six?" Larry's stomach knotted.

"Yes, there've been several calls about that incident with the blind man, and I've got to tell you Larry, Minister Saddleback is not amused at having a state-run radio station going viral as you've done here. It's most undignified."

"Oh, erm sorry, we didn't have much choice." By now Larry is losing fucks to give, "So that's it then?"

"Well assuming you've not raised the money for the frequency, it is, yes."

"What about our jobs?"

"Well, you'll have to get new ones won't you, Larry?"

"Just like that?" Tic

"Yeah. Just like that, Larry."

As he puts the phone down Larry lets his head thud down against the desk, as he cups his ears in his hands. Before he can do anything else though, the desk phone starts ringing again. This time it's Nazreen.

"Oh hi, Larry," She says, sounding out of breath, like she was in the middle of something, "I've been trying to call you for the last few minutes, but it was engaged."

"Yeah, I just had Lambartus on."

"So, he told you?"

"Yep, told me about the funding decision. Said the money's being withheld."

"Oh, Larry, I'm so sorry you had to find out like this. I told him I wanted to talk to you before he did."

"It's okay."

"Did he tell you about the sixth complaint?"

"Yep."

"So, I guess if it's going to auction, you'll need every penny you can get. How much have you raised now?"

"Six hundred thousand."

"How much?"

"Six hundred grand."

"That's an incredible amount, Larry." Nazreen is flabbergasted.

"It's not enough though, is it?"

"Well, I can tell you it might be."

"What, how so?"

"Remember the last time I saw you I said that neither UNZ nor Radiohub might not be bidding on it? Well guess what? It's wide open."

"Really?" Larry says with astonishment. These are the two main players. It's these two that kept the prices of frequencies out of all but the richest hands.

"Yeah. They're in the middle of a spending freeze, 'cos of the downturn."

"We seem to be living in a permanent bloody downturn."

"So, it'll still probably go for more than a million though. You'll have a job raising the rest of it."

"Well at least that's one positive, the donations do just keep coming in."

Chapter 59

THE CONSEQUENCE

Wednesday 22nd January - 16:50

Melody is run off her feet with international media expecting a pound of flesh. Every one of them offers an opportunity to promote the station's fundraising effort. It's exhilarating, and on an entirely different level of marketing to putting on a sausage sizzle outside the Countdown. But she does it, and, it is working, spectacularly. She's had a couple of calls from employment agencies in the last days too, head-hunters. Both have been rejected. There isn't time for any of that now. Besides she is in the middle of a fight.

In just ten days the station had raked in over half a million bucks in pledges. Fifty million views. It is unheard of. They are flush. Shit, even Sarin hasn't cancelled her direct debit, and another grand has come the station's way.

With the world's eyes on the radio station, Jay Dicks also finds himself in the spotlight, which, for him isn't a welcome addition at all. Unnamed in the video, but outed by Bento's X and TikTok-bots, the hashtags #TailstampingDouche, #TailStampa and #StampaDicks used against him. Now, news outlets worldwide clamour for his story, leaving his phone inundated with missed calls.

On Sunday, Jay was door-stepped by local comic, and celebrity praying mantis Guy Williams. The host of Tuesday night magazine show, *Back Paddock*. The mantis Williams is disguised as a dog and chases Jay down the street, camera crew in tow. He wants to ignore the attention and seeks advice from his lawyer Shep Funkhauser who reassures, saying.

"Lay low, let it blow over. Besides, there's no proof it's you."

Chapter 60

THE RACIST VOICEMAIL

Thursday, 23rd January

"Anything come up with those voicemails, Mark?" Larry asks.

"Nah, it's still all just drug codes and pocket dials. There's nothing there."

"Well, keep on at it. Hers and his."

Mark does as Larry has asked. Both phone numbers, thrice daily. Monday turns up nothing, nor Tuesday, nor Wednesday. Thursday is the day. It's the last thing Mark and Melody do before clocking off. Melody calls Sarin from a withheld landline at the station. Seconds later Mark calls from his mobile. As usual Melody's mobile records the audio.

You have one new message…

Message received Yesterday at 4:30pm

Yeah, it's me, babe, hey I've finally managed to touch base with our friend Mr Raghead. He's been in hospital. He'll be sweet though. We'll be all good for the auction. Birdie was right, neither UNZ nor Radiohub are bidding and I'm pretty sure the God Squad will struggle too. Look, give me a call when you can.

Chapter 61

THE RESURRECTION

Friday, 24th January – 09:34

All up, Mr Sidhu Singh was in the hospital for one month and one day and it was a period of reflection for him. During his convalescence, the Radio Punjab project was firmly on the backburner, with nothing to bring it to mind, the phone was lost in the house fall. He's not bothered reactivating a replacement. That was, until yesterday. Within an hour, a call came in. It was Jay Dicks.

Mr Singh is wheeled out of hospital, his left arm and his left leg both still rigid in casts. At the hospital door, a cab waits to drive him and his son, Prakash, down to the Auckland ferry terminal.

There, they catch the first boat to Waiheke, hire Eladio's wheelchair-accessible taxi and drive to Burrell Road where Eladio pulls over to the kerbside and from the vehicle's passenger seat, Mr Singh looks down at the site where the house had once stood. The remnants of the landslip still visible, so too the pile of broken bits of painted blue wood where the house in which he almost died broke apart and came to rest.

The second place they go, is the fire station. It's important to Mr Singh that he thank the person who saved his life. He knows who that is. Firefighter Bella Lasagne. When they arrive at the fire station, station commander, Samuel Jones, tells them that Bella is up at the radio station doing her monthly fire safety segment on the breakfast show.

"She'd love to have you on the air, go on, go up," says Samuel. "I'll call her now and tell her you're on your way."

Moments later, Mr Singh and his son are back in the car heading to the radio station. Once they arrive, they ring the bell, and Mark comes out to reception.

"I got your message," says Mr Singh. "You're a good man."

Mark is shocked. Mr Singh is the last person he expects to see. "It's good to see you, man. How'ya feeling?"

"Ah, still a bit sore but getting stronger every day."

"How can I help?"

"Well, I'd be dead if it weren't for that lady in there." Mr Singh coughs as he points through the studio window at Bella who is just preparing to do her on-air segment on the *Island Breakfast*.

She turns, recognises him, waves and motions for him to come into the studio.

Mr Singh is good as gold, wheezing his way through the five-minute piece, thanking her and lauding the work of everyone who helped him.

🐶

While Mr Singh is on the air, Melody turns to Mark and says in hushed tones, "Am I the only one who thinks this is a bit weird? He's out for our jobs and we're being all lovey-dovey with him."

"Look, just leave it for a moment." Mark says.

"Well, if you don't say something, I will."

As soon as the show is over, Mr Singh poses for a selfie with Bella, Bruce, Larry, Mark, and a sour-faced Melody, before Prakash posts it to *Facebook*.

Suddenly Melody speaks up.

"Excuse me, Mr Singh. Can I ask you a question?"

"Of course."

"You know that frequency you'll bid for? You know it's our frequency, eh? You do realise that if you get it, we'll all be out of a job?"

"No, it must be a different one."

"Yes, ours is going up for auction in February, 89.0FM."

Mr Singh's eyebrows raise up a good three hundred feet as he fingers his chin and settles on an arm fold. He turns away slightly, he looks conflicted "Mmm, I'll have to have a think about things. I'll have to have a chat with Mr Dicks. You see it's always been a dream of mine to do something for my people. It's very important to me to give the Punjabi community of New Zealand a radio station of their own. News in our own language, radio plays.

We work a lot, we listen lots. You, see? It's been a lot of work."

"But we carry a Punjabi show here every week. The podcasts get more hits than any New Zealand podcast. It's called Punjabi Time, most of the hits are in India."

"It's only one show though. It doesn't give news on the hour in my language. Besides you could continue on with an AM frequency."

"There are none."

"You could go online."

"Yeah, we could but we are an Access station. People need to know we're here, and they won't know if we're exclusively online. You don't just stumble on online radio. Besides, allowing access to traditional media for ordinary people is a function of democracy. That's what we do and that's our frequency."

"You know, I came here today to thank Bella, I hadn't come to talk business."

"You couldn't expect it not to be addressed!" Melody says, snapping back.

"You see, I have an obligation to Mr Dicks. He has put a lot of hard work into this deal."

"More than you know," Mark says under his breath.

"Yes?"

"Well, for a start he had his girlfriend do a show on our station and she's purposely been getting complaints so that we would be punished by New Zealand On Air and lose our funding, and frequency.

"Oh my, that's a lot of information."

"Well, that's what Dicks has been doing in the background."

"You know, there's always two sides to a story."

"There are two sides to Jay Dicks, Mr Singh. I don't think you know who he really is."

"Do you?"

"Well, if you remember, he was my boss at UNZMedia."

"And?"

"You know he's into the drugs?"

"What kind of drugs?"

"All of 'em, just Google '*Wrecked Magazine* - Caner of the Year 2008-10.'" Mark pauses, saying, "Is this the kind of person you'd want to be associated with? Really? You know he came to our station a few days before he came here with you?"

"Mr Dicks did?"

"Yeah, and he barged into a live radio show and threatened a blind man, on-air, in my main studio."

"He attacked a guide dog," Melody says.

"You don't want to know what he did to our toilet. It was out of order for three hours," says Larry under his breath.

"I ended up having to clean it," Mark complains.

"I told you there was something off about that guy, Dad." Prakash says, shaking his head.

Mr Singh exhales. It is pained, and he is irritated. "Look, I came here today to say thank you to Bella for saving my life. I'm actually very sick and you've ambushed me with this. As it stands, I've got an obligation to Mr Dicks. I can't just walk away from it. It's a matter of respect now. I will say no more on it. We are done here. Come on Prakash. Let's go, wheel me out of here." As annoyed as he is, Mr Singh says his goodbyes politely, but he has food for thought now and soon he'll be getting some recordings that'll give him a whole other bone to gnaw on.

THE AUCTION

Friday, 14th February – 17:05

As saturated as the Auckland radio market is, licenses for the region's full-power FM frequencies don't come cheap. In fact, under normal circumstances, anyone wanting to buy one would be looking at a hole in the pocket measuring over twelve million bucks. These weren't normal circumstances though, with just the three 'small fry' bidders, Waiheke Island Radio, Radio Christ and The Jay Dicks Syndicate. The conglomerate big boys abstaining.

"Don't Dream it's Over" by Crowded House plays at the station where Mark, Larry and Melody have gathered over beer. A mammoth effort, it's been, raising nearly one and a quarter million dollars. A miracle, but they know it's touch and go as to whether it's enough.

Shilbottle is amongst it. Sitting on his own, behind a locked door in the Portakabin next to the burnt-out husk that's all that remains of the *Radio Christ* headquarters. It's the moment he's been waiting almost two decades for. Tantalisingly close. His own full power FM frequency. A bottle of Russian Standard vodka stands guard at his desk. He's ploughed half of the bottle already, but he has a high tolerance for it because he is a secret boozer.

Unfortunately for Roger, the fire at Christ FM is still under investigation, and as a result, there's still not been a pay-out from the insurance company. Now, he's reduced to re-mortgaging his house and selling his Bentley. A loan shark had him on the hook for twenty grand too. Roger knows it'll be tight. He's shit scared of that loan shark, and he doesn't even know if he has enough.

Jay Dicks is with Sarin Murray at Quay on Brew at The Viaduct. They're quelling the nerves with cocaine and pinot gris, Jay worry-beading his phone from hand to hand since lunchtime. It is beginning to look like a tic. His guts have been impacted too and he's been in the bathroom for the last fifteen minutes, splattering the place. He needn't worry, the man has a war chest of close to six million bucks and with Mr Singh poised to sublet it, Jay would turn a hefty profit every year for the next fifteen years. For doing nothing.

At twenty past five, Roger makes the first move.

"They've put a bid in." Jay says, mincing out of the gents with his phone held high.

"How much?" Sarin asks.

"One million."

"One million?" She says incredulously.

"Yeah."

"Jesus, how did they raise that much money?"

"That video."

"Really, you reckon? Hey er, actually, is it really you in it?"

Jay is wired again, chewing, "You know, the more I look at it, the more I think it is me, yeah but there's something weird about it. You know what else is weird? I've been getting loads of missed calls lately, all from this hidden number. You ever get anything like that?"

"Actually, I do, most days lately. It'll be one of those hackers from China or India or some other shithole country."

"Yeah, probably."

In Larry's office, all are glued to the screen for the TradeMe auction.

"Jay's just gone in," says Mark, "one million."

"It'll be Shilbottle," Larry says.

"Well, what do you want to do? Do we go in now or what?" Mark, anxious.

"No, no. We'll wait for a moment. Never show your hand until the last possible minute." Melody knows how to play the game, "go in at one minute left."

Shilbottle pours himself another short over in Mount Eden. He cracks a packet of smokes too. Marlboro Lights. You have to ask for Golds at the dairy now. Sixty bucks a pack. Over at the Viaduct, Sarin and Jay are on the edge of their seats. Waiting for the next move. It is imminent.

"Okay, go now." Melody calls the play from Larry's office couch.

"Are we sure? One million, one hundred bucks."

The bid goes down and Shilbottle bites hard on his durrie when he sees it. He's at the edge of his means and he administers another neat vodka to cure his nerves. It works. He doesn't panic he just hits straight back, and twenty seconds later.

"Another. One million, two hundred bucks," Mark.

"Damn." Larry is glued to it.

"Let's go again," says Melody who places a bid for one million and three hundred dollars.

It's thrilling, they hold the lead in the auction for another ten seconds, and then a pattern starts to form with an increment of one hundred bucks.

"Ok, let's play our hand." Melody says, and with that, she places a bid for one million, two hundred and fifty-two thousand dollars.

Over at the Viaduct, Jay is confident. He is standing off. "What kind of low value individual increments in hundreds?" he says.

"Peasants," says Sarin.

Almost theatrically, "What to do? What to do?"

"Put them out of their misery, Jay," Sarin says.

"Yeah. I think I will." Jay faces his phone. "I'll stick the one point five down."

"Oooh!" Sarin purrs.

"Well, I wouldn't want to look like a bottom feeder, would I?" And with that, Jay pivots his index knuckle and taps away the future of Waiheke Island Radio in the process.

"Fuck." Chorus Larry, Mark and Melody,

"F-Bomb," Shilbottle in Mount Eden.

"We can't match that, Larry."

Larry doesn't say anything. He is reaching for his fridge again.

Down at the Viaduct, Jay and Sarin are delighted and celebrate with a line of Charlie and a fuck in the disabled toilet. As usual, Sarin is disappointed by the sex. Jay's little choad is no match for Derek Barnaby's foot-long baguette. Jay knows he is a selfish lover, but he doesn't care. He feels super smug. All that work, it is paying off. He reaches for his phone and sends a text message saying.

"GOT IT".

"I KNOW" comes the instant reply.

Twenty minutes later as Jay Dicks is reclining in his seat, the sound of *The Benny Hill Theme* blasts out from his pocket. He's wired as fuck, but keen to take the call outside.

"Jay Dicks," he says it in his Smooth FM voice, assuming Mr Singh is calling to congratulate him on the auction. He isn't.

"I saw your video, Mr Dicks," Mr Singh is abrupt.

"Which one, Mr Singh?"

"The one where you stand on the guide dog's tail and abuse a blind man."

"That wasn't me."

"It looks like you and it sounds like you and it's at the station whose frequency you're trying to buy."

"I'm not trying to buy it. I've already bought it. The auction just finished."

"Well, you're going to have to find another buyer because I won't be doing business with you."

"Mr Singh, Mr Singh, please, can we just have a little think about this? I've put in an awful lot of work on this deal."

"Yes, I can see you've put a lot of work into it. I can see from that video; you've been intimidating people. Well, I won't have that kind of behaviour associated with my family's good name."

"It wasn't me."

"It was you. I think you're telling lies, and I can't have mistrust with any of my business partners. Besides, I've heard some other things about you."

"Like what?"

"Drugs, racism."

"What! I'm not a racist. Who told you that?"

"You did. You think I'm a raghead huh?" Mr Singh is spoiling now.

"What, no, never."

"I have a recording of you referring to me as a raghead, Jay."

"But that's impossible. I've never called you a raghead. Can you play it to me?"

"I will email it to you."

Jay is confused, "but Mr Singh."

"Thank you, goodbye".

Jay is in a flap now, his guts are aching again, "Fucking ragheaded cunt."

Chapter 63

THE PLAN

Monday, February 17th - 09:30

Larry is writing redundancy letters when he stops what he is doing and gets up from his desk. Then, leaning on the frame of his door and facing the main office, he says, "You know how I said I had a feeling we'd get through this and that something would turn?"

"Yeah."

"Well, I've got an idea for getting hold of Dicks's phone," tic.

"Oh, come on, Larry. Let it go. We'll never get his phone. He's got no reason to come back to the island." Mark is becoming indignant. "He's got what he wanted."

"What if he had a reason to come over? What if we had something else he wanted?"

"Like what?"

"What if we could use the drug thing to get him over here?"

"He's not going to come to Waiheke to sell drugs. And besides, what drug dealer is going to sell to someone he hardly knows, let alone us?"

"What if it wasn't to *sell* drugs?"

"Eh?" Everyone's piqued.

"What if it was to buy them?"

"Oh, you're not on the dark web now are you, Larry?"

"No, no, nothing like that."

"Well, what of it?" Melody says.

"Truth is, I was a bit of a space cadet in my late twenties," tic "it's the reason I have this limp and this stupid bloody tic" tic, "I was a dentist, right?

And 'cos of that, I had access to all kinds of drugs. It attracts a certain type of person, if you have access to those kinds of drugs. Sometimes, with the drugs I could get, I was able to swap them for South African Quaaludes."

"Jesus Larry," Mark is stunned, "you weren't smoking it were you?

"Pill form."

"Quaa... what?" Melody.

"Sleeping tablets. You fight the urge to sleep, and you get really high."

"Okay."

"They mess up your motor skills though, don't they?" Mark.

"Well, *you* can't drive anyway," Melody says, "no change there."

"No, he's not talking about driving. He's on about not being able to control his face, his body, or his hands," Mark says.

"Not to mention the bowels." Larry chimes in, laughing.

"Oh my God Larry. You're not still into it are you?" Melody says.

"No, those days are over."

"What happened right, when I had my accident, I was high on Quaaludes. I left that bit out of my documentary." Larry pauses for a moment. He always does when he thinks of what that crash has done to his body. The emotional chokehold. "Anyway," he continues, "the rub of it is, I was clearing out my old clothes a few weeks ago and I found the jacket I was wearing the night of the crash. There was a bag of thirty Quaaludes in the pocket," tic, "I'd just bought them. I totally forgot about it."

"How long have they been there?" Mark says.

"About fifteen years," tic.

"Fifteen years? Won't they be past their sell-by date?" Melody asks.

"Quaaludes get stronger with age," says Mark.

"And you want to sell them to Jay?" she asks.

"I think he'd go for it. I mean, he *is* a drug dealer after all. He'll probably even try one himself, but I'm going to need one of you two to do the deal. I can't do it. If I get caught again, that's my third strike."

"I'll do it," Mark says without hesitation.

"Thanks Mark, you're a legend."

"But we need to make it as uncomfortable as possible. Make the bastard suffer."

"Larry!"

"He's right though. You know I was thinking about this the other day. On the two occasions that he's visited our station, he's gone to the toilet. Too long for a wee too. I reckon he might have that IBS. They were talking about it on *Better Living* a few weeks ago."

"Where are you going with this Mark?"

"I'm saying, maybe he's got that. Maybe he has to go for a dump when he gets stressed. Think about it. He got into it with you and Ken after standing on Sheba's tail. Then our toilet got messed up. Then during that visit with Mr Singh, he had to go out too. He would've been nervous for that. Said he was seasick. Had to go to the library, came back looking sweaty."

Part Five

Chapter 64

THE QUAALUDE OFFER

Tuesday, 18th February - 13:05

Jay is in Penrose when the call comes through. He's been trying to hawk the frequency off to the Asian broadcaster *Tsing Tao TV*, and as *The Benny Hill Theme* tune rasps out from his breast pocket, he considers the 372 at the start of the number and wonders why a Waiheke Island landline would be calling him.

Jay loves to prod 'low quality individuals,' always has. So instead of rejecting the call, he takes it. It is a call that ordinarily would be terminated within five seconds, but the opening line is solid.

"Do you want to buy some Quaaludes?"

"Who is this?"

"It's Mark Goodenough."

"Markie!!" Jay Dicks says with a condescending tone, "And why would you be wanting to sell me drugs?"

"Come on, everyone at UNZ knows about your reputation. I mean you were voted runner-up, Caner of the Year in *Wrecked Magazine* two years running. It's not like it's a secret."

"And?"

"And, I've thirty fifteen-year-old Quaaludes and I need the money."

Jay is keen. He's wanted to try a 'luude since he saw *The Wolf of Wall Street*. He knows they'll be worth a lot.

"How much do you want for five?"

"Well, they're a hundred and fifty bucks each, so if you want five then I'll take seven-fifty."

“How much for all thirty?”

“Three grand.”

“I’ll do it for two and a half.”

“Two eight.”

“Deal.”

Chapter 65

THE DRUG DEAL

Wednesday 19th February – 08:55

The very next morning, Jay Dicks is in the city, trotting across the scooter lane on Quay Street. Behind him, Commercial Bay, in front, Pier Eleven at the Auckland Ferry Terminal. A cruise ship is in, and the line for the Waiheke ferry is massive, consisting largely of three hundred overweight Australian pensioners coaxed into a quadruple hairpin arrangement by a series of retractable queuing belts. There's a separate queue for residents and in it, around one hundred Waiheke locals are waiting smugly. At the head of each queue is the vessel *Adventurer*. Her capacity of three hundred and ten would struggle to accommodate everyone there.

Jay has no intention of missing the boat, so he sidles to the front of the Residents' Lane and hovers by the Hop Card machine. To anyone watching, it's obvious that he has just cut in, and a murmur of unease is heard coming off the people near the front. Even before Jay jumps the queue though, Bento, running late, five places back, has already clocked him and recognises him, not through Jay's association with the radio station though. He recognises him from somewhere else.

See, as a kid, Jay Dicks was the star of a kid's TV series, called *Smithy*. A half-hour show on a rugby-mad kid from a place called Gore. He's been on *Shortland Street* too, and *Power Rangers*. The one Jay was most proud of was the time he was an extra in *The Lord of The Rings*." Bento hasn't remembered him from any of those parts, but he still wants his selfie, and he unclips the retractable belt from its metal stanchion post and monkey in hand, marches up the outside of the queue to ask the celebrity Jay Dicks for that photo.

"Hey bro, you'se that fella off that tampon advert, eh? Can we get a selfie?"

It is true. As Jay's star began to wane, he took whatever work his agent could get him. The low point was the role of *The Boyfriend* in an advert for the female hygiene product *Nu-Max*.

"Don't touch me cunt! I'll hurt you."

"Woah! Just a fan man, just a fan."

"Yeah, step the fuck back then, eh? Get that monkey back."

"No, all good bro, chill chill, all good." Bento laughs, open palms.

Jay is happy with the quality of his front. It isn't about to last.

Standing at position fifteen of the same Resident's Lane, Darcey Knight has just observed Jay's queue jump. They also saw the shove on the guy with the monkey that rode the dog at Larry's party. Now, Darcey has Jay pegged as a bully and Darcey hates bullies. As far as Darcey is concerned it's Alpha Time again, and advancing to the front of the queue, they go in to confront it. They aren't the only ones confronting it either. The Ferry Terminal's two security guards, Jacob and Marley are also confronting it and before he knows it, Jay Dicks is being stood over by two large Samoan gentlemen, and aggressed by a what he assumes is a transvestite, all while the glare of 400 eyeballs burn into the nape of his neck. Just then, the largest of the security guards leans in towards Jay's left and lifts the headphone, saying.

"There's a queue here, bro. You need to get to the back of it." Nodding the head, "now."

As Jay turns his head towards the security guard, Darcey Knight lifts the other earphone.

"Get to the back of this queue now, or you'll be riding stumps home, sistah."

"Oh, you reckon, do you? Maybe you should mind your own business." Jay says, confident. Fronting it out again.

"Remind my own business? Remind my own business? Me? Nah? Doesn't work that way honkey. Let's dance baby boy. Come on," nodding, "here. Now. Bully boy. If you die, you die." Darcey is right in Jay's face now, limbering up as though they were in the ring again. "You won't want to fuck with this pitch. I'm da motherfuckin' cycle-path." There's a real musicality in Darcey's fighting talk. That said Jay Dicks is having concerns with the intellectual rigour of their second sentence. The first one though had been a blinding bit of fighting talk. More was on its way, when, leaning in, and singing in a whisper, a little in the style of George Michael, *Careless Whisper*, Darcey sings the lyric. *"I'll take your eyeball out! Show you what your arsehole looks like."*

Jay notices the perfume on Darcey's neck. It smells divine. It triggers a boner. Confusing. The perfume, the closeness. He likes it, and then he considers the human likeability spectrum, and wonders whether upon it, the niceness ought to be counterbalanced with what may or may not have been a casual threat of mild cannibalism coming from someone he was beginning to recognise.

"Oi, come on, both of you. Hey, hey, hey," is what the second security guard says as he pulls Darcey back with an assertive arm, diligent in his religious and professional duty to prevent a live ocular transplant out there on Pier Eleven.

And then the lightbulb. Bing! Jay Dicks recognises the "tranny." It's a face from his old days training the producers on *Walt Hooper's Kiwi Sports Afternoon*. He was there the day Darcey came out as non-binary. Dicks was in the room when Walt Hooper choked on his *Pineapple Lump* and Martin Devlin gave him the Heimlich manoeuvre. He'd seen him first too, but he just watched on and waited for a good fifteen seconds for someone else to do something. It's a bit sick if you think about it. It wasn't like he'd froze or anything. He was just watching.

Jay knows that physically, he is no match for Darcey Knight. He knows that Darcy could have him in traction in a quarter hour. He pulls his head in. He chooses to loiter in the covered waiting room instead. He's still jumped the queue.

Dicks waits for Darcey Knight to get on the boat and then he hides from Darcey in a corner of it. Like a cockroach, hiding under a fridge. And then, by way of a taxi, arrives outside the radio station around an hour later. He approaches and sees Mark and Chunk, dominating the space at the station's front door. The dog is restrained on a tight lead and keen at Mark's side. Poised.

Jay eyeballs the canine. Looking it up and down. "What's with the dog?"

"The dog does what it wants." And it does. Except when it wants to express itself before the Patents and Appeals Tribunal Board about food dispensing inventions.

"Where's the merchandise?"

"Inside, come." Mark lets Chunk off the lead a little, giving the animal just enough rope for it to forget about his dreams and do something inappropriate. It sniffs Jay's bollocks and barges into his legs.

"Should've had it ready eh," Jay says.

"You don't get to call the shots anymore, Dicks," then, with a flick of the chin Mark says, "Phone. In the box." Nodding towards the letterbox.

"Nah, it's okay. I'm not going to use it."

"If you want those Quaaludes, you'll put the phone in the letter box. Now." Mark is on top here.

"What?" Jay says, incredulously, "but I've come all this way."

"Letterbox, Dicks."

"*Owe, Kaye,*" Dicks replies. He starts to think something might be up. He's paranoid and the dog freaks him out. His bowel is popping off again. It's been bubbling since the tranny attack on Pier Eleven. Now, it feels like his lower intestine is being drawn through a hand mangle. He isn't going home without those Quaaludes though, so he does as he is told, placing the battered auld Samsung in the letterbox, before entering the station.

🐶

Even though they were on the same boat, Bento is comfortably up at the station ahead of Jay after being picked up by Melody. He's set himself up in Larry's office, opened up his laptop and readied his tools. Everyone has a job. Melody's job is to get Jay's phone, and she sneaks out through the back door, quickly tiptoeing to the end of the path to retrieve it from the letterbox. Bolting back and slotting it through the open window to Larry who passes it to Bento for one last Hail-Mary-hack on Jay Dicks's phone.

🐶

Everyone at the station is in on it. Larry having primed them to stall and unsettle Jay Dicks as much as possible.

"Sit down here," Mark barks, pointing at the couch in reception, "I'll go and get it."

Jay sits down and he reaches for the copy of *Mojo Magazine* that has Coldplay on the cover. He loves Coldplay, especially their song *Feeding Tube Disco*. He loves P!nk too and appreciates the song *Don't Let Me Get Me* which is playing on the station as the pain in his gut intensifies. He's on edge now, nervous. It's hand-mangle time again. His fingers drumming his thigh, arpeggiating over and over.

In the On-Air studio Derek Barnaby and Barry Twelvedogs are finishing up from filling in on *Island Breakfast* and emerge through the partition behind reception, where Jay Dicks waits on the couch, looking at the pictures of Coldplay.

"MMMM up for a show, are youAAAAWWWW" Twelvedogs says, affixing his electrolarynx to his neck. Jay ignores him and carries on pretending to read the Mojo magazine.

"MMMM hello! Anyone home MMMM."

"Oh, are you talking to me?"

"MMMM well, I don't see anyone else in here. Do you? AAAAWWW"

"Sorry?" Waves of pain coursing through the Jay Dicks intestinal tract, condescension dripping from the voice.

Derek Barnaby enters the room, but it is Twelvedogs who's doing the talking now.

"MMMM can I help you?"

"I can't understand you with that harmonica you keep putting against your neck."

Derek Barnaby will always come in for Barry Twelvedogs on a larynx matter and this is one such occasion, "he's asking you if you're up at the station to do a show, or whether you're here to see someone else. He's about to offer to help you. Because, you know, he's kind enough to do that. And all you can do is ridicule his speech impediment."

"I haven't ridiculed his speech impediment. I couldn't understand him. I thought maybe it was Daft Punk or Benny Benassi or someone like that. Is it not?"

"No, it's not. He is clearly speaking English and you're choosing to be rude about it. What's with people like you?"

"Look, father, I don't want to get too invested in this conversation. I'm on private business."

Neither Twelvedogs nor Barnaby are too offended. They're just happy to buy time for the station so Jay Dicks' phone can be cloned to another handset.

🐶

Mark is the one to hand the bag of Quaaludes over to Jay Dicks, primarily because Larry wouldn't have been able to let them go. As soon as Jay takes them into his possession, he stuffs the Ziploc bag into the breast pocket of his blazer, as Chunk sniffs at his balls again.

"I'll count the money. You can count the pills, eh?"

"It's all there."

"I'm going to count it." Mark says.

"MMMM doing a drug deal?" Barry Twelvedogs says through his vocoder.

"I'd say," Derek Barnaby retorts, "we should probably go."

It's at that moment, that the *P!nk* song that's playing on the station segues into the new promo for *A Blind Bit of Difference*. This is the promo that inadvertently has the sound of Ken Oath's dog whistle in it, captured by accident after Bento had mindlessly blown it in the background when he'd recorded the voiceover.

It's the second time Chunk has heard Ken Oath's dog whistle. The first time was at the Christmas party after Mark had given it a test blow. Much like it had on that first occasion, the dog's tail immediately tucks between its two hind legs and the animal goes crazy, walking in small circles between Jay and the front door, growling and bearing its rank yellow teeth.

"I'll fucken do you ya cunt," says the dog in his Kiwi accent, for no human to discern.

"Get that fucking dog away from me, man. I mean it."

Starving the dog for a day had been the clutch move here, and, hangry, it can smell Jay's fear. The hangriness combines with the dog whistle and triggers Chunk. It's primal this time. The hackles are up. Snarling. Wide eyes. Vexed. Wild. Outside and off into the distance, dogs are barking by the score. The hardest cross-breed in Rocky Bay, the biggest boxer in Blackpool, and the fluffiest poodle on Church Bay Road.

Jay Dicks is frozen in fear, and inside his body, a bubble is rising through his colon. A bubble in a water-cooler. It loosens his whacked-out rectum. Bang. Touching cloth with a ten-tonne gut on a hair trigger ring-piece. It's happening again. He's going to need to pinch one off. Pronto.

"Where's your toilet?" Jay says as he clamps his sphincter with so much force it could drink from a straw.

The dog growls, snarling, angry.

"It's out of order. There's one at the library," Mark says dragging the dog back, "anyway I'm not finished counting."

"Look man, I can't wait here. I've got to go."

Pure desperation sends Jay running from the station. He grabs his phone from the letterbox, and sprints down the mobility ramp next to Ajadz, running over towards the library. When he arrives, he is horrified to find that the restrooms are all in use, and two people are ahead of him in the queue. He sprints back to the station in panic.

"I need to use your toilet man, please, come on." Meek now, the bravado having drained away again.

"Nah," Mark says, indignantly.

"Please, man. Come on. I've got a condition." For sure, Jay Dicks doesn't want to have to do it in a bush again.

"Nah," a pause, "jog on, you fucking idiot."

It is then that Jay Dicks notices Derek Barnaby's RV. The side-door of it is open and Barry Twelvedogs is standing next to it. Jay runs over to him and when he is close, Twelvedogs draws a fighting stance because he thinks he is about to be attacked.

"Hey, bro, mind if I use the toilet in your campervan, please? I've got a condition. IBS, I'm in a lot of pain."

"MMMM not my RV," says Barry Twelvedogs in vocoder dialect "AAAANNNNNMMMM"

"Whose is it then?"

"MMMM not my RVAAAAAANNNNN"

"Please, let me use the toilet. Please. I'm begging you."

"MMMM not my RVYA"

"Dude, please." Pleading to the cusp of tears.

"Alright Dogsy, you can let him through now. It's my RV and the lad's in pain," says Derek Barnaby, appearing from the other side of the vehicle.

"MMMM stink it out," cautions Twelvedogs.

"Thanks, father," Dicks says.

"Bless you, my child," comes the reply.

"MMMM problem gut," Twelvedogs' says.

With the green light, Jay Dicks climbs the two steps, enters the RV, opens the water-closet, throws down his trousers and relaxes his put-put muscle to let it flow.

"Ohhh, yes," says he.

Outside, Barnaby and Twelvedogs can hear the whole thing. It sounds like a concrete pour, and then, in short sporadic bursts, a scattering of slugs being thrown down a well.

"MMMM that's rank," says Twelvedogs.

Ten minutes all up was how long Jay Dicks shat for, and just as Twelvedogs had prophesised, he had indeed 'stunk it out.' Human excrement heavy on the rank, nutty on the notes and with the alkaline tang.

In the little space available to him, Jay tidies himself up and staggers to his feet. Just then he catches his trouser pocket on the wall panel that Barry Twelvedogs had broken late last year. It tears a hole in his trouser leg which runs along the seam. The priority now though isn't the trousers, it is the 'ludes and to make sure they're still there. He pats his inside breast pocket. They are. Things are good again. He's always wanted to try a 'luude. He'll easily sell the rest. Then, he strides out of the Barnaby RV, thanks his hosts and slings one of the Quaaludes down his throat.

Chapter 66

THE (REAL) 'FUCKING IDIOT'

Wednesday 19th February – 13:30

Jay is the last person on the one-thirty boat to the city. It's ready to go and he strolls up the pier, trousers-a-tatter. He doesn't run the last few metres like any normal person would, oh no. He just strolls aboard, entitled. The deckhands are annoyed, but Jay is buzzing, and he takes a seat up at the front of the main cabin next to the window on the starboard side. The boat's not busy, a couple of pensioners, a young mother, a small group of Christian teenagers. Once he is comfortable, he fishes in his trouser pocket for his phone. His fingering returns nothing. He checks the jacket. No dice. It sends him into a minor panic. Stomach pain again. He needs his phone. Always. And as the *Quickcat* slips her mooring, the window seat on her main deck is the last place Jay Dicks wants to be.

Five minutes into his forty-minute passage, Jay walks to the bar and buys himself a small bottle of Passage Rock's award-winning Syrah from the vessel's hostess, Joy. The wine is good, expressing notes of liquorice and anise. In moments though, the roll of the ocean is coalescing with the wooze of the wine. It brings on the Quaalude. If he can fight the drowsiness, he'll be flying. High as a kite.

By the time the ferry arrives back in Auckland Jay Dicks is fast asleep. Two independent strangers each tap Jay on the shoulder to try to tell him the boat is unloading. Neither succeed in waking him. He is still asleep as the boat offloads the last of her passengers. His snoring sounds like bursts on a dentist's suction pump. It is classic TikTok fodder.

Five minutes after the boat has off-loaded the last of her passengers, Jay is still there, sleeping at the front of it. He is surrounded by the hostess

Joy, the purser, and two of the deckhands. The four of them can smell the alcohol on Jay's breath and Joy confirms that she's sold him the empty bottle of Passage Rock, resting on the window ledge.

The purser calls over the captain who agrees with the 'alky' verdict. As captain though they have to follow protocol, so they call over the two security guards who are working at the terminal building. The pair of them manage to stand him up and they Jesus-walk him over to the indoor benches at the end of Pier Eleven. When he gets there, he slumps over and away to his left side.

"Brother!" Jolly, "It's that queue jumper from earlier," says Marley the security guard.

"The fella from the tampon advert?" Asks his colleague Jacob.

"Yeah. Maybe the cunt's got locked-in syndrome."

"Face is fucked, eh?"

"Trousers are ripped too."

"What d'ya reckon's happened to him."

"Dunno, man, munted off a wine tour, probably off that cruise ship they had in today."

"It's left now."

"I'll bet he's off it though."

Jacob pauses and then, with an indignant look down his left nostril goes, "he'll be an Aussie, man. Dogs brother. All of them."

"What, Aussies?"

"Yeah, man."

"Dogs?"

"Oath brother, there's no off switch with them. One minute they're on a wine tour, next minute, they're on a sex register and barred off the island for life. They don't fuck around. The cops will stick them in the slammer for an afternoon for a laugh, bro."

"Maybe Officer Hamilton's on leave today. I mean, this cunt got away, didn't he?"

"Maybe."

"Go on, give him a slap, my man. He probably deserves it. Slap him. Come on. See if it wakes him up. You can ask him yourself then."

"You slap him, Uce. There's cameras here, cuz. Need the job."

Almost at a whisper, "oh, come on, she'll be right, ma brother, just one little slap. Let him know you're there. These cameras haven't worked in years. Give him an elbow, I'll come in for seconds."

"Nah man, what if he's dying?"

"Nah, he's just sleeping, Uce. Pour some water over the cunt's face."

"Might shock him, brother. We don't want him having a heart attack."

"Well, we can't leave him here, like this."

"Maybe we should call the police."

"Yeah, cuz, they'll know what to do."

It might've been the word 'police' that triggered something in Jay Dicks, but at that moment, he lets out a large groan and a massive fart which follows through with a sliver of shit.

"Fuckin' hell bro, *what have* you been eating? Dog food?" says Jacob.

"Dog food?" says Marley, laughing, "Dog shit more like."

Again, Jay groans, and he lurches himself into a semi-seated position saying, "Whassh a rumpihgiks."

"What?"

"Whassh a rumpihgiks, milly baston."

"Let's get you up."

"Fuckin wasted, eh bro?"

"Call an ambulance. I think he's having a stroke. Listen to the way he's speaking. Might've shit himself too eh."

"Rone core ramburan."

Jay was trying to tell them that they should refrain from calling an ambulance, but it is no use, the words won't come out properly and so a call is placed to 111.

"Yeah, I think we've got an Australian tourist having a stroke here…" Marley says to the call handler. "The waiting room at the ferry terminal… Pier Eleven, yeah… if you could get here as soon as possible. I don't want him to die."

"Ron run rye," says Jay, refuting the suggestion that he might be about to pass away into the next life.

"You'll be right mate, just stay there, we'll get you back to normal," Jacob says.

Less than ten minutes later, the paramedics arrive. Immediately they are in Jay's space, grabbing at his arms, shining lights in his eyes, and talking to him as though he is a pensioner with wandering dementia. He is totally wasted. Slow to respond. Slower to move.

"Good afternoon, sir. My name's John and this here's Jude. We're with St John's Ambulance. We've come to see if you're alright," they are both looking him over, the way a sculptor looks at a block of clay.

"What's your name, sir?"

"Ray," says Jay

"Have you been drinking, Ray?"

"Been on a wine tour Ray?" asks Jude in full 'talking to a simpleton' mode.

"Ray, have you taken any drugs today?"

"Mo," Jay enunciates, "ashlin flerry mashed map, an a beshnitklev."

"Ray, are you experiencing any chest pain?"

"Mo, Shanna banna hush un tunna oh ro momegome," Jay Dicks is a mess, dishevelled, drooling, his face slumped to one side. "Ammazaz elastir eye o," Bell's palsy's fisheye lens. Hair unkempt, shirt untucked, blazer open. He stinks of shit too. It wasn't a fart.

Jude's eyes lock on Jay's half-open blazer. She's spotted the 'luudes. "Sir, I'm just gonna put my hand on your heart. I want to check you for an irregular heartbeat." She shoves her hand towards Jay's chest, but it takes a right-turn towards the blazer pocket and in a quick motion she pulls the bag of Quaaludes from it. "Well, looky here, what have I just found here, Ray? Is this part of the reason for your condition?"

Jay tries to say, *It's for my prescription.* but it comes out as "Mell us sess. Fhum ickson."

"And what do you take these for, Ray?"

"Have you had one of these, Ray?"

"Moh."

Holding the bag, John steps away, ushering Jude with him. "I don't think these are prescription meds," he says. "We need to call the Police, when they come in a plastic bag like this, they're usually illegal. Ray isn't having a stroke. He's on illegal drugs. Probably some opioid or something."

"Fuck! It's corrupted again," says Bento, angrily throwing the handset down on the table, "Why won't you work?"

"Oh no! Not again," Larry says, as he buries his head in his hands on the desk.

"So, I guess, that's it then eh?" Mark says, looking up at the clock on the wall, focusing on the second hand, aware that it is ratcheting the future of the station away with each tick. It's notched up a score of 2:05pm now and evidently, it is the second to last Friday of Waiheke Island Radio's existence. By way of musical accompaniment, the *autoDJ* has floated *Souvlaki Space Station* by Slowdive and this adds to the melancholy in the office.

"I think so yeah," says Larry, "was worth a shot though."

"Well, I've got that money from Jay Dicks here. Perhaps I could run across to the bottle shop?" Mark says.

"On you go! And Melody, can you pop to the butchers and get some meat?" Larry says, "Let's have a barbecue."

"Probably should've let him use the toilet. It'd have bought more time?" Mark says.

"Yeah probably."

Chapter 67

THE TUNE

Friday 7th March - 15:00

Within the hour, an impromptu wake is underway. Mark returns from the bottle shop with enough booze to float a battleship. Melody ferries a hundred bucks worth of meat from Carol at the butcher's shop. Larry changes the gas bottle on the rusty station barbecue, then sends a message to broadcasters telling them of free meat and piss.

"Can you look after this meat while I go and have a slash?" Larry says to Bill at half past three. He trots off to the washroom, leaving his phone on the bench where Mark and Melody are seated.

Mark is watching the meat sizzle when he feels Melody's hand touch his. The scent of her perfume fills his nostrils as she leans toward him. He feels her breasts brush his arm. He feels the warmth of her breath as she whispers in his ear.

"You know, Mark," she says, "I thought you were a bit of a dick when I first met you." She turns his head to face hers. She kisses him on the mouth. Lips then tongue. Everybody watches. She withdraws, her eyes smiling. "But I've probably been a bit harsh on you."

The pair hold eye contact. The energy is strong. He feels it. She feels it too. His spine tingles. A boner.

Left Shoulder – Just let it bake and think of her.

Over in Larry's office, the boss's phone buzzes alive, vibrating to the theme from *Curb Your Enthusiasm*. It is allowed to carry on ringing. It is getting close to rejection.

Mark picks it up, "hello, Larry's phone."

"Oh hi, it's me, Derek. Derek Barnaby who's this?"

"Oh, hello, Father. It's me Mark."

"Who?

"Mark."

"Mark who?"

"Mark Goodenough."

"Mark Goodenough?"

"Yeah, Mark Goodenough, the new PD at the radio station,"

"The radio station?"

"Yeah."

"W..w..well, which one?"

"Waiheke Island Radio."

"And who's calling again?"

"Mark Goodenough. PD. Programme Director."

"Oh right, right, right. Bless you, my child. Bless you, bless you. Mark Goodenough, of course. What's the matter my child?"

"Well, you phoned me."

"I did?"

"Well, *I* didn't phone you."

"I'm looking for Larry."

"He's in the bathroom, draining the snake, or so I'm told. We're still at the station. We're having a barbecue. I'm already drunk. You should come up."

"Really?"

"Yeah, free meat."

"Free meat?'

"MMMM free meat?" Barry Twelvedogs is heard asking in the background.

"Yeah."

"MMMM at the radio station?"

"Yeah," Derek says, caught in two conversations, "look, Mark, I was actually calling to see if I've left my portable hard drive up at the station, but I might just come back if there's free meat going."

"Free booze too, Derek," Mark adds.

"Free booze too?" Derek says.

"AAAANNNNMMMM free booze too?" Barry Twelvedogs says.

"Yeah."

"Now?"

"Yeah

"MMMM, probably should go and look for your hard drive, in person, eh?"

"I'll say."

"Are you coming up?" Mark asks, and in that same second, the unmistakable intro of *The Benny Hill Theme Tune* starts rasping out in the background at Derek's end of the call. Mark hears it and time stands still. Suddenly he's transported five or so months back in time and away to the memory of *The Dead Air Incident*, the sound of it playing out in the background of the call.

"Why is *The Benny Hill Theme Tune* playing Derek?

"Oh, not sure, boss. Gone off a few times since we left the station, so it has. Barry thinks it might be the Bluetooth speaker picking up a rogue signal."

"I don't think that's a rogue signal, Derek. I think you let our friend Jay Dicks use the bathroom in your RV when you were still parked here."

"Well, it was better than him doing it in the roses, Mark."

"MMMM stunk it out." Barry Twelvedogs again chiming in, in the background, as *The Benny Hill Theme* rings off. "AAAANNNN rank as fuck."

"Derek, I think Jay Dicks has left his phone in your campervan. Look er, I'm gonna call it from *my* phone now. Stay on the line caller. Start looking if you hear the music eh?"

"Ok"

"What if it's not the number?" Melody says.

"It's it, Melody, it's it," Mark says, excited.

In the Barnaby RV *The Benny Hill Theme* plays again and both of the van's occupants are looking for the phone. It's coming from the bathroom but neither want to go in there due to the stench of the Dicks's shit which has been looming for hours now. Barry braves the nutty cling, going in. He sees the phone vibrating on the floor between the toilet stem and the wall. Jay Dicks's phone is scared, lost and alone and trapped in the valley where piss-missers miss.

"MMMM, Jay Dicks' phone," Barry Twelvedogs says in his robotic voice, as he simultaneously receives a drop of piss to the cheek from the face of the phone.

"MMMM, I've got it. NNNN, I've got it. AAAANNNN, I've got it." Twelvedogs is jubilant.

"Give it to me," Derek Barnaby commands, dismissive, seeking a more authoritative witness.

"MMMMAAAANNNNMM shall I put you on?"

"Yeah, if you wouldn't mind putting me on that'd be brilliant."

"AAAANNNNMMMM I'll put you on then."

"Yeah, put me on the line. That's what I'm looking for."

"MMMMM I'll put you on the line then MMM especially now that you've asked me to put you on the line like that."

"Yeah?"

"MMMM Yeah?"

"Put me on then."

"AAANNNN Oh I'll put you on."

Barry puts Derek on.

"Thanks for putting me on."

"MMMM happy to put you on boss."

"Hello."

"Hello, father,"

"And this is?"

"It's me father. Mark. Goodenough."

"Ah, bless you, my child."

"And what did you say you wanted now?"

"No, I'm phoning to make sure that phone I've called belongs to who we think it belongs to."

"And whose phone do we think it is?"

"Jay Dick's phone."

"And, so it is. So, it is."

All of a sudden bedlam breaks out at Waiheke Island Radio. It is as if a goal has just been scored in the last minute of the World Cup final and New Zealand have scored it. An explosion of pure joy.

Chapter 68

THE HACK

Saturday 8th March

If it were an informant, Jay Dicks's Samsung Galaxy S20 would've fallen into the ranks of the super-grass. It sung like a canary, telling tales from his Photo gallery, his text and call logs, his calendar and his saved voicemails. The PIN for his banking app is the same as the one he uses for his phone too, so that is also wide open.

Viewing as a thumbnail grid, and scrolling back some months, a collection of images in his Photo gallery are a wash of blue. A pool party under clear blue skies, ocean as a background. Images of debauchery and drug use, someone whipping a cock out. It was Mark who made the connection. Checking off the dates, it all tallies up. The fine weather too. Labour Day. This was the party that Jay Dicks had been at during the *Dead Air Incident*.

Hundreds of text messages between at least fifty different numbers spoke in code about clandestine drug deals. The saved voicemails too, the conspiracy against Waiheke Island Radio. Gloating texts from Sarin after her first and second strikes. The crowing about Derek Barnaby's complaint and the messages that had been her and Jay's undoing.

> *It worked!! The cripple just announced the station is as good as finished!! LOL S XX*

> *Great job love, keep turning the screw JD XX*

On top of the conspiracy at the station, and the evidence of widespread drug dealing, there is something else on the phone. Something much more damaging for Jay Dicks. It is found a few days later by police in Jay's saved voicemails. A two-word message from the voice of a man they have in custody. A message despatched at 11:23pm on the night of Wednesday, December 8th. It is the only time that number has ever called Jay's phone, and the holder of that number is the prime suspect in the *Christ FM* arson.

Just one message of two words but it will end up costing Jay eight years in Mt Eden Prison. He'll also serve six months on possession for supply charges as well as a further six months for his part in the conspiracy against *Waiheke Island Radio*. The latter two sentences being served concurrently with his Accessory to Arson term. Sarin is lucky. She gets off lightly, handed a six-month suspended sentence and given a lifetime broadcasting ban for her part in the conspiracy.

🐶

It is Melody who finds the biggest bombshell. She cracks that one as the wake turns into a full-scale party. Recognising a wasted face from the pictures of the pool party. He is prominent in the photos is this person. Gurning at the camera, looking fried and snorting drugs.

"That's Jamie Saddleback."

"Fucken is too and he's doing drugs."

"That is not a good look for a Minister of the Crown."

It isn't just the face. Melody recognises Saddleback's voice too. It is in one of Jay's saved voicemails. She has Mark play it back.

> *"It's me. Greenlight. Call Bruce Bennett at Waiheke Council zero nine three seven two one two three. Tell him you want to view the station. Tell him the only time you can do the appointment is at ten on Friday morning."*

Adamant that it is him, she compares this message to an interview she finds on *YouTube*. In the piece Saddleback speaks about private schools.

> *"Well, I just think we owe it to our children to be able to give them the best education, and if that's done by paying for it, then I am fine with that."*

"That's him, that's the same voice. It's Jamie Saddleback."

"Oh, that crooked auld bastard. He knew the *NZOA* delegation would be arriving at ten. He did it on purpose. This is sabotage. Friday morning, he fucken arranged it. That bastard." Melody says.

❦

She is right. The Honourable Jamie Saddleback MP. He orchestrated the whole thing. In plain sight too. His position on Access Radio was never a secret. It horrifies him that the taxpayer has to shell out millions of dollars to minority media. He thinks it is nothing short of a travesty and if no one was going to do anything about it, he would.

There was a little kicker with the timing too. Jamie knew when he took the portfolio that four of these Access broadcasters were one year out from having their frequencies renewed with the government agency, *Radio Spectrum Management*. Quietly, he reshuffled the boards at the *Broadcasting Standards Authority* and at *New Zealand On Air*. Then he brought the two together to work in tandem on discipline. A move that led to the *Five Strikes and You're Out* rule.

Jamie knew that with *Five Strikes* in play, only a little bit of coaxing would be required to force the folks over at *Radio Spectrum Management* to de-register and dis-establish all four of them in short order. Jamie well knew how malleable people were, especially those attracted to the white light of Access Radio. His plan was to exploit it. Five steps ahead. Within nine months of implementing his new rules, he had undone stations in Te Anau and Te Puke. The latter, after (it turned out) Sarin Murray had influenced four fourteen-year-olds into hosting an on-air weed-smoking contest. She's given them the ganja. The former after (it turned out) Caleb McGill of the NZ National Front had stated, during the station's Health and Wellbeing Zone, between one and four, that Asian people were "like lice." It's his thing. Calling people lice. Lice and grubs and slugs. He usually does this when they look different from him. He also does it for those of a different political stripe than his. Dehumanizes them.

After Jamie recouped three million in frequency sales for the pair of stations, he was a media darling, playing brilliantly to potato-headed shock jock, Mike Hunt, and his audience of thumb-headed halfwits. That year, Jamie Saddleback was the smuggest man on campus, walking around Parliament like a dog with two dicks.

As soon as it gets out that he is crooked, the good times are over. Stripped of his portfolios and forced to resign from the ACT party with immediate effect. Politicians disavow him, the media won't touch him, even *Yesterday's News Tomorrow* host Duncan Farmer won't go near him. The mantis Guy Williams still takes the call though.

A police investigation finds Jamie Saddleback central to the plot against Waiheke Island Radio and when the case is tried, he is given six months in Tongariro/Rangipo with a further six months suspended.

Chapter 70

THE PAY OFF

Five days was as close as it got in the end, but *Waiheke Island Radio* never actually goes off the air. As soon as the evidence on Jay Dicks's phone is brought to the attention of Nazreen and Hone at New Zealand On Air, the auction is voided and, for a month, the frequency is held by Waiheke Island Radio in a caretaker capacity. Eventually after a thorough investigation and a reshuffle of the NZOA board, all but *A Dozen Dildos at Dinnertime* is struck from the record of upheld BSA complaints. With only a single complaint against the station's name, all funding is unlocked, and it is business as usual. Well almost.

They're flush now. Not from the *GoFundMe* page, those donations were never called in. The real money-spinner is the English, Punjabi and Mandarin versions of *Blind Radio Host Triggered after Guide Dog hurt by Hipster*, which cumulatively have earned over a quarter of a million dollars each on views alone. They keep the station house too. Bruce at the council lobbying hard on their behalf. He is a good sort is old Bruce. Solid as a rock.

Almost everyone at the station has seen their profile rise and hits on each of the show's podcasts are through the roof. The GLITFAB Crew have used the exposure as a springboard into the music industry releasing a fidget-house version of the *Pet Shop Boys* classic, *Shopping*. It is a banger alright, massive on *Spotify*. They'll be going out on the festival circuit soon. Darcey has no interest in the musical venture. They're too busy putting out exercise videos to their audience of two million on TikTok. They've also opened a non-binary clothing emporium called 'Neutral Mode Boutique' it's in the space where Greatest Friend used to be on the Oneroa Strip, a few shops up from the WINZ office. Sam Smith opened it.

Ken Oath's profile has gone through the roof too. For him, it started with an interview in the *Gulf News*. Then radio interviews in Australia, Canada, South Africa, Malta, Zimbabwe. Eventually his brothers in the old country heard him via BBC Radio Scotland. Now he is raking it in with a long list of endorsement deals to his and Sheba's name. Sunglasses, dog food, folding canes, dog harnesses, pet insurance, all kinds of things. Sheba is a bona fide celebrity in her own right now too, right up there with Schnorbitz, Lassie and Beethoven.

Derek Barnaby struck gold, though no-one quite knows quite how. Someone must've spread word about his massive knob, no one's owning up about it though. Now, he's under contract to Australian underwear kings, *Python Briefs*, modelling boxers, jockstraps and trunks 'for men with a massive mate.' Derek doesn't wear the clerical dog collar anymore. He is over that stuff now. He's moved on, got his head straight.

Mr Singh recovered from his accident and in exchange for a generous monthly donation has sponsored *Punjabi Time* for nine months. He's also been sponsoring *Punjabi News,* a daily current affairs bulletin broadcasting to the inner Hauraki Gulf for Punjabi speakers. Its numbers are sky high and he is happy.

Chapter 71

THE END

On the day of Larry's annual Christmas party, Mark climbs the wooden steps into the Onetangi bottle shop. This is last place to buy alcohol before the rolling hills and the winding road out to the bottom end. He passes through the shop door, Mark Goodenough, scanning the two narrow aisles of booze that lay before him. The spectrum of intoxicants, the wine through Scotch, the gin through the port. At the back of the room there's a walk-in beer-fridge. Its door is flapping back into place as a woman walks out of it. It's her, Liz. She is carrying a bottle of Sav and a box of beers. She looks different since he'd last laid eyes on her. There seems to be something manic in her energy. It's how she used to be when she was embarrassed.

Left Shoulder – Well, what do you expect? This is the Bottle-O.

Liz is so embarrassed that she's angry with it, no pleasantries this time, no offer of a coffee, no, *I miss you.* She does acknowledge Mark though, using ten judgemental words. "I saw your video, the one on TikTok. How embarrassing." Then, without leaving time for Mark to reply, she scuttles to the counter to pay for her booze.

By the time Mark comes back out of the cold room, Liz is gone. There is no singularity about the throat this time, no yearning, no spiral. He doesn't feel anything, just ambivalence. He's dodged a bullet. His life is looking good, and as he returns to the passenger seat of the silver Mazda, he looks over at Melody in the driver's seat and they exchanged a smile and a lingering look.

Behind them, on the backseat, Bento notices the energy as he manspreads, wolfing the Carl's Junior burger that he's just bought at the new drive-thru in the carpark outside Placeys. It'd been open a month now. The people said 'yes'. Sure, some people said 'no' but *most* people said 'yes'. The monkey is strapped in next to Bento. It is resting his elbow on the sill of the open car window, watching the world pass by. Out of the two of them Bento is the main fidgeter.

"Seen Liz coming out the Bottle-O there, bro, eh?"

"Yeah?"

"Gee, that'd have been awkward, eh?" Bento, still fishing.

"Nah."

"Yeah, whatever."

"*Nah.*"

"She say anything?"

"No," Mark lies.

"Cold."

"We've all moved on, mate."

"Seen those yoga pants though, eh?" Bento is going there.

"Yeah, what of them?"

"Couple-a bulldogs fighting in a bin bag yeah?" Pause for effect, "Called it."

"You did."

"Bento! You can't say that." Melody, calls out, "no wonder you're single."

"Who says I'm single?" Bento retorts.

A year is a long time, and how things can change as it passes. Mark was better now. Through it. He'd been working out at the gym. Keeping it regular. Trying to eat better. He was sharper, noticing it in himself. No longer did *The Walk-In* or *The Dead Air Incident*, or *Waster in Emu Suit Looks for Drugs in Own Vomit* live rent free in his head. Silent are the shoulders telling him he is worthless. Now he has other things to think about, and while Melody Longs gearboxes her silver Mazda up Waiheke Road and the Still Corners number *Strange Pleasures* plays out from the stereo, Mark reaches over and places his hand on hers, as it rests slender on the knub of the gear selector, waiting between changes.

"Called that too," Bento shouts from the backseat.

🐶

Three hours later and Larry's Christmas party is pumping at dusk. *When a Child is Born (Korky Pinks Drill House remix)* by Johnny Mathis is playing. It is one of Holly's. Pablo, Lalo and Nacho Techno have put her onto it. Eighty guests all up. There's friends, broadcasters, and prominent local faces dotted about the garden and deck. The weather is fine, and the mood is jubilant. As usual Chunk is in his element scavenging meat from all of Larry's guests. Mark stands on the deck, beer in hand. He's in a conversation circle with Bento, Melody Longs, Larry Minto, Derek Barnaby, Barry Twelvedogs, Big Bill Tong, Darcey Knight, Lynn Mall and Sylvia Park. They always seem to gravitate to one another at these events these days do Darcey and Bento. Some people think they're together now. They'd bonded over the monkey.

As the universe would have it, talk turns to the cricket, moving in the conversation between a current game that's showing on Larry's big screen and then back to that classic game at World Cup semi-final from the previous year.

"What a match that was. Walt Hooper's radio commentary was choice." Derek is drunk again, but happy.

"O-oh," Bento says shooting a look over at Mark.

"Was it just me, or did some people start talking during that broadcast. It went off as I recall, for like, ages man, right at the best bit of the game too. The climax. Couldn't believe it at first. Ended up waiting about five minutes for it to come back. When it did, the game had finished. Ropeable, I was. Spewin. I'm telling you. I ended up having to go to my next-door neighbour's place. He's got Sky. It was finished by then."

"MMMM I was there. AAAAANNNN Eden Park AANN" says 8-bit voiced Barry Twelvedogs, "NNNN left early for the last boat home."

"Whoa! That's right, I remember that. There was Benny Hill music playing in it eh?" said Big Bill.

"Must've been a technical glitch with the equipment." Mark's arsehole is going ten to the dozen now.

"I mean you'd have to have halohaiku to make a gaff like that eh?" Darcey adds.

"Probably got the sack for it," Bento, sarcastic as Mark eyeballs him, furrowing the brow, pursing the lips and faking the grin.

"Nah, probably got a promotion the way the world works these days," Derek says.

"You know, arv heard it too." Larry slurs with a chuckle.

"Oh, sounds like it's worth hearing," Sylvia Park.

"Oh, you've not heard it?" Bento says to Mark, grinning. Well, I've got the audio of it on my phone. Why don't I just flick a copy of it to you now. Do it for anyone else here if ya want? Just give me your email address and I'll pop it over."

Both shoulders – Fuck you.

THE END

ABOUT THE AUTHOR

Jonathan McQuillan is a writer and factotum. He's managed a theatre, hosted radio shows in Auckland and Hamilton, and worked as a radio programme director. He jobbed as a professional Santa Claus, a London tour guide, and a club DJ in Cape Town. Originally from North West England, he now lives on Waiheke Island with his family. Over six years of daily ferry commutes, he wrote his neurotic debut novel, *High Impact Insensitivity*, tapping out the bulk of it on his phone.

9 781991 083289